I0736856

PRAISE FOR CAROLYN MILLER

Praise for the Original Six series

"I LOVE THIS BOOK!! I love the uniqueness of the characters - we don't see too many hockey player heroes which is a true shame because THOSE KISSES!!"~ *CARRIE BOOTH SCHMIDT, Reading is my Superpower blog*

"I loved the dialogue and the hero and heroine, the very authentic and real challenges they faced and the unique setting and hockey slant." ~ *RACHEL MCMILLAN, bestselling author*

"A touching romance set on the breathtaking shores of Canada's Lake Muskoka. Sarah and Dan are so vividly drawn they practically leap off the page! Their sweet, slowly evolving friendship deepens into the kind of lasting love Christians long for. A must read!" ~ *MEGHANN WHISTLER, award-winning author of The Billionaire's Secret*

"I have been waiting for TJ's story and am so glad it's here! It's perfect...This is truly a story about loving the unlovable and the blessings that come as a result." ~ *GOODREADS review*

"There is nothing like a wonderful redemption story where someone changes their life and becomes a better version of themselves. It is a good reminder to me that God offers incredible grace to all of us." ~ *GOODREADS review*

"Carolyn Miller keeps on turning out these beautifully written, tender hearted books!... There was humor and brilliant bantering conversations, heart stopping romance, as well as exciting descriptions (and sometimes dangerous passages of play) of hockey games. Well worth the late night/early morning read!" ~ *KAYE'S REVIEWS & NEWS*

"A sweet love story that continues the Original Six Hockey series by Carolyn Miller. The setting of Montreal with the Gardens and all the French woven throughout was delightful!" ~ *GOODREADS review*

"I am emerging out of my book hangover after reading *Checked Impressions* by Carolyn Miller....The romance, humor and themes of identity are so enjoyable and make for a great read!" ~ *BECKY'S BOOKSHELVES*

"Adrenaline, chemistry, romance, and lots of wooing!...You do not have to be a fan of sports or even knowledgeable in hockey and short track to appreciate *Love on Ice*." ~ *GOODREADS review*

"Carolyn Miller scores another win with *Love on Ice*, the second book in her Original Six Hockey series. I absolutely loved the faith thread in this story. It's message that success does not lie on what we do, but who we are is powerful." ~ *GOODREADS review*

"*The Breakup Project* is a fun, charming, and faith-filled contemporary romance with adorable characters set in the competitive North American ice hockey world. Highly recommended." ~ *NARELLE ATKINS, Author of Solo Tu & Her Tycoon Hero*

MUSKOKA CHRISTMAS

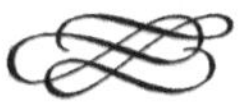

CAROLYN MILLER

Visit Carolyn Miller at www.carolynmillerauthor.com

Copyright © 2022 by Carolyn Miller

All rights reserved.

This book is a work of fiction. References to real people, events, establishments, organizations or locales are intended only to provide a sense of authenticity, and are used fictitiously. All other characters, and all incidents and dialogue, are drawn from the author's imagination and are not to be construed as real.

No part of this book may be reproduced in any form or by any electronic or mechanical means, including information storage and retrieval systems, without written permission from the author, except for the use of brief quotations in a book review.

Cover design by KT Design

Edited by Elizabeth Lance

ALSO BY CAROLYN MILLER

The Original Six hockey series

The Breakup Project

Love on Ice

Checked Impressions

Hearts and Goals

Big Apple Atonement

Muskoka Blue

Muskoka Romance series

Muskoka Shores

Muskoka Christmas

Muskoka Hearts

Muskoka Spotlight

Northwest Ice hockey series

Fire and Ice

Trinity Lakes collection

Love Somebody Like You

The Independence Islands series

Restoring Fairhaven

Regaining Mercy

Reclaiming Hope

Rebuilding Hearts

Refining Josie

Historical:

<u>Regency Wallflowers</u>
Dusk's Darkest Shores
Midnight's Budding Morrow
Dawn's Untrodden Green

<u>Regency Brides: Legacy of Grace</u>
The Elusive Miss Ellison
The Captivating Lady Charlotte
The Dishonorable Miss DeLancey

<u>Regency Brides: Promise of Hope</u>
Winning Miss Winthrop
Miss Serena's Secret
The Making of Mrs Hale

<u>Regency Brides: Daughters of Aynsley</u>
A Hero for Miss Hatherleigh
Underestimating Miss Cecilia
Misleading Miss Verity

'Heaven and Nature Sing' from the Joy to the World Christmas
novella collection

e

MUSKOKA CHRISTMAS

Clouds menaced above, wet leaves spattered through the air, and wind pummeled the stone fortress atop which she stood. Fiona held her breath as the howling intensified, clattering the shutters. She would be safe, wouldn't she? He could not find her here, she had taken all proper precautions. But if he did... Her heart throbbed with uncertainty. She would have to hope and pray that her knight would rescue—

"Staci?"

A shriek accompanied her jump as her half-full flute of champagne sloshed over her dress. "Max! How many times have I told you I *hate* being sneaked up on? Look what you made me do." She exchanged her glass for the handkerchief he held out, and dabbed ineffectually at her emerald-green, velvet dress.

"At least it wasn't red wine."

Was that his way of offering an apology? She narrowed her eyes, but kept her lips shut. The lights of Chicago stretched in glowing spiderwebs before her, silently mocking her lack of bravado. But it wouldn't do to antagonize her editor, not when she needed a favor.

"Did you try the salmon blinis? They're simply divine. Here, let me grab you one." He clicked for a black-and-white dressed server to approach, silver tray in hand, and scooped up three palm-sized plates of tiny caviar-dusted pancakes, before holding one out to her.

Typical. Two parts for him, one part for her. "Thanks, but I'm full," she lied.

"Oh well." He shrugged. "Waste not, want not."

As he shoved the food into his mouth she wondered, not for the first time, how someone who could dance with Gene Kelly-like finesse around words could have the social aplomb of a four-year-old. Not that she could ever afford to point this out. Literally.

She inched one Louboutin heel behind the other. Why had she ever thought such frivolities necessary? Too tight, too tall, too expensive, even at the fantastic online discount they'd proved way beyond her means. Honestly, who spent their entire advance on a pair of shoes? She would simply need to wait until he was slightly less sober before putting her proposition—

"So, how's Fiona going these days?"

Staci stumbled. He grabbed her arm, steadying her balance as she muttered, "Thanks." Apparently Max wasn't the only one lacking some grace here tonight. What to say, what to say…

"Well?" He eyed her, and she was reminded of the crows that used to line her grandmother's vegetable garden, waiting until Gran's back was turned before pecking holes in the produce, seeking whatever they could. Strange. She hadn't thought about Gran's garden for years. She should probably call and see how Gran was doing—

"Staci Everton! Hello? Is something the matter?"

She blinked. Oh, yes, something was the matter all right.

"Where is Fiona up to?"

A smile gritted out. "She's getting there." Understatement of the year. Fiona's story would get there if Staci ever got the time to figure out her character's goals and internal motivation. But it was hard to be excited when Staci didn't even care. How long had she been doing this for now? So many stories, so much marketing, she was exhausted trying to find a fresh spin on the old story of boy-meets-girl that leads to their happily-ever-after.

"So, I'll have something by Christmas?"

"Of course." Though it might be indigestion. And not just the kind caused by eating too much food.

"You sure? For some reason you don't seem too excited by this story."

That was because there was currently no story to be excited by. "Have I ever missed a deadline?"

"No, because you're the best." He hugged her, releasing an internal shriek of protest, before he stepped away with a grimace and half-laugh. "Sorry. Forgot."

She followed his glance to where Bryan Flanagan, chief editor of Flame Publishing, watched them, arms crossed, as if wondering whether his speech just half an hour ago about harassment and the #metoo movement had been for naught. She eked out a stiff smile and raised a hand she hoped conveyed ease—the company's cocktail party formality did not seem thumbs-up friendly—which he acknowledged with a nod, before pivoting to talk to Davis Scott, the eager-as-a-puppy newbie author whose debut novel was being promoted as the Next Big Thing.

She tried to stifle the stab of jealousy. Failed. Decided to roll with it instead. How *could* Flame prefer Davis to her, she who with ten books now had *always* met her deadlines, had achieved very reasonable sales for a company of Flame's size (so her agent Bronwyn Matthieson told her), yet who had never been honored with a sandwich plate let alone a cocktail party. It wasn't fair. Just because Davis had spent years cultivating the acquaintance of Marco Fischer, whose NYT bestseller status was unquestioned (even though she couldn't understand the attraction of a story with no romance – seriously? What did those gritty hyper-realistic fictional people do all day? Where was the fantasy element for the reader, where was the escape in *that*?) and now Davis had Marco's glowing endorsement gracing the cover of his new release, well, why did Flame get all excited about that, rather than rewarding the consistent efforts of one of their lead authors who had met EVERY deadline EVER!

Until maybe this one.

Uncomfortably aware that Max was saying something, she schooled her features to assume interest and not like she hadn't been indulging in Pity Party #779.

"Hello? Staci? You seem even more vague than usual. Is something wrong?"

Nothing that a completed manuscript wouldn't fix. And finding a way to overcome this stupid, pointless jealousy. "I think it's probably time I left." She tried out a smile she hoped could pass for sweet. "You know me, working, working, working."

His brows met. "I *do* know you, which is why you should stay here relaxing, relaxing, relaxing."

Like that was going to happen. Relaxing was something that seemed to belong in the vague shadows of her childhood. Her smile took on gritted teeth status. "Thanks, Max, but I really should—"

"Hi, Staci."

She closed her eyes for a second, prayed for strength, and that her now *truly* gritted-teeth-smile looked pleasant enough. "Davis. Hello."

"Isn't tonight just amazing? Booking out the restaurant, all the fancy food, all the great speeches. I can't believe they did all this for me."

That was one thing they agreed on at least. But no good would come from her desire to speak filter-free. Best she looked like a team player. "It's certainly something I've never seen before." She gave Max a pair of raised brows that probably didn't look too team player-like but seemed to get the point across as he flushed satisfactorily.

"I guess it's not every day Flame has one of Marco's protegees launch a book."

"No indeed," she mumbled, as a fresh lightning bolt of envy zapped through her. Was this Davis trying to be humble? If so, he had a lot to learn. Was he able to walk into a deal on the Marco name alone or did his being a man have anything to do with it? She studied him from under heavily mascaraed lashes. Maybe it was the eager beaver puppy dog eyes and Pollyanna enthusiasm that had Flame salivating and offering a contract larger than anything they'd offered in history, or so the industry gossip whispered.

"Hey, I heard you have another book coming out next year," Davis said. "Congrats."

"Thanks," she unstiffened enough to say. Well, that was surprising—

"Flame's just offered me another contract. For another three books! Isn't that awesome?"

No. Awesome was seeing Westminster Abbey and being struck with the majesty of God. Awesome was standing in the Canadian Rockies, or the Grand Canyon, stunned by vistas of great beauty. Awesome definitely wasn't hearing this. She mumbled something appropriate and grabbed Max's arm. "Sorry, Davis," sorry but totally *not* sorry, "gotta go. People to see, things to do. Congrats again." She faked another smile and pulled Max to a quieter alcove.

Max chuckled. "Green doesn't become you, my dear."

What? She glanced down at her emerald wrap dress. Her Celtic coloring meant she'd always worn—

Oh. She huffed out a breath. "I can't understand why Flame loves him so much," she grumbled.

"Really." The lower-pitched second syllable denoted dryness.

"Look, my books have been steady sellers for years now. Granted they're not exactly Pulitzer-prizeworthy," like her covers would ever grace such hallowed halls, "but my readers *love* me."

Well, most of them. Apart from the sanctimonious ones who wrote to object to the salacious content and the provocative covers and felt inclined to point out the errors of her ways. Like she needed them to do that. She shook her head. Like she should even pay attention to people who were obviously hypocritical enough to judge a book by its cover then go ahead and read the whole thing. Hello? Talk about a disconnect.

"But your books have never graced the NYT list."

"But neither has—" she gestured to Davis, even now schmoozing his way through the powerbrokers of Flame.

"Actually…" He pulled out his phone, tapped the screen a few times, and held it out to her.

She squinted, heart plummeting as she recognized the title halfway up the list. "How?"

He shrugged. "You know how preorders work. And Marco's name does seem to hold some sway."

The burn in her chest reached the back of her eyes. She pressed her lips together. She would not cry. She would not!

"I'm sorry, Staci. You know I think you write really well, and I've loved working with you." He paused.

The giant green mass writhing within suddenly panicked and scrambled up her throat. "But?" Was this to be the end of her writing career?

"But you know readers like something that suggests 'same, same, but slightly different'. Once they've read all your backlist they want someone new. And if that person has Marco's blessing, well…" Another shrug.

"What are you saying? Doesn't Flame want me anymore?" She drew in a sharp breath, conscious her voice held a note too high to project confidence.

"Staci, calm down. Nobody is saying that."

But would they be saying that soon? "You've always said Flame needed me to write the same kind of story. I've been begging Bronwyn to try something different for years, but she always said Flame just wanted more of the same. I have other stories in me."

"Not historical bodice rippers?" He raised a skeptical brow.

"Good stories. Wholesome stories." Well, they would be once she cut a few scenes. "Stories someone's grandmother or daughter would love." Stories that maybe even Gran and her cronies could approve. "Come on. You *know* I write well."

"And I know you have a contracted book to deliver by December twenty-fourth."

Why, oh why, had she agreed to such a stupid date? Just because Max was alone and without family and preferred to work rather than take a few days off over Christmas like normal people.

The panic reared again. How on earth would she get this written? She exhaled an anxious breath—she hoped silently—but from the pitying look Max gave her it apparently wasn't silent enough.

He patted her arm. "Look, send me the manuscript you're contracted for, then maybe it might be a good idea for you to take some time out to relax, refuel the batteries. What are you doing for Christmas?"

"I'm not sure," she hedged. Gran had invited her—as she always did—back to Muskoka Shores, but while pretty, the small town was exactly that: small town. There'd be no hiding from her past there. Not when everybody knew everybody and liked to know everybody's business. What Staci *would* like to do would be to stay cooped up inside her Lakeshore Drive condo wearing PJs, watching Hallmark movies, and imbibing chocolate in all forms. No expectations. No obligations. No stupid deadlines. She sighed.

"Look, submit it and I promise, we can take a look at something new."

"You can, or you will?" she pressed.

"Stace, I don't know why you're so insecure—oh, is that Marco? I thought he couldn't come." Without further ado he pushed past her to join the crowd swelling around the slight, graying man, the crowd who were snapping photos, taking selfies, their excitement as voluble as what she imagined pigs might be like at feeding time.

"Staci."

She pivoted, toes pinching in the slightly too small heels. She would *never* go shoe shopping online again. "Hello Bryan."

They exchanged air kisses. "Max behaving himself this year?"

"Of course. You know that was just a rum punch-induced one off."

"If you say so."

She eyed the Marco and Davis crowd miserably. "I should probably go." Somewhere far away. A spark flickered. Maybe she should go visit Gran, but earlier, like next week, and hide away in her spare room that she was always begging Staci to use. That way she could write her blessed story and fulfill her granddaughter duties while avoiding the Christmas chaos. The idea held so many possibilities. Quite possibly good possibilities. "I really *should* go."

"You don't want to meet Marco?"

Not particularly. But before she could find a polite rejection she was being drawn forward, was being introduced, was having her hand clasped by Marco NY-flippin'-T Fischer. Her hand was firmly grasped. Sweatily grasped. Ugh.

"Miss Everton writes too. Historical romance."

"Ah, of course. I believe I've seen your work."

Seen, not read. But hey, at least it was something. Bronwyn would be impressed.

Davis whispered something in Marco's ear, and the legend's eyes lit. "The racy ones, like Fifty Shades."

"Not exactly." Not at all. She preferred to have her characters engage in meaningful relationship building. "The covers are a little historically inaccurate, but..." Conscious of Bryan hovering nearby, she couldn't explain Flame's decision making with certain aspects of marketing.

Marco's fingers, which still had not let hers go, pressed warmly, before taking on a caressing motion across her palm. Gross. Why did people always assume that her stories equated to how she wanted to be treated in her life? She pulled her hand free, stepped back, and subtly wiped her hand down her hip. "Well, nice to meet you."

"And you." He slung an arm around Davis's shoulders. "I'm so proud of this one. Have you read his book yet? It's wonderful, simply wonderful. I wish I had such talent at his age."

Davis's face grew pink and shiny as he nearly exploded with pride. She really shouldn't be the one to puncture the happiness. Best she leave now. Best she get the book written. Best she get away from this stupid scene so she could *get* the book written. Best she call Gran tomorrow and find out if her perpetual spare room offer was still on offer.

"Gotta go." She faked a smile and nodded at Max, Bryan, and a few other editorial staff, before forcing her gaze to Davis's general direction. *Be a big girl. Be a team player.* Treat others like you'd want to be treated, and all that. "Congrats again."

Spinning on her heel she strode away.

Words had never tasted so sour on her tongue.

MUSKOKA SHORES still looked the same, but then it always had, for as long as he remembered. James Wells huffed out a breath that puffed into a white cloud, as he carefully skirted the patch of icy sidewalk on his journey beside the lake. What a contrast to his former world. No desert sands or drought concerns here.

"Hey, Doc," a fellow lunchtime jogger called.

James nodded, gave a quick smile, and continued his slow run. Would he ever grow reconciled to this new life, the one that harkened back to feelings of being trapped inside a snow globe? The life with no way out, save for what a career in medicine could offer, first in hospitals in the city, and then when burnout loomed, a career half a world away serving the poorest of the poor. Until a near breakdown had sped him home.

He released a long, chill-laden breath. Maybe he didn't have what it took. Maybe he should simply stay here and settle down. He knew Mom would be pleased. But what then? Did he really want to settle into a facsimile of Frank Lewisham's life? Or had James failed in his one big sip of the greater world's delights?

He forced himself to plow on—his legs were tired now, too much sitting on a plane—and hit the main street of Muskoka Shores. A stream of tourist shops and quirky stores beckoned for dollars that could save a child's life in other parts of the world. He shook his head at himself. Reverse culture shock, that's what they called it. He shouldn't judge. He'd been that way too, six years ago.

The Coffee Blend had twinkling lights festooned around its window, and he took up the silent invitation and hurried to the warmth inside. "Hey Suzy."

The woman behind the counter glanced up with a smile. "Well, look who's back."

He smiled, accepted the inevitable as she hurried past the coffee machine and gave him a tight hug. "It's good to see you."

"And you." He gestured to the rustic chic adorning the walls. "Love what you've done to the place."

"It's a bit different, isn't it?" she said, hands on hips, surveying the interior. "But the plastic tack had to go."

He settled in at the stool. "Didn't fit the vibe of the town these days, huh?"

"You noticed?" Her nose wrinkled. "We need our tourists, and they need their creature comforts." She patted the coffee machine. "Now, what'll it be? We've got all sorts of options on offer here, pumpkin spice, caramel, peppermint."

"Just give me something tall and dark to go."

"Still keeping healthy, huh?"

"Gotta practice what I preach."

"Just a splash of milk?"

He nodded, and she grinned and surveyed his height.

"You Wells boys never liked things too complicated, did you?"

No. But that hadn't stopped complications from following them anyway. A pang of sorrow crossed his chest, and he glanced away.

The coffee machine roared to life, saving him from further conversation, and he took a moment to calm his thoughts, to look around. The coffee shop held a contented buzz of tourists and locals, some faces he recognized from years ago. A few quick greetings and then Suzy called out, "One TDH to go."

From the way she eyed him, he guessed she meant his coffee was ready. But "TDH?"

Her grin was like a Cheshire's cat. "One tall, dark, and I bet I don't need to tell you what the 'h' stands for, do I?"

"Honest?" he suggested, sliding out the bills to pay.

"Put that away, James. I'm not charging you on your first day back in town."

"Not quite my first day."

"You know what I mean." Her expression softened. "It's good to have you back. You've been missed."

"Thanks." He held up the coffee in a salute. "Appreciate it, Suzy."

"See you soon."

He took a sip, the caffeine hitting his bloodstream like liquid gold. "I'm sure you will. This is really good."

"I know." She gave a smug smile which tugged out his own, the boost in spirits chasing his steps back to the clinic. Perhaps this time here would not be so constricting, nor feel like a punishment. He shook his head at himself. First world problems. He should really get a grip. For how could anyone not enjoy Christmas at Muskoka Shores?

CHAPTER 2

he carriage trundled under the large overhanging branches of the tree-lined avenue leading to the village. Gray skies lapped deepening shadows, the snowdrifts of several days ago browning into slush, something that had taken her by surprise. She should remember the early December snows. What else had she forgotten in the years since she'd been away?

The wheels clattered over the wooden bridge, the carriage drawing nearer, up the steep incline to where the church steeple pointed to the heavens. Fiona's chest tightened. The posted sentries straightened, their eyes following her slow progress. Would she be remembered as the conquering daughter of a king or as the despised maid who had sold her soul—

Bang!

Tires skidded. A gasp escaped. Heart pounding, Staci clutched the steering wheel even more firmly, muttering a prayer for protection as the car jerked and shuddered, before grinding away into the street curb as it finally drew to a pause. She exhaled. Thank God she hadn't hit anyone. Thank God she hadn't hit anything. What a homecoming that would've been.

She heaved in another breath as her heartbeat slowed and

her white knuckled-grip eased. Well, she was wide awake now. Had that been caused by a moment of travel-induced weariness? Maybe leaving in the wee small hours and trying to drive ten hours today wasn't her smartest idea. She wrenched open the door, and Muskoka Shores welcomed her with icy breath. A glance at the back wheel revealed a deflated tire. Awesome. Welcome home, indeed.

Shivering, she slammed the door shut, huddling in the driver's seat, willing herself warm as she summoned up the courage to get back outside and change the tire. The frigid temperatures were just one of the many reasons she'd been happy to leave all those years ago. But university in LA had led to a job that scarcely matched the blue skies on offer, forcing her to the Midwest for a better pay rate, even if little else attracted initially. But she'd ended up enjoying Chicago, the architecture, the museums, the fact she could order food delivery any hour to the condo her parents' bequest had bought her. She had especially enjoyed when her small magazine editorial role had taken a turn to the right and the historical story she'd been tinkering on for years had been snapped up by Bronwyn at a writer's conference, then soon sold to a publisher with a fledgling imprint called Flame. She'd kept working for a year or so, before demand for her books had grown so loud she'd been able to quit the magazine and focus full-time on writing. Flame had been good to her. At least in the beginning. She hoped they remembered it when this stupid manuscript finally appeared. If she could ever figure out what to write.

A knock came at the window, startling her.

"Miss?" An older man's weathered face peered in at her, gesturing that she lower the window.

She pressed the button, but the car engine had been switched off too long. Sighing, she switched the car back on, and the engine shuddered back to life, along with the car accessories. The car window zipped down, releasing more coolness inside.

"Hey, missy. You seem to have a flat tire there."

"Yes, it seems I do."

"You gonna fix it, or hope an angel will come along?"

"I was planning on fixing it, but if you happen to know of any handy angels…"

He chuckled, then motioned her outside. "Come on. I'll help you."

Gratitude at his offer relaxed her tight smile into real. She hadn't planned on tire fixing when she'd dressed in her suede boots, leggings, and oversized orange sweater in Chicago's predawn darkness.

She popped the trunk and stared at the fabric-lined cavity. Where was the spare?

"Look under there," the man pointed to a corner.

She peeled it away. Lo and behold: the spare tire.

"You can change a tire, can't you, missy?"

The goodwill from earlier evaporated under a tide of feminist defensiveness. "Of course I can. My grandfather taught me when I first started driving."

"Your grandfather? Not your dad?" He peered at her more closely. "Hey, wait a minute, aren't you the Everton girl?"

"Anastacia Everton." She squinted at him, but her memory came up empty. "And you are…?"

"Mitch Wells. I used to teach at the high school. But that was a long while ago." He bent down and retrieved the mechanics kit, and drew out the jack and a lug wrench, the latter of which he handed to her. "Know how to use one of these?"

"Yes, sir."

He positioned the jack and wielded some muscle power to heft the vehicle higher. "There you go."

"Thanks." She squatted down and began working the first lug free as he drew out the spare.

"Jenny, my wife, taught English."

"Oh, I remember Mrs. Wells! She was my favorite teacher. I think I got my love of words from her classes."

He glanced over at her, brow creased. "That's right. Jenny has talked about you. Aren't you a famous author now?"

"Well, I don't know about famous." She flashed a smile. "In fact, I'm pretty certain I'm not."

"That's not what she said."

Well, everything was relative.

"Jenny said you live in the big smoke now." He snorted. "Never understood what it is with kids wanting to get away from here. God's own country, this is." He gestured to the snow-dusted trees and distant bluish hills.

"It's certainly very pretty, especially at this time of year."

"At any time of year."

Sensing he would not be particularly receptive to her reasons for leaving, she turned the conversation back to his wife. "How is Mrs. Wells these days?"

"Survived her second bout with breast cancer," he said proudly.

"Oh my goodness!" Guilt strummed. How could she not have known? "That must've been so challenging."

"It certainly hasn't been easy."

She pocketed the lugs, and eyed the tire, then eyed her hands. It had been a long time since she'd changed a spare. Oh well, it wasn't as if she really needed manicured nails…

He motioned her to move, which she promptly obeyed. She wasn't about to let feminist principles stand in the way of keeping warm and dry and clean. Men needed opportunities to feel good about their masculinity, after all.

"You have…" she paused, trying to remember as she rubbed her hands together briskly, "two sons, or is it three?" The Wells boys had always been a few years ahead of her at school. Church had been their only common circle.

"Was three. John got killed in the Middle East two years back."

Her heart wrenched. Poor, *poor* Mrs. Wells. Why hadn't she known? Oh, she knew why. Such was the price of wiping off the small-town dust from her wannabe designer-label clad feet. "I'm so sorry."

"Now we have Jem and Jeffrey."

"And what are they up to?"

"Jeff has married, and lives in Nebraska. Jem is just back in town after being away. Good to have him home." He tugged the wheel free with a grunt, then motioned for her to roll him the spare. Ice and rubber assailed her senses, eliciting a wince.

"I truly appreciate your help, Mr. Wells."

"Mitch, please. I've been retired these past five years." He pushed the spare into place, gesturing for the lugs then tightening them in place.

She collected the scattered tools as he shifted the flat tire to her trunk.

"There you go."

"Mr.—I mean, Mitch, thank you. I can't tell you how much I appreciate you."

He chuckled. "And I thought you were supposed to be good with words."

"Well, I suppose I could try." She eyed the nearby row of stores. "Is The Coffee Blend any good these days?"

"Not too bad."

"In that case, I'd love to buy you a coffee and muffin—unless of course you want an early lunch—and try to more fully explain the depths of my thankfulness, if you are interested." She grinned. "Or even if you're not."

Laughter rumbled from his chest. "I could be persuaded. But I have a better suggestion. I know Jenny would love to see you. How long are you in town for?"

Her smile grew strained. "A few weeks." At least until her

book was written. Then it was back to the big smoke to escape the small-town Christmas craziness.

"Then I hope you'll join us for dinner sometime soon."

"That'd be wonderful. But I feel you're the one doing me another favor."

He shrugged, smiled. "Never hurts to be a good Samaritan."

"At least let me buy you a coffee now to warm up."

"I wouldn't say no."

She retrieved her purse and beeped the car locked, joining him on the slippery sidewalk to where the coffee shop's twinkling lights beckoned.

The door opened, releasing a huff of caffeine-scented air. Instantly her taste buds kicked to overdrive, her stomach releasing a growl of anticipation.

"That sound reminded me of my boys," Mitch said with a laugh.

That sound reminded Staci that she'd skipped lunch after her obnoxiously early escape from the city. She glanced about her. The Coffee Blend was nothing like what she remembered. Instead of the 80s plastic vibe, the room was dressed in earthy tones, with timber floors, recycled painted chairs, and large polished wood offcuts as bar tables. The walls were lined with memorabilia: antlers, battered ice skates, and black and white photographs of long-ago Muskoka Shores. She drew closer, studying a print of a wooden shack with smoke curling from the chimney, positioned between two grand poplars. She'd seen that place before…

"Hey, Suzy. Look who I found. Muskoka Shores's own famous author."

Staci glanced up, moving to the counter which encompassed a refrigerated display case of cupcakes, muffins, cakes, and slices. Her stomach's protest rumbled again. "Hi."

"Sounds like someone needs a sugar fix." The blonde woman

in her fifties smiled. "Hey, I'm Suzy. I saw you seemed to be having some car trouble out there."

"I'm Staci." She gestured to the room. "Is this your café?"

"Sure is."

"It's fantastic. Really inviting."

"That's what we aimed for when we bought it five years ago." She wiped her hands on a cloth. "I saw you had a visiting angel before."

"Mitch was a godsend, for sure."

"He often is. Now, what'll it be?"

"This is my treat." Staci glanced at Mitch and raised a brow.

"Just my usual, thanks, Suzy."

"One TD coming up. And for you, precious?"

It must be the sense of cloying sweetness permeating the room that pricked her eyes. No one had called Staci by that endearment since her last visit in town. "I, er, oh…" She blinked away the moisture, tilted her chin and adopted an expression she hoped conveyed city cool. "What coffee flavors do you have?"

A plastic-sleeved menu was placed in front of her, and she studied the options. Pumpkin spice?

"Sorry, Suzy, better make mine to go." Mitch glanced apologetically at Staci. "I just remembered Jenny had asked me to pick up some things which I plumb forgot about."

"Oh, but—"

"Sorry, Staci, but I better scoot." Mitch nodded as Suzy handed him a to-go cup, which he collected with a murmured thanks. "Now don't forget about dinner. I know Jenny will be tickled pink to hear you're back in town. I'm sure she'll call you soon to arrange the details. You staying with your grandma?"

"Yes."

"Okay. Well, be seeing you both. Thanks, Staci." He lifted his cup in salute. "Much obliged. See you later, Suzy."

"Sure you don't want a pastry?"

"I do, but better not. Jenny's trying to keep sugar-free, and I don't want to lead her astray."

"Fair enough."

"Thanks again, Mr. Wells," Staci called.

"It's Mitch. And you're very welcome. See you around."

He held up a hand in farewell, then drew open the door, nearly colliding with someone coming in, where they stopped and exchanged greetings.

Staci sighed, returning her gaze to the coffee menu. What a friendly man Mitch Wells was. And she hadn't exaggerated before. She did thank God that he'd taken pity on her and deigned to help a lady out. When she looked up Suzy was smiling at her again. "Sorry. I seem to have lost all decision-making ability."

"No hurry."

Just as well. She bit her lip, wondering about the pumpkin spice flavor. Should she? Oh, for goodness sake! "A pumpkin spice latte please."

"Regular, tall, or grande?"

"Um, tall?"

"To have here or to go?"

So many decisions! She probably should have it to go. She was already later than what she'd told her grandmother. But she really needed some form of sustenance if she was to face the barrage of love sure to be her fate. "To go, thanks."

"And something to eat?"

She paced back to eye the delectable goodies on display, almost colliding with the newcomer, a man of curly dark hair, a five o'clock shadow, and a bemused expression who held up his hands. "Sorry."

"No worries." His voice was low, holding a rich, soothing timbre. No, holding *mellifluous* tones.

Since she'd been a little girl, certain phrases had called to her, begging her to remember. She closed her eyes. Mellifluous tones. She really should write that down. It totally matched the warm expression in his dark green eyes. And totally suited Fiona's hero.

"Miss?"

A touch on her arm jerked her eyelids open. "Oh!" What a fool she must look. Refusing to look at the man anymore she hastened back to the counter to where Suzy waited patiently. "And a chocolate croissant, please."

"As it comes or heated?"

What to choose? "Uh, heated would be nice, thanks."

"Coming right up."

Staci paid, then pivoted, nearly colliding with the man a second time. "Sorry." Heat flushed her cheeks as she refused to look at him, instead moving to the collections of pictures on the wall to study the cottage photograph from before, as a low-voiced conversation continued behind her. What *was* that wisp of memory?

A ding sounded.

"Staci?" Suzy called. "Here you go." She pushed a paper bag across the counter top toward her.

Staci hurried past the man who was looking at his phone and ripped the bag open. The scent of freshly baked chocolate croissant reactivated her hunger. She might have moaned as the first mouthful melted against her tongue.

The dark-haired man's mouth twitched, as if suppressing a smile. She raised her brows and turned away, as the sound of the coffee machine rumbled again.

"Those things will kill you, you know."

What?

The low tones she'd imagined might belong to her—no, *Fiona's*—hero came again as she shoved the last corner of pastry in her mouth. "Chocolate croissants are considered to be the number one food to avoid if one wants to live a healthy life."

He was talking to her? She swallowed creamy deliciousness and wiped either side of her mouth. "I beg your pardon?"

He smiled, his gaze descending to her lips, before meeting her gaze again. "Not from the sugar or the butter, but from the risk of choking when being eaten so quickly."

Was he teasing her? She was about to ask whether he worked in the health industry and was therefore qualified to make such assumptions when Suzy called, "One pumpkin spice and one tall, dark and handsome to go."

One *what?*

Ignoring the twinkle in Suzy's eyes, Staci thanked her and grabbed the coffee marked PSL on the white lid and hurried to the exit. If the coffee proved good, she suspected this place might prove handy to refuel her creative juices. She pushed open the door, conscious of Mr. Croissant-hater behind her, and met the icy breeze just as she took a sip of coffee.

Ugh. Her taste buds protested the lack of sugar, the lack of milk, the lack of anything but what tasted like pure unadulterated caffeine.

A choking sound behind swung Staci's gaze to the man who objected to her eating habits, whose wince seemed to mirror hers. "This is foul."

"No, *this* is foul."

He glanced at her, frowned. "Did you get my nearly black coffee?"

"Your what?"

"Did you get my coffee by mistake?"

She peeled off the lid and stared at the very dark brown contents. "What did you call this?"

He sighed, his breath making a huffing white cloud in the cool air. "It's Suzy's little joke. It's not black coffee because it's got a splash of milk, so she calls it a tall, dark..." his words, his gaze faltered.

"Tall, dark, and handsome, wasn't it?" How had those words

slipped out? Though that was what Suzy had said. Just because he fitted that description didn't mean... didn't mean *anything*. Heat renewed its dance along her cheeks.

Heat she felt sure matched the color filling his. "Suzi likes to tease." He shook his head and handed her his coffee, tinted a warm dark golden hue. "I think this is yours, Pumpkin Spice."

"Thanks." She eyed it. Took a sniff. Wait—what had he just called her? She frowned up at him. "Did you just call me Pumpkin Spice?"

His mouth twitched. "Maybe. Sorry. I'm caffeine-deprived so I can't be fully aware of what I say."

Again his gaze flickered to her mouth. Despite her misgivings, she knew, as any good romance author did, just what that meant. But seriously? He wanted to kiss her? They'd only just met. She didn't even know his name!

"Um, I think you should know..."

She didn't have time for this. He might have a lovely voice, and be handsome, in a rough-around-the-edges kinda way, but she had no interest in a small-town holiday romance. "Do you want your coffee then?" She held out the cup. "I've only taken one sip. One sip was more than enough."

"Do you have cooties?"

She blinked. "What?"

"Cooties. Do you have them?"

"Are you five-years-old?"

"No. I'm just health-conscious." His head tilted to one side. "So do you?"

"What, have cooties?"

"Or any other communicable disease?"

"No!"

He chuckled. "It's fine. You can have the rest."

"But it's disgusting. I don't want—"

"Oh!" Suzy burst through the door. "Oh, I think I muddled

your orders. I'm so sorry. Here, come back and I'll make you another one."

Staci glanced at her watch. "I really need to go."

"I can't believe I got it wrong." Suzy looked genuinely upset. "Please, next time you're in it's on the house. That *plus* a pastry. I can't have visitors thinking I don't know the difference between a latte and a long, almost black."

And Staci couldn't afford to get the locals offside. Not if she was going to stay here for a few weeks to get the manuscript done. "Sure. Thanks, Suzy."

"Thank *you*." She turned to the man. "And you, want your freebie now or later?"

"Later is fine," he said. For some reason his eyes were still fixated on Staci's mouth.

A surprised feeling of gratification—a feeling that feminist Staci should probably despise—swelled her chest. He must have the hots for her quite badly.

Suzy peered at her closely, then swatted his arm. "Really, James, what kind of gentleman are you letting a girl walk around with chocolate beside her mouth?"

What?

Staci slowly echoed Suzy's mimed wiping beside her lips, which revealed that yes, she did seem to be wearing some of the chocolate from her croissant... from how long ago? She forced out a gritty sounding laugh. Far from having the hots for her, he seemed only to have the knack to make her feel like a fool.

"Thanks a lot," she muttered. Her gaze shifted to Suzy. Probably wouldn't be back for the make-up coffee, after all. "I need to go."

"Sure, precious." Again that word pricked unwanted emotion. "Hope to see you soon."

Not if Staci could help it. She nodded, hurried to her car, and slammed the door, pride keeping her head stiff as she refused to glance at Mr. Croissant-hater, still watching her from his place in front of The Coffee Blend. She muttered a prayer of thanks when her car started without incident, keeping her gaze averted as she carefully drove onto the snowy street.

And saw, in the rear-view mirror, the dark-haired man swivel to watch her drive away.

REGRET CROSSED James's heart as he watched her drive off. Seriously? Suzy was right. How had he let the redhead go on speaking for so long with that drop of chocolate by her mouth? Except it had seemed more of a beauty spot than a smudge, something that begged him to pay attention to pink lips that seemed as quick to smile as pout, her words drawing an urge to banter, the repartee something he'd thought long days of hard work had rusted quite away. Not that he thought he'd managed the banter very successfully. Cooties? That was the best he could do? Not that it mattered. He really should not be thinking about a stranger he'd likely never see again.

James drove to the clinic for his afternoon session, and soon forgot her in his focus on patients who came with colds and boils and pains. The work was satisfying, and not too strenuous. More challenging cases could always be referred to Muskoka Shores's small hospital, where he worked the three days he was not rostered here. This was not like Africa. Poverty did not present in the same way, yet he noticed his role as listening ear remained the same.

A knock on the door preceded his call of, "Enter."

The receptionist, Anna Morely, poked her dark head in, her smile warm. "How are you doing, James?"

He dimmed back his own smile a notch. Anna was sweet and all, but the way she looked at him sometimes made him wonder if she hadn't read the handbook on workplace protocols. "Fine, thanks."

"Okay, well, your last patient is here. Miss Jemima Taylor."

He nodded. How he hoped this wasn't another of the eyelash-fluttering types who had visited in recent days, almost like they'd heard a new doctor was in town. "Send her in."

He braced as a murmur of conversation and soft laughter came from beyond the door, yet more proof of the small-town vibes that lent itself to personal exchanges beyond medically-related conversation. The door opened again and in walked a small redheaded girl followed by a woman, presumably her mother, who explained Jemima had been complaining of a sore throat. The little girl soon proved to also have a cute lisp, no doubt further embellished by her missing teeth. He bit back a smile at his earlier presumptuous thoughts.

"You look as though the tooth fairy has visited recently," he said.

The redhead nodded proudly. "I'm weally witch now."

"She means really rich," her mother whispered.

He vaguely recognized the woman from church. A glance at the file revealed her name: Rachel Taylor. He nodded and returned his attention to the small girl. "It's nice when tooth fairies are generous."

She shook her small head. "No, there'th only one."

"Only one—? Oh, only one tooth fairy, of course. My apologies," he said. "Now, open wide."

He peered inside her mouth, but there was no sign of tonsil redness, or anything that might construe illness. Just a sniffly nose, and an over-anxious mother. After taking her temperature, and asking a few more questions, he stood to wash his hands at the china basin in the corner and dry them before reseating himself.

"Now, Miss Jemima, I think you're going to be fine, but you need to stay warm." He glanced at the mom, tilting his head at the jar of candy, and received a nod. "Now, do you think you can manage to do that?"

Jemima nodded seriously.

"Do you think you might like a piece of candy?"

Her blue eyes lit. "Oh, yeth!"

He pulled out a wrapped candy and dropped it in her hand and glanced at the mother. "Don't worry, we have a reciprocal arrangement with the dentist up the road."

She chuckled and ruffled her daughter's red curls. "Now, what do you say to the nice doctor, pumpkin?"

He blinked, barely hearing the sing-song, "Fank you," and farewells as his mind backtracked to hours earlier, to another redhead. What was she doing? Would she remember him? He grimaced, remembering his all-too-charming small talk about cooties and the like. Yeah, she'd probably not forgotten, had probably decided to avoid him like the plague. How weird that the role that drew some people like a magnet led others to regard his conversation topics as a loss.

Oh well. She'd been cute, with her big eyes, flaming curls, and orange sweater. Stylish, too, which likely meant she had expensive tastes, like his sister-in-law, who'd drawn Jeff from an unpretentious background to workaholic to pay the bills. He'd never understand how someone could justify paying thousands for a pair of shoes.

He pushed back in his seat, scrubbed his hands over his weary face. How tired must he be to even be thinking like this? No. He needed someone grounded, someone who valued life as he did too. Especially now he knew how easily such life could be stolen away.

CHAPTER 3

He was a cad. A loathsome cad. She would never forgive him!

Lord Lucius drew near, dark eyes smoldering. Fiona lowered her lashes and turned away. She would not fall prey to his wicked ways, ways that were whispered in court as having resulted in more than one unfortunate girl being cloistered away for months on end. She would not fall prey to his advances. Even if his smile made her heart beat erratically, and his scent made her want to swoon. She would stay strong. She would be brave. She would be—

"Anastacia?" Gran's voice.

Staci pried open her eyes. The heavy drapes shrouding the room released the slightest rim of daylight. She shifted her head to the partly opened door, and the click of canine toenails on the tiles in the hall.

"Annie?" Her grandmother's abbreviation of Staci's name.

"Hi, Gran." Her voice was croaky, like she was a three-pack-a-day smoker. One would think her enormous drive yesterday would've meant a thorough night's rest, and it might've, if she hadn't stayed up way too late trying to corral each idea as they invaded her sleep.

"Breakfast is ready when you are."

"Thank you."

And so the smothering began.

To be fair, she had *loved* yesterday's reunion with Gran. It had been way too long since she'd been in town, and guilt had repeatedly stabbed deep as she recognized changes in the house, the yard, and the weathered features of her only relative. But the memories had not allowed for much peace, last night's tossing and turning as much about pain from the past as it was about promising story ideas. Thank God that Gran understood. Or at least said she did. Her graciousness these past years in allowing Staci to freely ignore home had proved a soothing balm. Especially on holidays and anniversaries she'd rather forget. But knowing Gran was gaining in years jabbed new awareness both that Gran might not see too many more, and that some might see Staci's flight from the past as more selfish than self-preservation. Not that she wanted to care about what people here thought. Though some of them, like Mrs. Wells...

She groaned, forced her body upright, and staggered from the bed. A quick shower later, a brush through tangled curls, clothes appropriate for writing and not being on show, and she padded out to the kitchen-diner, where Gran sat at the round table reading her Bible, Penny the poodle snuggled at her feet.

"Good morning," Staci murmured, pressing a kiss to her cheek. The scent of lilacs lifted from her grandmother's skin, a scent that drew renewed longing for what could never be again. How long had she missed the feel, the scent, of love? She wrapped her arms around Gran's shoulders, bent in a posture her yoga teacher would decry but which she knew was long overdue. Just breathing. Being. Two Evertons in this world. "I love you, Gran," she whispered.

Gran reached up and gently clasped Staci's arm. "And I love you. I'm so glad you're here at last."

"I am too."

For in the hustle-bustle of her crazy life, in the efforts that threatened Staci's hard-won independence, she knew underneath the heavy, at times smothering, blanket of her grandmother's loving affection lay another quality for which she yearned.

Peace.

She drew it in now, willing the calm of her grandmother to permeate the chaos cluttering her heart. How good it would be to return to Chicago with not only a finished manuscript, but a way of facing the new year with some peace. She sighed.

Gran patted her arm, and Staci eased from the embrace to slump into a wooden chair. As if jealous for attention, Penny whined at Gran's feet, which earned her a half-hearted pat, before Gran's attention fixed on Staci again.

"That sigh sounded serious."

Staci shrugged, eyeing the purple leather cover of the Bible. When did people first discover leather could be dyed? She forced her ever-curious thoughts to still, to focus.

"Want to talk about it?"

"It's nothing new." She met her grandmother's worried blue gaze with a self-deprecatory smile. "Just what I mentioned yesterday. I need to finish this manuscript, but I can't even decide what period to set it in, let alone what should happen. All I have is the heroine's name, and the knowledge that there needs to be a happy ending."

And the sound of the hero's voice. She blinked. Shoved that thought away.

Gran studied her, love in her eyes. "Annie, precious," again that word caused Staci's eyes to sting, "You can do this. You've done it many times before, you're so talented. Besides, I'll be praying for you."

"Thanks, Gran. I think I need it." Staci pushed back the chair with a creak. "I also think it's cup of tea time."

She moved to the kitchen, almost tripping over Penny as she

did so, garnering a small canine growl for her effort. Staci kept her own growl behind her teeth. Gran's fluffy, little new best friend hadn't exactly welcomed Staci's arrival, baring her teeth whenever they were alone. "I don't understand," Gran had said yesterday when that introduction had not gone as smoothly as envisaged. "Penny is always so placid with me."

Just as well she was, Staci thought, eyeing the pampered pooch. She didn't blame Gran for getting a companion dog; it was more evidence that she'd been lonely. Although now she remembered, Granddad had always expressed reluctance about having such a pet, claiming a dog would only chew the furniture and dig up his garden. Penny was just another sign of change.

She switched on the kettle; another difference. Gran had always used a stovetop kettle. Another new thing to get used to.

She fished out two English Breakfast teabags from the red Twinings box and fixed a bowl of cereal as the water boiled. She ate mechanically, eyes on the garden visible from the window above the kitchen sink. The conifers were bigger now, yet their perfect shapes remained the same. "Have you been trimming your trees, Gran?"

"Oh no, I have help for that. A local handyman comes every two weeks. Not in winter, of course, unless there is something in particular that needs attention. But it's been nice to know things are being maintained as they ought."

Guilt pierced again. She should have been here. Should have helped—

"Annie, please, don't feel bad you haven't been here. I know you needed time away. I'm just glad you're here now."

The rumble of boiling water drew attention then the kettle switched off. Staci's chest was tight as she poured the water into the mugs and watched the teabags stain darker. A splash of milk then she placed a mug in front of her grandmother. "It won't be so long next time."

"I'm glad."

Much more of this remorse and she'd be in too much of a mess to get anything written. She moved her empty bowl to the sink, rinsed it.

"Leave it. I know you have work to do."

"Thanks Gran." She pressed a kiss to the top of the white curls and picked up her tea and moved to the spare room, closing the door against the curious canine peering in the doorway. There came a whine, then a scratch on the door, followed by her grandmother's reprimand. Plonking down on the desk-chair, she opened up the laptop. Thirty new emails. Opened them. Delete. Delete. Delete. Save. Delete. Reply. Delete. Delete.

She really needed to unsubscribe more often to more emails. Or at least sort out her filtering processes. Her Mac gave a ping of notification. Facebook. She opened up her account and saw two comments from her last post. Only two? And—she peered at the screen—had the number of page likes fallen by five? What was happening?

A groan escaped. Social media was yet another space in which she felt inadequate. What happened to readers who just loved reading good books? Why did publishers seem to think readers needed to be lassoed into buying, or at least considering her books, or leaving a review, and could only be persuaded to do so with whimsical professionally-designed images and constant sell messages, messages that made her want to scream. She much preferred to connect with readers, to pose questions and respond to answers in a way she hoped felt genuine. It felt genuine to her. She really *did* care about her readers. Of course, someone like Davis Scott probably knew all the tricks of social marketing. He probably had Marco whispering in his ear just what he should tweet. Tweeting? Instagram? Ugh. Twits.

She shut down Facebook, making sure to switch off the notifications. She couldn't afford the distractions—or the comparisons and sense of inadequacy Facebook always seemed to evoke. How did someone get on the NYT bestseller list anyway? Surely Davis hadn't had that many preorders. Did Marco's name really hold that much influence? Maybe she should find a mentor, someone whose coattails she could ride until—

"Enough! You're acting like a child. Stop it." Talking to herself had always aided focus. "Now, let's get this done."

Staci opened up the document and stared at the page. Wrinkled her nose. What she'd written wasn't great. She slipped from her seat and retrieved the notebook she'd scribbled in last night whilst in her bed. Squinted, in a vain attempt to read her writing. Was her handwriting truly that bad, or did she now need glasses?

Despite feeling hopeful that she'd collected a few drops of gold whilst dreaming in the dark, nothing seemed to suggest that this morning. So she scrolled back and read from the beginning.

Yawned. Read some more. Took a sip of her cooled tea. Wondered about Facebook. Read another chapter. Propped her head on her hands. Glanced out the window. Reopened her email. Deleted two more vacation website invites she couldn't afford. Stared at the screen.

The words blurred, dissolved. Her head sank lower. Then jerked. This was ridiculous!

History had taught her the importance of maintaining 'butt in seat' while smashing out a first draft. But she'd always been excited about her previous stories and had always had a vague-to-precise idea as to what would happen in the end. But now...

Past stories floated through her memory. Historical romances that covered every period from King Arthur's court to WWII. Her publishers hadn't minded the varying eras; they'd just been happy she could produce stories so quickly. There'd been a few loose series among them: a three-book Georgian-era pirate family legacy, a two-book Tudor deal. Should she add a third? No. She'd never really cared for Henry VIII. Elizabeth? She shook her head.

"I can't do this."

Her email pinged again. Hadn't she turned it off? She clicked it open, heart sinking. It was like Bronwyn had her superspies out. Did she know how hard Staci was finding this?

Hi Staci,

Just sending a friendly reminder that deadline day is only three weeks away! I know you've spent your advance on those gorgeous new shoes, so we don't want to be obliged to miss your dates. Looking forward to seeing another wonderful manuscript soon!

Bron

Her shoulders slumped, pressure digging into her neck and head. She wasn't a machine. What did people want from her?

Another glance out the window revealed the sky was blue. Maybe she should hazard a run. Yes, a run would clear her head, and fuel fresh inspiration. It had worked in the past, hadn't it?

Within two minutes she had changed and was lacing up her Nikes. She gathered her phone, earbuds, cap, and sunglasses. Out in the kitchen she found her grandmother, Penny at her heels, writing on the sticky note shopping list attached to the fridge.

"Hey Gran, I'm going for a run."

"Have you been getting some good work done, then?"

"Not exactly. I just need to clear my head."

Gran nodded. "Of course, dear. Stay safe, then."

"See you soon."

She opened the front door, bracing as the cold air rushed her skin. Maybe she should have applied a second layer of moisturizer this morning. Maybe she should exchange this thin black hooded sweatshirt for something warmer. Oh well. A quick run and she'd be right.

Staci turned to the left, then slowly picked up her pace. How long since she had jogged? She probably needed to take things easy, especially with these temperatures. This wasn't exactly a treadmill in a warm Chicago gym.

But oh, how much prettier than any fitness center was Muskoka Shores.

She padded past the houses lining Gran's street, all single story cottages with gardens that hinted of yesteryear. She knew some of these were owned by city folk and used as weekenders or vacation rentals, but they had maintained the old-world charm with the picket fences and gardens that would look glorious in spring.

A turn to the right led into Maple, and the neighborhood that surrounded the high school. Breath exhaled in white swirls as she neared the administration block. Well she remembered the day in the principal's office, when the school counselor came to tell her—

She pushed the thought away. Concentrated on her pace. On her breathing. On the blood pulsing in her ears. On anything, except *that*.

The school athletics field drew near, along with the memories of weeks of running track, of discovering a twisted sense of joy in beating her body into submission, that she could control some things in life at least. She recalled the surprise lining Ms. Hewett's face, her gym teacher's astonishment that the nerdy bookworm actually could run okay, given a chance. The shock of her peers when they saw the same. They hadn't really known what to say when it had happened, and neither had she. Running and studying and planning her escape had proved effective enough walls. When she'd finally left town, nobody had tried to chase her, nobody had ever called. Her lips twitched. Of course, she hadn't made things easy, forcing Gran to keep her new contact details secret, to her grandmother's protest.

"But they are your friends. They'll want to stay in touch."

"They were my peers, not my friends, Gran. I want a fresh start with people who don't know me, who won't judge."

And Gran, God bless her, had not argued.

The tightness in her chest eased a fraction as she continued her stride. She glimpsed the lake framed by snow-laced trees, the gray clouds ensuring the lake looked as bleak as her chances of finishing her story today. She ran along the poplar-lined path, past a playground that seemed new, but was devoid of youngsters today. Not that she blamed them. Breath rasped to form pale puffs. It was really cold.

The path continued to edge the lake, but she veered away toward the commercial district. Interposed with residential blocks were occasional businesses: attorneys, architects, a medical practice. Staci glanced at the sign. Surely Dr. Lewisham had to have retired by now? But no. He was *still* there. Although —she squinted at the carefully handwritten sign—only working three days a week now. A Dr. Wells worked the other two.

Dr. Wells. She snickered. Who wouldn't hold high expectations of recovery with a doctor named that? Another name to add to her collection of career nomenclature. Not that she could see anyone called Dr. Sick being employed for long. Or Dr. Death. A chuckle escaped. Back in California she'd had a roommate whose dentist father held the unfortunate title of Dr. Meaney. For some reason he'd proved surprisingly popular.

An intersection made her pause, stretching out her legs as she waited for a big Ford truck to cross. She pulled her cap lower. She had no desire to be recognized any more than she already had. Her lips flickered again. Of course, if anyone was looking for her, her hair color swinging in a ponytail might give things away.

Once the road was clear, she hurried across, conscious the brief stop had allowed the slight burn in her chest to ignite. Not that she'd get sick. Her last asthma attack had been nearly two decades ago.

Two decades ago.

Swallowing the metallic taste in her mouth, she slowed her pace as she drew nearer the town's commercial heart. Storefronts she vaguely recalled were interspersed with newer businesses that seemed designed to favor tourists: a chocolatier, a store called 'The Nuthouse,' a vintage toyshop, a bar that promised the world's best gin and tonics. There was McPherson's pharmacy. The grocery store. The Fish and Chophouse. Her lips quirked. Cute. Each window held twinkling lights and Christmas decorations, though it was only the first days of December. But Muskoka Shores had always enjoyed the holiday season.

Dodging pedestrians, she rounded the corner to where the civic square was positioned, its bandstand overlooking the playground she'd passed earlier, and the lake beyond. A large spruce centered the space, no doubt destined to be decorated before the great tree-lighting ceremony began, a time when the Christmas festivities really notched up a gear. Something she'd be really pleased to miss.

Past the civic square she jogged along the road that curved to another stretch of storefronts. Brandi's Books & Gifts was swiftly followed by the scene of yesterday's car troubles. God bless Mitch, and Suzy, too, though she had no desire to step inside The Coffee Blend today. Not when she was sure to have a bright red face from exercise. And especially not when she might run the risk of bumping into Mr. Croissant-hater. Not that those two things were related in any way at all.

Stop it! She huffed out a breath. Think about the story. The *story*. Fiona. It was Fiona who needed a hero, not Staci. Fiona… who would be brave. Who would take on the men and beat them. Could she be a queen? A noblewoman? Yes. What about a noblewoman who had been mistreated because she was a woman, because men thought they could get away with such things? Then she returns…

But wait. To be a romance she'd need a hero. But not someone to rescue the damsel in distress. Staci had written so many of those stories and they always felt a little disempowering. Of course she knew women had very few rights in previous eras, but her previous research had revealed surprising tales of courage and rebellion against the status quo. Maybe Fiona could be a noblewoman disguised as a servant, someone able to fight her own battles, but who needed the hero's help to secure her true identity. Not that the hero should be her boss; she might need a happily-ever-after, but it didn't need to be too cliched.

Maybe she could shape it to be a gothic romance, something with a castle, and a moor—no, wait, it would be better located near the sea. Then maybe one of her pirate stories could be loosely linked, which could provide an excellent cross-promotion opportunity...

Excitement pulsed within. Her feet pounded the pavement. Now to get home as quickly as possible to capture this shimmering haze of possibility. She still didn't have a hero, but he would come. He always did. But her readers loved the strong heroines she presented, loved feeling like they could identify with her characters' flaws and triumphs. And Fiona would be one of her best. Feisty, but in the best possible sense. Not too pretty, or else readers found it difficult to relate. Not too sassy, otherwise she might come across as rude. But Fiona definitely wasn't a pushover. Principled, but not straitlaced. She'd have to have a good sense of humor, perhaps be quick with repartee. A chuckle escaped into the wind. Maybe she could finally write a story that her grandmother would approve.

Another jogger drew near, someone moving with more technique than speed. She lowered her gaze but offered a pleasant smile as he muttered a "hey," leaving a faint trace of Old Spice in his wake.

She coughed. A dull fire swept her chest. For a moment she

felt lightheaded. Surely she wasn't coming down with something? She jogged on, but soon slowed to a walk, rubbing at the pain surging through her side. A check of her phone map indicated she had two blocks to go. She could do this. Follow Elm, then turn into Maple and she was nearly there. She just needed a distraction, something to keep her from thinking about the pain in her legs and the stitch in her side.

Her story. *Fiona's* story. Fiona's hero. What should he look like? Complementary to Fiona's Celtic beauty—she would have to possess Irish or Scottish heritage with a name like that—or someone very different? Someone more Mr. Rochester-like, all impassioned fury, or should she aim for a sunshiny Mr. Bingley to contrast with Fiona's hidden pain? Who would suit her better?

Staci's last boyfriend had been her Scandi opposite, with blond tanned height to her auburn curves. They'd met at a bar, so it probably shouldn't have surprised her to learn Alex was at his most fun after a few drinks. Neither should it have surprised her when after a few more drinks he turned mean. It hadn't taken her long to realize he was someone who cared more about scoring sports tickets than remembering it was the day of her latest book release. Granted, book ten didn't exactly warrant the same celebration as that of her debut novel, but even after all this time it felt like her books were still a part of her, something she'd lived and breathed for months, and for Alex to ignore this part of her life had felt cold. Taking a leaf from her heroines, she'd eventually manned up enough to tell Alex they were done, their interests too disparate. The fact he had to ask her what that word meant sank the final coffin nail. She should have realized sooner, but maybe she'd been too needy. Regardless, she had no desire to be taken advantage of again. Nor for any of her characters to experience the same.

Fiona. Her hero shouldn't be too obvious, should probably be more Rochester-like, after all. Someone dark and complicated, whose motives might leave the readers guessing, someone who spoke in deep, melodious tones.

The signpost indicated Maple. Thank God. She couldn't wait to get home, to write this down, to let the words she could already feel itching to leap from her fingers finally run free. Having this run had been a great—

Pain sliced her leg, and she twisted to one side, meeting the icy ground with a loud "Ow!"

A vehicle screeched to a stop in the middle of the road. "Miss?"

She groaned, pushing herself upright, vaguely aware of a car door slamming, but mostly just aware of the tremendous pain in her ankle. Surely she hadn't twisted it again?

"Miss?" Low, mellifluous tones. "Can I help you?"

Her heart beat strangely. She glanced up. Behind her sunglasses' protective screen she saw him. "Tall, dark and handsome."

Mr. Croissant-hater's brow wrinkled then cleared. "Pumpkin Spice. I didn't recognize you dressed like a ninja." He offered her a hand to rise.

She accepted, standing with a wince. "And here I thought maybe it was the lack of chocolate smudges that made it hard."

"About that—"

"Ouch." She grabbed his arm for balance. "Sorry."

"You okay?"

"I'll be fine." She tried to walk. Gasped at the pain.

"Or maybe not. Here, sit down. Let me take a look at your ankle."

She didn't have the heart to argue so she obeyed, propping her sunglasses onto the top of her head. "Are you some sort of medic?"

"You could say that." He gently felt around her right ankle, his gentle prods eliciting a hiss of pain. "Hurts there?"

"Yep." She pressed her lips together to hide the wail. She'd embarrassed herself enough around this man. There was no need to add any more.

His gaze found hers again, and she was conscious this time of his long dark lashes, and the dark green eyes that today seemed filled with something that wasn't mockery or bemusement. If she didn't know better, she might think that expression could be called compassion.

"I'm sorry you're in pain," he said. "Here, let me take you to the medical clinic. It's not far away. I think your ankle will need to be wrapped, but it might be best to get it x-rayed."

But that would cost time she didn't want to waste and create a sense of obligation to this man she really didn't want. Not this man, with his disconcerting kindness after yesterday's hard-edged tease. "I'll be fine. I've sprained my ankle before so I know what to do. I'll RICE it and it'll be better soon."

"You sure?" He frowned.

"Yep. Thanks for coming to my rescue." She glanced over at his battered Ford truck, the driver's door flung open that blocked a car behind. "You better go before the natives get restless."

"Don't move. I'll be right back."

She watched him race to his vehicle, something that looked like it had passed its use-by date ten years ago, and, ignoring his advice, slowly pushed to her feet. She bit back a groan, and then swallowed another one, as he steered to the side, parked, and hurried toward her again.

"Hey, don't move." He laid a restraining hand on her arm.

She shook it off. "Thank you, but I'll be fine."

"Is this your house?"

"Yes," she lied.

"Funny. I could have sworn it belonged to the Thomases. I didn't know you knew them."

"I'm a second cousin, twice removed."

"Is that so?" He eyed her, his lips twitching in that irritating manner she recalled from yesterday. "It's just that you don't look much like the rest of the family."

"You shouldn't judge."

"Forgive me." He gestured to the door. "Should I see if they are in? It's strange you should collapse here and none of them come out to check on you."

"It *is* strange," she agreed, working to stifle a spear of panic. "But I promise I'll be fine."

"Still, I'd feel better to know you were in safe hands."

She watched in horror as he hurried to the yellow painted door and knocked. What if someone was in? What would she do now? Maybe she could hobble away, or at least hobble far enough away to hide behind a tree.

Before she could hobble anywhere the door opened, and there came the sound of voices, of greetings that suggested her unwanted rescuer really did know the house occupants. And then he shifted, and she saw why he had smirked at her comment about claimed heritage.

The middle-aged couple had skin as black as night.

CHAPTER 4

Fiona stilled. How had it come to this? Were her lies about to be revealed? How could she have ever thought her disguise safe?

Stop it! Staci screamed at the voices in her head, mind whirring as she wondered what to do.

He motioned to her, and she lifted a hand weakly. How to explain, how to explain…

They shook their heads, and her coffee shop nemesis thanked them, and drew close, smirking. "It's funny, but neither Gordon nor Ella claim to know you."

"It's not that funny really, because I don't."

He laughed, a warm, whole-hearted sound that trickled ease into the situation. "Really?"

"I think I might have been confused."

His mouth opened, as if he was going to say something, then closed. Wise man.

"Now I think about it, I'm pretty sure the house is on the next block."

"And will that be where we find your second cousins once removed?"

"Twice removed," she corrected meekly.

His eyebrows rose. "Truly?"

"No." She smiled at his look of confusion. "But it is where my grandmother lives."

Another chuckle escaped him. "And may I take you there? I know we've gotten off on the wrong foot, but I really don't want to see you further injured, just because I was ungentlemanly yesterday." He offered a smile that held a tinge of sheepishness. "Sorry about the chocolate smudges."

Her chin tilted. "I'm sorry, too."

His eyes widened. "Hey, I meant it when I apologized—"

"I'm sorry that I wasted such good chocolate when it would have been far better eaten." She swallowed a smile as relief washed his features. "Even if some people are prejudiced when it comes to certain pastries."

"I'm not prejudiced. I like croissants as much as the next guy."

"Unless the next guy is French, perhaps."

He laughed again. "You're kinda funny. Here, let me get the door."

She hesitated. So she wasn't twelve, but stranger danger did still matter to a girl, even if she hadn't been a girl for two decades. Serial killers lived under the radar, had neighbors and friends who spoke on the news saying just how much they'd never suspected John or Jim or Harry could have ever done such a thing.

"Do you want to call someone to get you?"

Mental head slap. Why hadn't she thought of that? But calling Gran to come collect her when she was only a block away seemed so silly, would put her grandmother to such trouble… "It's fine." Conscious that sounded ungracious, she added, "Thank you for the offer, Mr.…?"

"Call me James."

James. What a perfect name for Fiona's hero! Maybe she

could set her story in Scotland. Not every Scottish hero needed to be called Angus, after all. Speaking of her story, she *really* needed to get back to it. She had so much new material to write down after all.

She glanced at him. He was still studying her, with that lazy amused expression she recognized from yesterday, like he didn't know what to make of Klutzy Girl. She had definitely gotten off on the wrong foot. Or feet. A chuckle escaped.

"What?"

"Nothing." Nothing worth repeating, anyway. "Thank you, I would appreciate your help, James."

"Okay." He opened the passenger door for her and she slid inside with the grace of a newborn giraffe as she tried not to put pressure on her ankle. He shut it carefully, leading her to wonder if maybe he had gentlemanly tendencies after all, and moved into the driver's seat. The cab was clean and smelled slightly of spiced oranges. She closed her eyes. Bergamot. That should be his signature scent. That way Fiona could recognize him even when—

"If you'd like me to take you somewhere you need to tell me where it is."

Her eyes flew open. He must think her a dunce as well as a klutz! She peered across at him. "You mean you don't have telepathic powers?"

Half grin. "No."

"Well, in that case you'd better just take me to the next street."

"Certainly, ma'am."

She bit her lip. Did she sound too officious? Why was it she could arrange her characters' lives so well, but understanding the subtleties of real people was so hard? You'd think exploring the complexities of the human condition for so many years would make her better at this.

He drove smoothly, two turns barely enough to study him or

think of what to say so she didn't sound quite so bossy. So she kept quiet, taking in his details. He must be mid-thirties at least, his clothes seemed to hold a casually professional vibe, and now she noticed it, the five o'clock shadow from their previous encounter definitely wasn't making an appearance today. He looked much smarter. She peeked at his hands. Definitely no wedding ring.

He glanced across and she pointed halfway along. She didn't want to give him her grandmother's address in case all this solicitude was designed to give false assurance of his 'safe' status before the kidnapping. Or worse.

The vehicle slowed, stopping outside Gran's neighbor's house. "This you?"

"Yes, thanks." Near enough, anyway. She opened the door. "I should let you go. I'm sure you have things to do. Thank you again."

"No problem. Promise to remember to rest, ice, use compression and—"

"Elevate my ankle, yes, I promise. And if it doesn't improve I'll seek medical attention."

His brows rose in skepticism, but he only said, "Well, it's been nice to see you again, Miss...?"

But she didn't want to give him her name. Granted, he didn't look like one of the serial killer types, but they didn't exactly go around advertising their occupation, did they? Hence why they were *serial* killers.

"I thought you knew my name."

His brow wrinkled.

"It's Pumpkin Spice, remember?"

And with a smile and a gentle slam of the door she limped her way to the drive, before turning to wait for him to leave.

He studied her a moment longer, before finally putting the vehicle in motion. She lifted a hand in farewell, willing him to drive away. The last thing she needed was for the Changs to come out on their front lawn to prove she'd fibbed again.

The truck turned around the corner and she hobbled across to Gran's house, knocking on the front door before discovering it was unlocked. Really, how could Gran live this way? Didn't she know there were bad people out there?

"Hi, Gran. I'm back."

Staci winced as her ankle made its presence felt again, and limped to the freezer, grabbing a handful of ice, and wrapping it in a tea-towel. It'd be best to get this sorted before Gran had time to worry.

She hurried to the spare room, sat down on the bed, and was carefully removing her shoes and biting back the cry of pain when Gran appeared in the doorway, Penny scampering at her feet. "What's happened? Are you injured?"

"Just a slight sprain. I'll be fine."

"I'll get some bandages, and maybe some of the tiger balm ointment Mrs. Chang recommends."

Resistance was futile. "Thank you."

Within ten minutes, Staci's ankle was bound, iced, and propped up on a small cushion, and she was trying madly to write down all the details she remembered from her productive morning excursion. She might not have too much of a plot just yet, but she had the essence of her lead characters, and it was always in their histories that a story could be found.

WHAT SEEMED like just minutes later, but a glance at the clock revealed was actually over an hour, Gran was knocking on the door, asking if she'd like a sandwich. "I'm not too hungry, Gran." These creative spurts meant she often lost weight as she tried to grasp the elusive tendrils of imagination. It was editing that always brought her health goals undone, with chocolate a very necessary addition to sweeten her editor's razor-like comments.

"A nice cup of tea, then?"

"That would be wonderful, thank you."

Within a short space of time a fragrant cup of hot tea was placed on the bedside table beside her. "Thanks, Gran."

The feathery lines beside her eyes crinkled as she smiled. "I'm glad you're finding your time helpful again."

"Me too."

"See? Prayer works."

"Yes." Well, maybe Gran's prayers worked. Staci didn't remember actually praying about this at all.

"Speaking of prayer, I was hoping you'd want to join me tomorrow at church. Now, before you say anything, I know you're busy, but I really think it would be nice for you to see some of the people who remember you from years ago. They're always asking me how you are, and it would be wonderful if you could say hello. We needn't stay too long after if you don't wish."

More of the silken noose of obligation. But she had to get these ideas written down now. "Sure."

Gran's look of surprise melded into relief then delight. "I'm so glad. Very well, I know you're busy. I shan't disturb you any longer. If you want dinner, I plan to eat at six, but if you don't come out it can be reheated as leftovers."

"You're so good to me, Gran."

"I love you, Annie."

"I love you, too."

Gran pressed a soft kiss into Staci's hair, the tenderness sparking memories and the heat of tears. Staci's smile felt a little wobbly as her grandmother gently closed the door. Gran was so good to her, letting Staci stay, cooking her meals, taking care of her. Such things were markers of real love.

Real love.

She eyed her scribbled notes that now filled half an exercise book. Maybe she could twist this story even more and have the hero's affection proved not in his physical prowess, but through his actions of care and concern for Fiona. Her readers usually expected the formula of the first kiss at the quarter mark, with escalating degrees of passionate encounters at regular intervals after that. But what if she withheld all that and forced Fiona and James to focus on really caring for each other and kept things really sweet. That might well send Max and Bronwyn into a tailspin—although she suspected Bronwyn never read the entirety of her manuscripts anymore—but it would be a way of honoring a woman who had enjoyed fifty years of marriage with a husband who had cared for her in a similarly demonstrable way.

"I don't want cheap," Granddad had said on more than one occasion. "And I don't want disposable. When I said my vows I meant it, for better or for worse, in sickness and in health. And keeping my promises to Rose and to God has been for the better, let me tell you, even when it's been hard."

Like when their only son had died with Staci's mother in the plane crash.

Staci shook away *that* memory, focusing instead on her grandfather who had instead proved his love for Gran in a million different ways, ways she'd witnessed when she'd come to live here in her sophomore year. The rose garden he'd built for Gran. His encouragement of Gran in her various crafting projects. "See this piece, Annie?" he used to say with his slight Irish accent. "Isn't your Gran simply grand?"

Heat moistened her eyes. He used to say that about her, too. "Oh, Annie, that's grand," he'd say when she'd come home with a first in an exam or an A on a paper.

Such statements had gone some way to easing the pain shrouding her soul.

How she missed him.

Shaking off the emotion, she returned her attention to her story, mind ticking, ticking, ticking. Perhaps her grandparents' attitude of self-sacrifice and encouragement should lead to the significant plot points, the grand gestures of love rather than the cheap gestures of desire. She chewed her lip. This could work. She could feel it. But what would her readership and publishers say?

~

"Hey, James, how are you?"

"Brandi," he nodded to his brother's former fiancée—or was she more his former brother's fiancée?—and then sent his mom a surreptitious eyebrow rise to which she shrugged, as if replying, "I don't know why she's here, either."

Still, Mom could never turn away a stray. Especially the girl who had been part of John's life for many years. Maybe Brandi thought by staying entwined in their family it somehow kept him alive. Or maybe the blonde's regular visits were a habit from which she'd yet moved on. Although—he frowned—it had been two years since John's death from an IED. How long was too long?

"How was the clinic today?"

He sank onto the kitchen stool, snatched up a carrot straw. "Busy."

He was tempted to mention the incident with Pumpkin Spice, but didn't, hugging that bit of news to himself a little longer. He had no desire for Mom to conjecture, nor for Brandi to insist on details, as seemed to be her way.

Another exchange of glances with Mom, then she turned to Brandi. "So, Brandi, are you joining us for dinner tonight?"

"That'd be great, Jenny. Thanks."

He drilled Mom with a stare that only made her smile and

move away. He suppressed a sigh as the other stool was soon occupied.

"How was work today?"

"Oh, fine." Brandi started to chatter about some of the window displays at the bookstore—apparently the local chamber of commerce was sponsoring a contest for the best Christmas display. Politeness was a strange balance between interest in the person and feigning interest in stuff he had no interest in at all. Not that he wanted Brandi to think he was too interested in her. Or even interested at all. That would be too weird.

"…don't you agree?"

Shoot. "Agree to what? Sorry, it's been a big day."

Brandi's engagement ring flashed in the overhead lights. "Oh, never mind. I know you're not much of a reader."

True. He'd always been too busy studying or working to have much time for fiction. Although after the past few years he could understand the appeal of escaping reality.

His dad's return put paid to more fiction-based conversation, as his parents discussed the return of another of Mom's former students—another topic of little appeal. His parents had taught so many students over the years he'd be hard-pressed to know or care about most of them.

"Oh, that's wonderful! Rose must be so pleased."

His dad's low rumble continued. "…invite to dinner sometime."

"Oh, yes, we must do so." His mother glanced at James.

Uh oh. He'd seen that look before and had no desire to be set up. Well, whenever his mom issued such a dinner invitation, he'd have his excuse set. And simply be too busy.

CHAPTER 5

Fiona walked down the aisle, head held proudly, eyes fixed firmly on the front. She would not give a moment's satisfaction to those who must be wondering how she dared walk into such a place. Hadn't she betrayed them all? Didn't they all believe that she had traded goodness for evil, her actions allowing blackness to creep over the land? Perhaps she was a fool, but she hoped this place would still remember its duty as a sanctuary, a place of respite, a place where one could find a tiny grain of peace...

Nerves roiled through Staci's stomach as she made her way down the aisle. She hadn't stepped inside a church in years. Hadn't stepped inside *this* church since Grandad's funeral. Returning stirred a mix of bittersweet memories of her youth group days with the harder, harsher ones, those moments that had encased her heart in cold pain, memories that had eventually subsided to disinterest.

She wobbled, ankle paining, in Gran's wake to the pew Staci recalled from decades ago. Some things never changed. The carpet certainly hadn't, although it looked like it needed updating years ago. And a paint job wouldn't go astray. And while the musicians looked four decades younger than what she

"

remembered, the melody they played held notes of familiarity. She moved past gossiping congregation members, her chin raised, her lips lifted, to not give Gran any reason for doubting her earlier assertion that she was fine. But her ankle *really* hurt. She'd be hard pressed to keep the façade from splitting if she didn't find a seat soon.

"Ah, Rose, how lovely to see you." A woman Staci was sure she'd never seen before clasped Gran's hands with a gentle shake, before her attention slid to Staci. "Oh, don't tell me, you must be Anastacia."

She forced her cheeks up to approximate a smile. "Hello."

The gray-haired woman leaned forward. "I'd recognize that lovely auburn hair anywhere. You know you have your mother's eyes."

What? How could this stranger—

"I'm Dorothy Hollis. My granddaughter Anna lives on Rose's street. I think you went to school with her." The name rang no bells. "She's usually here in services—oh, look! There she is now." Dorothy pointed to a brunette laughing with four other women, one of whom held a baby.

Staci's chest clenched. They looked like the kind of tight-knit group she'd never known. She kept the smile pasted on.

"Anyway," Dorothy continued, "I'm one of your grandmother's prayer partners. I've seen your pictures in her living room."

That last posed photo of her parents with Staci, taken when she had a bad haircut and scowl to match her teen attitude, in pride of place centering the fireplace mantlepiece. Such a contrast to the photo next to it, a publicity shot taken two years ago, artfully designed to make Staci look younger and thinner and highlight her Celtic coloring of red, white, and green. Yep, kinda hard to miss.

"You've certainly been the subject of quite a few prayers, my dear."

Wonderful. Staci murmured something appropriate before

eyeing her grandmother with raised brows. Gran flushed a little, murmuring a "sorry" as Staci shifted past her to take her seat further away from the aisle—and Dorothy. Gran's conversation with Dorothy resumed, leaving Staci free to focus on the church bulletin. A welcoming message from the pastor, someone whose name she didn't recognize, but whose words conveyed friendliness. Notices about an upcoming ladies' Christmas lunch. A playgroup. Expressions of interest in forming a young adults group. Memories flickered of the one and only time she'd attended youth group, back on a day when she'd felt foolishly brave. What had happened to the others? Did they still believe? She peeked behind her. Were any of them here? Was Hope still dyeing her hair blonde? Had Dwight ever found a sense of humor?

Curious eyes soon returned her attention to the front. Would anyone here recognize her? How many attended now? Did they still accept high school seniors or was it more aimed at young professionals now? She was still under 35, so she could attend, if she wanted. Which she didn't. No way in—she glanced at the empty cross gracing the sanctuary and swallowed her first response—heaven.

A scan of other items listed the church's involvement in various outreach programs and missions. For a small town this seemed to be a thriving church, enough that they could justify an assistant pastor. Maybe that's where their money went, instead of fixing up the place. Which was good. How it should be. Probably what Jesus would do. If she'd found a church like this in LA or Chicago then maybe she would have gone more. Her lips curled. Well, very likely there had been churches like this that seemed to practice what Jesus preached, but after her first couple of half-hearted attempts, she hadn't bothered trying any more.

The rustle of people moving into the seats behind was soon drowned out by a man in his late fifties who introduced himself as John McPherson, the pastor, and then welcomed people to the service. Apparently, today was the second Sunday of Advent. Who knew?

He began to pray, and she closed her eyes, listening as he spoke. This pastor also had mellifluous tones, a soothing quality that took the edge off her earlier irritation with Dorothy and helped the tumble of her heart find a foothold of ease. He sounded like he knew God in a way Staci had always longed for. Probably it was the effect of being in ministry. One *should* expect a church minister to be on good terms with God.

"Amen."

She echoed it weakly, then grasped the pew in front to help her stand. Stifling the wince, she gave Gran a gritted smile of reassurance, and focused on the song being played. She didn't recognize the melody, so could only mouth along with the words. Fortunately, the people behind had enthusiasm to spare and could drown out her pitiful efforts. Why did songwriters make their songs so hard to sing? Surely not every song needed two key changes and the vocal range of Mariah Carey.

The words flashed up to a second song, one whose words and tune she did vaguely recognize: a Christmas carol about shepherds and angels singing from on high. It was a key a tad too on high for her, and for most of the congregation judging from the way the general volume dimmed in the chorus, though the enthusiastic congregation members behind her didn't seem to mind singing out of their range.

At the song's conclusion they were invited to sit, and after a couple of Bible readings the sermon began. As Pastor McPherson continued speaking, her attention wandered around the room as she eyed quilted depictions of Bible verses hung on the walls, the trails of a ceiling cobweb dancing softly in the push of heated air, the heads of congregation members concentrating—as she probably ought. She returned her attention to the front, listening as he spoke about the gift of the first Christmas, and what the 'Christ' in Christmas really meant.

"It's the gift of life, the gift of hope, something we can all experience anew each day."

Something within her tugged to respond afresh as he prayed. She needed hope, needed life. Or at least her story did, though she could probably do with some herself, too.

"Amen."

She mouthed the word and took a second to realize the others were already on their feet. She dragged herself to a standing position as the musicians ascended the stage and began the opening strains of a very familiar melody.

Amazing Grace. Now this was a song written by someone who knew something about music and congregational singing. She'd included a slave trader in one of her pirate books, and research had taken her to a website about John Newton. What an amazing life he'd led. It wasn't any wonder his words held such profound meaning for so many people over hundreds of years.

The music continued, the congregation singing wholeheartedly, as the words ascended to the heavens. *I once was lost but now am found, was blind but now I see.*

She bet her next contract that Gran was hoping those words would prove apropos for Staci. Probably that's what she and Dorothy and the rest of their little praying club had been doing this past however many years long. Staci knew how these things worked. She'd been in church—in this church—before.

The music concluded, and another prayer was prayed by a younger handsome man, before announcements were given followed by a final song she didn't recognize. This seemed to be the offertory song, one where two older men passed plates around, so the congregation could see who gave and who didn't. Her lips twisted. No pressure there. Should she give something? Would that be hypocritical? It wasn't like she never gave to charities; she had even once participated in a charity fun run for cancer patients. Besides, she rather thought God was big enough to not need her scraps of an offering.

The plate passed by, the bearded gentleman giving her a mild look of reproach. Finally the song finished, and they were released with a blessing to be a blessing. Her lips curved. The biggest blessing would be to get out of here as soon as poss—

"Well, how did you find the service, Annie?" Gran asked.

"It was, er, good."

Gran smiled in a way that suggested she didn't quite believe her, but said nothing more, simply moving to greet the couple turning from in front of them. Staci followed her unspoken command and tried to look interested as Gran introduced them: Joel Wakefield, the man who'd prayed before—the assistant minister, apparently—and Serena Williamson, one of the laughing women from before.

Serena's eyes flashed with recognition. "Of course! You were ahead of me at school."

She was? "That feels like a lifetime ago," Staci said. A lifetime that still felt too close.

Not that it mattered. As soon as she finished writing this story she'd be leaving this town. Again.

"I remember now. My former roommate loved your books," Serena said kindly.

Staci's smile grew wry. Serena's roommate had. Not Serena herself.

"That's right," Joel said. "I think my sister has some of your books too."

Huh. Well, one didn't expect an assistant church minister to admit to that. Maybe people weren't as quick to judge here as she'd thought.

"Well, if it isn't our famous author."

Staci's shoulders dropped, her smile relaxing into genuineness as her rescuer from her arrival appeared. "Hi Mr. Wells."

"It's Mitch, remember?"

His grin evinced her own, as she peered behind him. "Is Mrs. Wells with you?"

"Not today. She wasn't feeling too well this morning and needed her rest."

Staci joined the others in offering sympathy. "I'm looking forward to meeting her again soon."

"Well, that offer for dinner still stands." His brow furrowed. "I think we're pretty clear this week so pick the day and we'll make it happen. I know Jenny's eager to catch up with all the news about her famous student."

Another woman Staci had been introduced to before—whose name she'd already forgotten—leaned forward interestedly. "Excuse me, but did I hear Mitch say you were a famous author?"

Staci managed a laugh. "Not famous, but yes, I'm an author."

"And what sorts of books do you write?"

None that should be mentioned in a church. "Historical fiction. Romances, actually."

"Oh, I love romances! I'll have to look you up."

"I, er," how to explain she wrote for the general market, so some of the content might be considered a little objectionable? "Um, don't be too put off by the covers," she felt it necessary to say.

"Oh." The look of disappointment on the woman's face stiffened Staci's smile back to artificiality. Looked like she wouldn't make that sale any time soon.

"We best be going," Gran said, as if embarrassed by Staci's admission.

Yes, that was probably best.

"Don't forget to let me know when you can come for dinner," Mitch said. "I'm sure Rose has our details."

"Will do. Thanks again."

Staci nodded goodbye and followed Gran into the aisle,

forcing her expression to pleasantness as Gran stopped innumerable times to introduce her, almost as if she thought Staci would be staying long term and she needed to know everyone's life story and how they fitted in the great web of church relationships. Maybe when they got out of here Staci should sit Gran down and tell her straight that she could only stay long enough for this story to be written. She didn't want Gran being hurt by unmet expectations.

They'd reached the door now, where the church minister stood shaking hands. What would he say when he learned what she did for a living? Nothing good, she bet.

A voice several congregants behind arrested her attention, drew Staci to glance over her shoulder. Her coffee swap inveigler stood there, looking far more handsome than the last time she'd seen him, smiling down at a perky blonde who had her body pressed against his side.

Well! Look who had a girlfriend. Or a wife. She glanced away quickly before he noticed Staci's interest. Not that she was interested. Not that it mattered in the least. Except if Staci had a boyfriend, she certainly wouldn't want him acting almost flirtatious with another woman. Is that what he had been?

Staci peeked back, and encountered those dark green eyes she remembered, those dark eyes now widening in surprise, before one eye closed in a wink. Her pulse spiked, and if she hadn't been a twenty-first century woman she would have blushed. She turned her head away, ignoring the strange thudding sensation pounding through her bloodstream, and forced her thoughts to her previous ruminations. Was he a flirt?

She thought back over their past encounters and was trying to recall exactly what had been said both verbally and non-verbally, when she became aware that Gran was introducing her to Pastor McPherson, who had his hand outstretched expectantly.

"Hello, Miss Everton," he said. "Welcome to Muskoka Shores Community Church."

For some reason his welcome bothered her. "It's not exactly my first time here," she said. "I used to come all the time when I was younger, but not since I moved away."

"Oh," his eyes widened—had she been too abrupt?—then he said, "Well, it is good that you are back then."

"Christmas is the season for miracles," she murmured, adding a smile she hoped counted for nice points, then followed her grandmother to another room where the introductions continued among cups of coffee and cookies, leaving her jaw sore with the effort of all those smiles. Mr. Coffee was nowhere to be seen, nor was Mitch. Conscious of a mingling sense of something that felt a little like disappointment and a lot like relief, she refocused on the conversations around her. Finally they were released and she followed her grandmother to the car.

"Thank you my dear," Gran said. "It was wonderful to have you there at church, feeling like a family again."

Remorse struck anew. She should have come back more often. Even if Staci's work demands meant they'd never be the cozy family unit Gran seemed to want. Those days were long gone.

After lunch, she squirreled away in her room, tapping furiously to get the day's impressions in her computer before the sights and sounds faded. Not that she would directly transpose today's events to her story, but that feeling when she saw Mr. Coffee with his arm around the girl—*that* feeling—she wanted to capture. How would Fiona feel if her hero succumbed to the charms of a fair maiden? Would it feel similar to this churn in her chest? She closed her eyes and imagined, willing the emotions to rise, to fully form. How would she feel if the man she dreamed about had eyes for another? What did betrayal feel like?

Fiona stood, watching as Lord Markworth smiled down into the blue eyes of the petite blonde beauty. A savage kind of pain roared across her chest. How dare he look at Gwendolyn that way? Her fingers clenched. He should be hers!

Her eyes snapped open, and she hurried to tap out her thoughts on the keyboard, working to capture the emotion and not lose a drop of feeling, all the while conscious that underneath was this niggling question as to why thoughts of Mr. Coffee had elicited thoughts of belonging and betrayal at all.

∼

"It's good to finally have a chance to talk," Joel said over dinner that night after church.

"Thanks for the invitation." James pushed back his plate and eased back in his chair, grateful for the chance to connect with someone nearer his age, whose offer of friendship wasn't merely rooted in the past, with whom he could be as real or as filtered as he chose to be. The conversation had been easy so far: sports, church, family. James had learned the assistant pastor was fairly new to the area, having moved here in July with his sister, an artist. She—and her baby—were out with friends, including Joel's girlfriend, Serena.

"Your parents mentioned that you're back here on leave."

"For six months." Unless his break proved longer than that, and he was discharged permanently.

"And you're working at the hospital and clinic?"

He nodded. "Dr. Hollis has been gracious to allow me to work here in the interim. It helps that he's known me for years. One of the perks of small-town life, I suppose."

"Are you enjoying it?"

James straightened his knife and fork. "I suppose I am. To be honest, I didn't think I would too much at the beginning, but I gotta admit it's nice to be somewhere where I don't have to worry about whether I'll be shot at, or whether the clinic will be burned down."

Joel's eyes widened. "When you put it like that then life must seem pretty tame here by comparison."

"Not tame, exactly," he said, recalling the thudding of his pulse when he'd been grabbed by Pumpkin Spice yesterday, something that might have left fingernail indents in his skin but also an impression that here was someone he'd like to further know. An impression only heightened when he'd seen her at the service today and experienced a kick to the heart that made him realize just how opposite to dull his stay here could be. He'd looked for her later, until an emergency page had taken him to the hospital, delaying his meal with the assistant pastor until now.

"And when do you return to Africa?"

"*If* I return," he corrected gently. "That depends on the board and their assessment of my emotional functional capacity."

"Ah, I see." Joel looked at him, sympathy lining his features. "It's hard to wait on the unknown."

James nodded, then started sharing about the list of incidents that had led to his enforced "mental health break," something he'd loathed to comply with, but now could see he'd desperately needed. It wasn't normal for a man to wake with night terrors, bracing against possible compound invaders. It wasn't normal for a doctor to carry a concealed weapon, in case of robbery. Not in Muskoka Shores, anyway. The burnout that had beckoned while working long shifts days on end in city hospitals had only grown exponentially by these past years of tension, both with work and family suffering. "It's actually nice to feel I can breathe here," he admitted. And feel like the sharp edges of his fear were slowly smoothing away.

"And maybe think God still has good things in store for you?"

"Maybe," James said. "Christmas is the season for miracles, after all."

"That it is," Joel agreed, his mouth curved as if thinking of his own miracle. "Well, I'll be praying for you."

James offered his thanks, and soon left, but couldn't help wondering what had caused the twinkle in his pastor's eye.

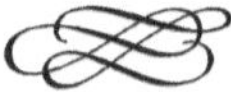

iona stood atop the battlements, gazing at the scene below her. Now she knew that all men were fickle, that none could be trusted, she needed to secure a marriage that would bring security, both political and financial. She would not throw herself away on a man due to misguided notions of love. Such things were for commoners, not for the daughter of a king. Her lips twisted. Even if the king refused to acknowledge said daughter…

The words were flowing now that Staci had a greater sense of place and purpose. These past four days—well, three and a half, actually—she'd forced her backside to remain in her chair hour by hour as she tapped out nearly thirty thousand words. At this rate, she'd be well and truly done by Christmas Eve, and would even have time for a pass or two to review and edit. It had helped that Gran had basically let her be, only rapping on the door occasionally with reminders of a meal. These she basically inhaled, more out of desire to get back to her writing than from any real hunger; she had little appetite for food when in the midst of creative throes and hated to lose the headspace of her characters. It could be so hard to wrestle back.

And the story had to get out. *Had* to. She could feel it inside her like a living being, clawing its way to escape. It always amazed her that the faintest breath of an idea could so quickly take on form and substance, given enough time and space. If only her fingers worked as fast as her thoughts flowed. If only—

"Annie?" Gran's muffled voice came through the closed door. "There's a phone call for you."

Staci groaned. How many times had she asked Gran to hold her calls? She frowned. Actually, maybe she hadn't asked, as she hadn't really thought she'd need Gran to. Nobody knew where she was staying or knew her grandmother's phone number. All her city friends and work colleagues would contact her cell, or via messenger or email, all of which she'd conscientiously switched to mute. So who could be calling her now?

She pushed back her seat and padded barefoot through the thick carpet and opened the door. As if recognizing her foe, Penny bounded along the tiled hall, barking madly.

"Stop it," Staci commanded, in a voice she hoped conveyed alpha-dog status.

Which obviously didn't work as Penny kept yapping.

"Penny!"

The dog quieted at Gran's voice, enabling Staci to move toward the phone.

"Who is it?" she murmured as Gran handed her the phone.

"Jenny Wells."

"Oh!" She lifted the phone to her ear, smiling a thank you at Gran who disappeared to her sewing room, Penny trotting self-importantly at her heels. "Hello, Mrs. Wells."

"Anastacia Everton, oh how good to hear your voice!"

Staci closed her eyes, as memories of high school English flooded in. Times of solace. Times of feeling a rare sense of worth. So much had gone wrong in her world, but English always had a way of making things a little bit more right.

"Mitch told me you were in town, and I was so sorry to have missed you on Sunday. How are you, dear?"

"Fine, thank you. It's good to hear your voice, Mrs. Wells."

"Oh, Jenny, please. Now, Mitch tells me you are planning to come for dinner."

Guilt streaked across her chest. "Well, he mentioned it, and I was planning on it, but I'm afraid it kind of slipped my mind. I've been a little busy, so I'm very sorry I haven't contacted you before."

"No problem at all," Mrs. Wells soothed. "I just wanted to find out what day might suit you."

Staci thought about what remained of her week. If she could finish the scene today then maybe... "Would tonight work at all?" No, that was too last minute. "Or tomorrow night?"

"Tonight is fine. I'm planning gravy beef. I hope that's okay. You're not vegetarian or have any food allergies, do you?"

"No, I'm pretty easy to please. Grateful for anything I don't have to cook." She winced. That didn't sound especially gracious, did it?

"Wonderful. You remember where we live?"

"Yes."

"Then is six-thirty okay?"

"That would be fine. What do you want me to bring?"

"Please don't bring anything, just yourself."

They ended the call, and Staci returned the phone to its cradle above the microwave. "Jenny Wells asked me to dinner tonight."

Gran looked up from her knitting magazine, her face brightening. "It will do you some good to get out and see people. You've spent a lot of time isolated in your room."

Staci sighed. "It's the only way I can make sure I can get this book written."

"I understand."

"And that understanding nature is part of why I love you so," Staci said, pressing a kiss to Gran's hair.

"Go on with you," Gran said, swatting her hand. "Go and get your writing done. I'm looking forward to having some time with my granddaughter once her head is clear of this imaginary world."

Guilt twisted again as she murmured acquiescence and hurried down the hall. She really should spend more time with Gran. Well, she *would*, she promised herself, just as soon as this blessed story was finished.

STACI KNOCKED ON THE DOOR, juggling the fresh flowers and bottle of premium apple juice. Her breath wisped white in the evening air, her down-filled jacket doing little to cut the cold. The porch light trembled as a creak behind the closed door suggested shifting weight, then light poured onto her as the door opened, and Mitch's cheery face smiled down at her.

"Ah, here she is at last. Come in, come in."

Staci followed him inside to cozy warmth, glad to be relieved of her burdens as she was encouraged to remove her jacket. Mrs. Wells—looking a little thinner and a mite older than Staci recalled—came from a room beyond, from which delicious smells emanated.

"Anastacia! At last!" Staci was enveloped in a hug. "Oh, how good it is to see you."

"And you, Mrs. Wells."

"Jenny, please. You're not in school anymore." She glanced at Staci's offerings, a mock frown crossing her face. "And didn't I tell you not to bring anything? You're a very naughty young lady."

Staci smiled. "Oh, I didn't bring them for you, Mrs.—ah, Jenny," it seemed so weird to say, "but for your husband here."

"Mitch?" She turned to her husband. "Have you been charming the ladies again?"

He shrugged, a twinkle in his eye. "Can I help it if I'm popular?"

"Mitch helped me when I arrived last week. My tire blew out."

"Oh, I remember now." Jenny nodded, her graying bob swinging.

"But the flowers aren't really for him. I got them for you." Staci handed her the flowers.

"They're lovely," Jenny said. "Thank you."

"Well, I can't begin to thank you for all your help with my writing when I was at school. If it hadn't been for you then I wouldn't have believed in myself enough to try to make this happen. So, thank *you*."

"Oh, Annie, it wasn't me. It was all your own talent and hard work. Now, come inside and let me dish up dinner and you can tell me all about it."

Staci followed her through to the kitchen. Her offer to help was refused, and she was invited to sit at the dinner table, where she busied herself with straightening the placemats and silverware as Jenny and Mitch finished preparing the food.

It was while doing this that Staci noticed a fourth-place setting. "Are you expecting another guest?"

"No. Well, we hoped Jem might make it, but he's been so busy lately. I like to keep a place set for him in case he can make it, but more often than not he's caught up at the surgery."

"Is he a vet?"

"No, a doctor."

Staci nodded. Why couldn't she remember this? Had escaping into imaginary worlds made her such a bad person she didn't know what was going on in the real world? Wait—the fact this was a single place setting… No. Surely Jenny and Mitch weren't trying to matchmake, were they? Jem would have to be a few years older, and if the table was set for only him that suggested no wife or girlfriend. She glanced around the room, but no photos appeased her curiosity, save for some very old ones that must have been taken at a scout camp sometime last millennium, and showed three curly-haired, dark-eyed boys with arms wrapped around each other, grinning at the camera without a care in the world.

Her heart sorrowed, emotion clogging her throat. No wonder Jenny set a place for her workaholic son; she would never have her eldest son join them for a meal again.

She eyed her hosts, both so happy, slipping little comments between them as they served up the beef stew atop mashed potatoes with a side of steamed vegetables. How had they managed these past few years? She knew—only too well—how grief tended to eat at people until they turned bitterly twisted or vagued out in disconnection. She'd found solace in creating imaginary worlds, places where she could control what happened, and every story was guaranteed a happy ending. Her lips twisted. If only life could be so sure.

"Are you sure you don't mind beef?" Jenny eyed her worriedly.

"I love it."

"Good. Here you go, then." A plate of steaming food was placed before her.

Mitch and Jenny seated themselves, then held out hands. "Shall we pray and ask God's blessing?"

She nodded, closing her eyes, and listening as Mitch prayed. Perhaps this solid trust in God was what had buoyed them these past years.

"Amen."

The first taste of beef stew was heavenly, the second was divine.

"Oh, this is so good," she mumbled past a mouthful of creamed potato.

"Jenny could have been a chef, but always loved her books too much."

"Something I can't be sorry about," Staci said, with a smile.

"Nor I," Jenny admitted. "Especially since retirement, I've had plenty of time to indulge my love for creativity with food. But that's by-the-by. Tell me, Annie—oh, I keep forgetting, I should call you Staci, that's what you go by now, isn't it?"

"Yes." It had been yet another way to forge her new identity beyond the memories of this town.

"Tell me about your writing. I've only heard snippets from the newspapers and from your grandmother—how proud she is of you—but I can say I have read your first novel."

Ah, *Secrets of the Wind*. The tension in her shoulders eased. That particular title was not too titillating, at least.

"I can't say I have much sympathy for pirates, so I have to admit I never read any of the others in that series, and then I became ill, and time did not allow for reading very often, I'm afraid."

"I was so sorry to hear you had been sick."

"It was a difficult time."

Staci caught the exchange of glances between husband and wife. Had this also been the time when their son had been killed? But she couldn't ask such a question. A writer might view conversations as meat for future stories, but she was loath to delve too deeply in the tragedy of her former teacher's life.

"But Jenny is better now, praise the Lord," said Mitch.

"I'm so glad." Staci smiled at her hostess.

"As am I," Jenny said. "I never realized how much I took my health for granted."

"I think we can all be that way," Staci offered, thinking back to when she had first realized her knees and ankles would never be the same as when she was a teenager. Running had a lot to answer for. "I think we all have a natural tendency to be complacent."

"Very true," Jenny said. "Now, you'll need to forgive me for not knowing all the details, but I'd love for you to tell me some more about your writing career and what happened and when."

Staci obliged, skirting around some of the less wholesome aspects of her stories.

"So you write for the general market?"

Staci shrugged. "That's what my agent represents." And, to be perfectly honest, she'd never really thought about writing for the Christian market. Readers wanted a good story, an opportunity to escape, not a sermon.

"And you're happy with how things are going at the moment?"

"Sure."

Except that wasn't really true. Just prior to coming tonight she checked her email and discovered a message from Bronwyn, with the news that Davis's new story was climbing the charts. Such news had soured the anticipation of the reunion tonight. No, she wasn't precisely happy with how things were going at the moment.

"Judging from that look, I'm not sure that I believe you," said Mitch, wryness tugging at his lips.

"Now, now, don't tease the poor girl. She must do what she feels led to do."

Led to do? Unease crossed her chest, then clambered up her throat. It was only recently she'd ever wondered about whether writing the books she had was what she should be doing. What if she'd been wrong, and wasting these past years? Was that why she was left watching other people's careers steamroll ahead while she was stuck changing a tire on the side?

Noticing another exchange of glances between her hosts, she figured it was time to change the subject. "Would you tell me something about the past few years? I have to admit I'm surprised at how well you seem to be taking things. I would have thought that with a cancer diagnosis and family troubles you would have found these past years extremely trying."

"Well, to be frank, it was. But it was also a time when we learned to more fully rely on God and remember His love, and to realize what matters most in life."

"Life doesn't always work out as we plan, but we always have the choice to draw back and close ourselves down in fear or press on and trust in the love that we can find."

Mitch's words echoed in Staci's heart. She could feel the tendrils of memory, of long-ago assurance, curling round her mind. Was this what real love really looked like? A protective trust beyond the immediate, that trusted in the outcome being *for* good rather than merely feeling good? What a brave kind of love that was.

The quiet challenge resonated. Had Staci shut off love from those around her? Well, she'd run away from Muskoka Shores as soon as she was able, and while she'd never shunned Gran and Granddad, she'd not exactly let them love her. Her breath suspended, her chest grew tight, moisture lined her eyes.

Jenny reached across and grasped Mitch's hand. "I knew in my dark hours that this man loved me, that God did, too, which buoyed me in those hardest days."

Mitch cleared his throat. "And we took comfort in the fact that we knew John was with Jesus in heaven. He'd made a commitment when he was younger and serving in the military only made him realize the precarious nature of life all the more. He'd been reading his Bible every night, so one of his buddies told us."

She nodded. Well, that was some comfort at least.

"There is power in the written word."

Jenny's smile was probably meant to assure, but Staci still felt the admonishment. She knew the power of words to rouse the reader to fantasies they probably shouldn't indulge in. That was what her publisher wanted, what her readers wanted, what her agent expected. She couldn't very well start writing Amish stories now, could she?

Could she?

The thought teased like an elusive perfume. She didn't want to write stories about the Amish—there would be too much to research, and to be honest, she'd never had much interest in trying to understand that particular section of society—but what if God *was* interested in her writing career, and wanted Staci to explore something new? Could she write to please her agent, please her readers, *and* please her grandmother?

Mind spinning, she barely heard Mitch's enquiry about whether she would like dessert. She nodded and got up to help clear the table.

The phone rang. Jenny offered an apology and took the call in a room beyond.

Mitch scraped the remains into a composting bin and loaded the dishwasher. "Thanks for saying yes to dessert. We only have it when we have guests, so it's a bit of a treat for me."

"Happy to help you out."

Although the waistband of her jeans wouldn't be too happy if she continued eating this way. She might have been losing weight while writing her first draft, which had led to an overly enthusiastic attempt to fit into skinny jeans which were now proving a tad too snug. But disappoint Mitch she would not. She would just have to work dessert off tomorrow. Although not by running.

Memories flashed of the last time she had gone running, thus necessitating her rescue by the handsome stranger. The man with the blonde she'd seen at church. Who *was* he? Mitch must know; she'd seen the two having a conversation at Suzy's diner. But how could she display blatant interest in a man whose last name she didn't even know? She had no wish to question Mitch, who, though kindly as he was, did not seem averse to indulging in a spot of local gossip. She had no desire to be the next subject of speculation over coffee and pastries.

"Here you go." Mitch handed her a bowl of heaped stewed rhubarb. "One scoop or two?" He motioned to the tub of vanilla ice-cream. "Or would you prefer cream?"

"Cream is good." She helped herself to the glass jug of pouring cream, arcing a trail of dairy goodness on the glossy dull red stalks.

"Oh, good," Jenny said, reentering the room. "You found the dessert. I hope you like it. I've been trying to avoid too much sugar, and I've made this with honey which Mitch assures me is still packed full of sugar, but I like to think it's more natural that way."

"I'm sure the bees agree," Staci offered, obeying Jenny's gestured invitation to resume her seat.

Jenny laughed. "You'll have to forgive me for being longer than I thought. That was Jem apologizing for tonight. He'll be a bit later as he has an emergency down at the clinic. Apparently one of the Taylor boys broke his leg while chasing their cat. You know, Bobby? The curly-haired lad from church with a cheeky smile?"

"Boys will be boys," Mitch said.

Staci spooned in some of the rhubarb and cream. Bit back a moan. Was there anything Jenny couldn't cook?

"I'm sorry you won't get the chance to meet him," Jenny apologized to Staci.

She swallowed an overly ambitious mouthful of dessert. "Meet Bobby?"

Jenny laughed. "No, Jem. I think you'd find him a tad more interesting than some of us who have lived here all our lives."

Her earlier suspicions now confirmed, there was no way Staci was going to encourage her former teacher in this regard. She changed the subject.

"So, what does Muskoka Shores do these days for Christmas? I heard the minister mention something about a Christmas lunch."

"Yes, that's been going these past five years or so since John and Angela took on the church. We do a similar thing at Thanksgiving, too. These are wonderful opportunities to help those who are lonely feel a sense of community and connection."

"Jenny has been basically running the show the past few years."

"What does that involve?"

"Oh, I don't exactly run things. I help Angela, the pastor's wife, with organizing and planning the menu, the volunteers, and whatnot. Well, last year she had family commitments so couldn't help, but we still had close to one hundred attend, with about half as many volunteers."

"That's impressive." Big city kind of impressive.

"Well, after our family circumstances changed, and Jeff got married and moved away, we just felt it was the right time to do Christmas differently. And being with lots of other people certainly kept us from being too sad and focused only on ourselves."

Staci bit her lip. The same could not be said about her. Pizza party with a side of pity was her usual speed. "Well, I am sure it must be a highlight of the year."

"Judging from the comments we received last year I believe it is," Jenny said.

"There are so many lonely people out there," Mitch said. "Even in a town like Muskoka Shores."

Staci nodded. Even in a heart like hers.

"We must do what we can to help. And focusing on others always helps to take away the personal pain, don't you agree?"

Again Staci nodded, feeling like a fraud. Somehow she didn't think daydreaming about characters for her stories was what Jenny meant with her talk about focusing on others.

Speaking of… She glanced at her watch. She probably should go home. She'd enjoyed reconnecting with her former teacher but sensed all had been said that was needed. And if she left now she'd be able to miss being forced to meet Jenny and Mitch's son of mystery.

"You need to go soon, Annie?" Jenny asked.

"I'm sorry, but I probably should. I'm on deadline, and I really need to get this story submitted before Christmas, which means it really needs to be written."

Jenny chuckled. "And you never liked to miss a deadline, did you? Very well, we'll let you off the hook this time. It's been wonderful to catch up and find out your news. You know we're very proud of you, don't you?"

Would Jenny say that if she had read Staci's other books? Somehow she didn't think so. "I've enjoyed catching up with you, too," she managed. "I'm so pleased that despite the past challenges you both seem to be happy." Although happy wasn't quite the right word. Maybe content fit better.

"Perhaps after you've met your deadline we can do this again."

"I'd like that." If there was time afterward. "I do plan on getting back to Chicago for Christmas though."

"Oh." Jenny's face fell in disappointment. "I thought for sure you'd be staying here with your grandmother. She's been so excited about having you home."

Except Muskoka Shores was not really her home anymore. And the guilt associated with obligation was something she'd rather not feel. "Well, we'll have to see how things go."

"Of course. And if by some chance you do end up being around at Christmas, we'd love to have your help at the community Christmas lunch."

"I'll keep it in mind."

Her jacket and pink scarf were collected, her cheek kissed, and she farewelled her hosts and headed out to her car. White beams of headlights indicated a vehicle turning into the street. She hurried to her car, beeped it unlocked, and turned the ignition, reveling in the heat as it warmed her. She pressed the windscreen demister and the windows blasted transparency in twin V-shapes. A vehicle slowed then pulled into the spare driveway parking space of the Wells' place. Was this the son she just missed? Good thing she was leaving now, then.

She plugged in her phone, whose battery had drained to low while she'd been having dinner, as the door opened and a figure got out. A tall, lean figure. A dark-haired figure. One sure to be the grown-up version of one of those sweet-faced boys from that picture inside.

Urgency compelled her to leave, but before she pressed the indicator, she snuck another look at the man hovering at the Wells' front door. To see him looking in her direction, hands on hips, as if his eyes were straining through the darkness.

Her skin prickled, she wrapped her scarf around her throat, and urged the car away.

"OH, JEM, YOU JUST MISSED HER."

What a shame. "The clinic was busy." He hung his coat on the rack by the door and moved into the kitchen. Pressed a kiss to his mom's cheek. "Something smells amazing."

"Annie appreciated it."

"Annie?"

"Annie Everton, Rose's granddaughter? Do you remember her from school?"

"Nope." And he had no intention to.

His mom looked at him sadly, as if she guessed his unspoken thoughts.

"What? I'm sorry I missed dinner," sorry for his mom's sake, not his own, "but sometimes stuff happens."

"Kinda remarkable how many times stuff seems to happen whenever a young lady is around," his dad murmured.

"I don't like being set up by my parents, okay?"

"This wasn't a set up," Mom protested.

"Right." He fought the inclination to roll his eyes, concentrating on dishing out the food onto his plate instead.

"Most men your age are married by now, enjoying life with a young family."

"Maybe they are, but they probably haven't done some of the things I have."

"We just want you to be happy, son."

"I am," he said, eyeing his father firmly as he shoved in a piece of beef.

"Are you really?" Mom asked quietly.

He swallowed, wishing he could swallow the sudden thickness in his throat. Well, to be honest, maybe he wasn't happy. A little nervous about the future, a little uncertain about what his past meant for his present. Once upon a time he'd believed his life choices had been the best decision. But now…

"I sensed Annie was a little lonely."

"I did too," his father agreed with a nod.

"Mom, can you seriously see any woman from around here being able to cope with my life in Africa?"

"You learned to cope," she pointed out.

"Because I wanted to."

"And what makes you think someone wouldn't be willing to do the same?"

"To please me?"

She nodded. "If she loves you…"

He snorted. "Thanks Mom, but I don't need your help."

"Have you found someone?" she asked, hope lighting her eyes.

"No." He thought of the way Pumpkin Spice had smiled up at him, the way her touch had caused a hitch in his pulse. "Maybe."

He only realized he'd said this aloud when Mom's breath caught. "Oh, who is she?"

"Nobody you need to worry about." Nobody he should even mention. For how could he, when he still did not even know her name?

iona studied the manuscript before her, eyeing the gold leaf embellishing the script with a frown—

No. Actually, that was Staci eyeing the words with a frown. Would Fiona really study a manuscript? Young ladies in those days did not do nearly as many things as modern-day authors liked to suppose. Historical accuracy had always been important to Staci, and while she knew she had occasionally got things wrong (thanks to some very assiduous readers who seemed to take great pleasure in pointing out such things), she knew such inconsistencies were far less than some authors and editors allowed for. Why, once she'd read a Regency novel where the heroine had said, "Wow." Imagine Elizabeth Bennett saying such a thing! Staci simply couldn't, which is why she simply couldn't read the rest of the novel.

No. Fiona wouldn't be reading a manuscript. Perhaps she could be studying her nails? Too boring. Perusing the view from the window?

Oh, what did it matter? Staci stretched, heard the muscles in her shoulders crack and pop as they protested the hunched position of the past hour. She needed out of here. Her brain was turning to mush.

"Gran, did you need anything at the store?"

Her grandmother sat at the kitchen table, and for once Penny was nowhere to be seen. Gran seemed a little pale. "Gran? Do you feel okay?"

"I didn't sleep very well last night."

That made two of them. Staci had barely caught a wink as she tossed and turned over the conversation with Mitch and Jenny Wells. What if she was to write a different type of story? What would it look like? She'd wondered before about writing something more sweet. Could she write it without the racy elements she was now known for? What would Bronwyn say? What would her publishers say? She'd even dared pray and ask God for His opinion.

Not that she heard any reply. But she had felt a mite reassured, that if God did care at all about her future, that He now knew she would like His involvement. At least regarding what to do next. And honestly, the idea of creating a page turner without the salacious content did hold a measure of interest. It would be a new challenge, a good challenge. Something more worthy of the wordsmith tag than the authors she was usually associated with. And perhaps, instead of merely offering a happy ending, if she could offer something of hope, something of real commitment—something like what she'd seen modeled in her grandparents' or the Wells' marriage—then maybe she could feel her writing was more than just a sop to bored housewives.

"Is there anything I can get you? A cup of tea?"

"I just had one, thanks dearie. I think I'll be fine, just sitting here for a while."

Staci worried her bottom lip. Should she go out, or stay here and watch over her grandmother? Anxiety rose. What would happen if Gran was to get sick—or worse?

"Is there anything I can do for you?"

"Did I hear you say you were going to the store?"

"I don't have to go if you would rather have me stay."

"No. That would be helpful. I was thinking I need to go but just can't summon up the energy to do so today."

"I'll go. What do you need?"

Gran pointed to a notepad on the refrigerator. Staci ripped the list free and stuffed it in her purse. "I'll be as quick as I can."

Gran chuckled softly. "I don't know how quick that will be, with Christmas getting ever closer. The stores seem so busy now."

"Then it's best to not put it off any longer." Staci eyed her with concern. "Is there a friend you want me to call? Someone to be with you while I'm out?"

"I don't need babysitting, Annie."

"Okay." Staci grabbed her sweater. "I'll be back as soon as I can."

"See you soon."

Staci pressed a kiss to Gran's cheek and hurried out into the frigid air.

In the car, on her way to the grocery store, she muttered a prayer for Gran. *God keep her well, God protect her, help her to rest, keep her safe—*

The car almost skidded into another. Stupid snow. If she was back home she wouldn't be having to face such things, one of the benefits of city public transport.

But then if she were home she would not be spending time with her grandmother. Or getting new ideas about her story.

She must be halfway through the manuscript now, thanks to Gran's hospitality. Guilt gnawed. Had Staci being here proved too much? She'd never really regarded her grandmother as frail, but there had been something in her features this morning that spoke of great weariness. "God, be with Gran," she muttered.

The grocery store loomed, and she pressed on the brakes

and veered to the parking lot. Beeping the car closed, she hurried inside, relishing the relative warmth as she grabbed a shopping cart and attached the sticky note grocery list to the cart's handle. Milk, eggs, bacon, fruit, bread, dog treats. Maybe Staci could buy Gran her favorite imported tea, and some of those fancy English biscuits she only ate at Christmas. Digestives, she thought they were called. Not the American sort, but the proper English kind.

A few minutes later she was hunting through the cookie aisle, the plethora of choices amazing as always. Quadruple choc chunk cookies? Yes, please. Although, maybe with a job that involved sitting down much of the time wouldn't be the way to maintain her weight. Or stave off diabetes. Maybe it was best to leave them on the shelf.

A brunette about her own age stooped to snag a package of the death cookies. She glanced up, noticed Staci watching her and gave an apologetic grin. "They're for work."

Sure they were. Eating a pack of those cookies would provide plenty of work alright—in the gym. Staci gave a polite smile and said, "Do you happen to know where the digestive biscuits are kept?"

The other woman's brows rose. "Do you mean the imported cookies?"

"I guess. They're for my grandmother, and she's part Irish, and I thought it'd be a nice treat for her."

Why was she saying all this? This poor woman didn't need to know her life story. But chatting with people her own age in Muskoka Shores had proved slightly problematic. Most people had kids, or at least were coupled up, and she'd met few singles she could identify with at all. Not that she needed a friend, not when she was leaving soon anyway. But it would be nice to occasionally have the opportunity to talk with someone who might enjoy Coldplay more than the Beatles.

But the woman didn't seem to mind; in fact, was offering a

nice smile of her own. "The imported foods section is down the next aisle. It's not really an aisle, more like a quarter of one, but you should find what you need there."

"Thanks."

"Excuse me, but you look a little familiar."

Staci's gut twisted. Was she a fan? Someone who had heard Muskoka Shores's slightly infamous author was back in town? She glanced at her clothes, worn for writing comfort not promotion duties, that looked baggy and drab in comparison to the woman's business attire. Was she someone who had read Staci's books, and would judge both on her content and her dowdy appearance?

"That's right." The slight furrow in the other woman's brow cleared. "You were a year ahead of me in school. Annie, Anna something right?"

"Anastacia Everton, but these days I go by Staci."

"Well, you probably don't remember me. I'm Jackie." She gave a self-deprecatory smile. "Oh, I remember now. You were a good runner, weren't you?"

"Once upon a time. Back in the day."

"That's right, I saw you at church the other day, too. Well, that's nice you are back for the holidays. I bet your grandmother is pleased."

"Yes." Understatement of the year. Speaking of... "I really should get going. It was nice to see you again, Jackie."

"You too. See you around."

Staci hurried to the checkout, adding a pot of African violets from a nearby display. Gran loved African violets; her kitchen window held numerous pots. This mauve would be a pretty addition to her collection.

She shoved the bags into the car, then glanced at the coffee shop across the street. She could really do with a cup of coffee. Maybe it was time to finally give The Coffee Blend another go. Suzy might have a different barista serving today.

Staci pushed open the door, the scents of caffeine and baked goodies slapping her senses alive.

"Well, lookee, she's back! I was sure I'd scared you off last time, so I'm relieved you're here again." Suzy beamed. "Staci, isn't it?"

"Hi again," she said weakly.

"What'll it be this time? Another pumpkin spice latte? Another pastry? Remember, it's on the house."

"Sure, that'd be great, thanks. The same as last time. To go," she added, as the coffee machine roared to life. Although perhaps she could take Gran home a piece of lemon slice. Gran had always enjoyed any baked goods containing lemon. "I'd like a lemon tartlet instead of the croissant, this time, please."

"No problem."

As she had last time, Staci surveyed the scene, but this morning there were no unnerving encounters with handsome men with intense dark green eyes, nor overly helpful older gentlemen. She turned to study the picture on the wall. What *was* it that seemed so familiar?

"Here you go. One pumpkin spice that you can actually enjoy yourself this time, instead of sharing it with one of Muskoka's most eligible bachelors."

The sip she'd been enjoying suddenly spurted up her nose. So her mystery coffee guy wasn't taken?

"Careful, Staci. I have a reputation to uphold, and the way you keep choking on my coffee makes me think you'll never truly appreciate its quality."

Suzy's eyes held a twinkle that suggested tease. Staci's shoulders inched down as she relaxed. Maybe this would prove a nice choice of venue for a break. Better than McDonalds, anyway. But she still wasn't completely convinced by the pumpkin spice flavor. It tasted kind of...dirty.

Offering a farewell she hurried back to the vehicle, taking care not to slip in the snow. After settling the coffee snugly in the cupholder, she started the car, thanked God aloud for the seat warmer, and steered back onto the road. She took a different course home, one that followed the same route she'd used for her run last week. Something she probably should get back into doing—if it wasn't for the blessed snow.

She finished the coffee as she drove; probably not a flavor she'd try again. Maybe a simple chai latte might prove a better bet. There was the architect's office, there was the medical clinic. Was that the one where Jenny's son worked? Of course—mental head slap—that was his name listed. Weird she hadn't realized that before. A few more turns and she was back on Maple, was pulling into Gran's drive, and was tugging out today's purchases. She beeped the car locked, then hefted her packages to one hip as she balanced the African violet with her keys. A twist of her hand and she stumbled inside to blessed warmth.

"Whew! It's getting cold out there."

No answer.

"Gran? Hello?"

A barking sound suggested Penny was trapped in the laundry. Good. She could stay there.

"Gran?" Where was she? Maybe she was in the bathroom or something. "Hey Gran, I'm back. I brought you something."

But the something Staci had brought slipped from her nerveless grasp with a loud crash as she spied the slumped figure of her grandmother on the kitchen floor.

CHAPTER 8

"Gran! Gran!"

Staci rushed to her side, knees buckling as she knelt beside her grandmother. She leant down, one ear pressed against Gran's chest. Was that a heartbeat? She couldn't hear anything save the fear rushing through her ears. How could she tell? Oh, her pulse. She placed two shaking fingers on Gran's throat. Was that the right spot? Why couldn't she feel anything? Surely Gran wasn't—

Swallowing a sob, Staci reached for Gran's wrist. Again, her fingers found no reassuring evidence of a heartbeat. But was she doing it right? Oh, this was so hard! Why hadn't she paid more attention to first aid courses? She'd always thought write-from-home authors barely needed to know first aid. Seemed she was wrong. How else was she supposed to know—

Breath. Of course. She placed a trembling finger under Gran's nose. Felt the faintest whisper of moved air. "Thank God." Staci exhaled shakily, then stumbled to her fallen bag, and retrieved her phone. Checked the screen. No battery.

An unladylike exclamation escaped, and she hurried to Gran's phone atop the microwave. Stabbed the numbers for emergencies. "I need an ambulance. It's my grandmother. She's… she's had a heart attack or something and is not responding."

A few answered questions later and Staci resumed her vigil on the floor, one hand clutching Gran's as she willed her to live. "God, don't let her die, not today, not now. I need her. Please God, *please* let Gran live."

Long minutes dragged past, before finally there came a knock at the door. Lunging up, Staci yanked the door open and hurried the medics inside. "I'm so glad you're here!"

"What happened?" The female paramedic's shiny brown ponytail swung as she crouched beside Gran. "Hello, ma'am?" She pressed her fingers to Gran's wrist. "Ma'am? You're going to be okay."

Staci's heart grabbed onto her words. *Please God, let Gran be okay.*

"What happened?" The other medic, a balding man in his thirties whose badge named him Michael, looked up at her.

"I arrived home to find Gran like this. She wasn't moving, and I couldn't find a pulse for the longest time."

He gave a sharp nod. "And what's your grandmother's first name?"

"I…er," For the life of her, she couldn't remember. Tears pricked. "She's always just Gran to me," she sniffed back the emotion.

"Hey, it's okay. We're going to need to take her to the hospital. Do you think you can pack a small bag with her essentials? And if you find any medications, bring them out here, it may help."

"Sure."

Staci jumped up, thankful for something to do, and hurried to Gran's bedroom, packing her nightwear, some underclothes, her Bible, and the Helen Steiner Rice devotional beside the bed. She moved to the bathroom, tugged a toiletries bag from the cupboard underneath the sink, and shoved the various bottles and packets of pills inside, along with the other toiletries items she'd likely need. Then she hurried back to find Gran being strapped to a stretcher, her body looking shrunken and frail.

"Here." She thrust the bag at Michael the paramedic, who looked at her with a slight frown. "Oh, you wanted the medication, didn't you? Sorry." She dragged out one of the bottles, glanced at the information. "That's right, her name is Rose. I can't believe I forgot! I think this is the bottle she used for heart medication."

He glanced at it, nodded, then barked orders at his partner, and they lifted Gran out to the waiting ambulance. By now a small group of neighbors had gathered and were watching proceedings like concerned vultures in thick coats.

"What's happened to Mrs. Everton?"

"She's unwell," Staci managed. How could she reply when she didn't yet know the truth?

A tall brunette in her late twenties drew nearer. "I'm Anna Morely." The woman from church. "I live two doors down. You're Rose's granddaughter, aren't you?"

"Staci," she managed.

"I know Rose was very happy to have you back home with her. If there is anything I can do—"

"Miss? Do you want to go in the ambulance with us?"

"Oh, yes!" Staci glanced at the gaping front door. "I just need my purse."

"You got thirty seconds."

She nodded and tore back inside, scooping up her purse from where she'd dropped it beside the smashed African violet and the eco-friendly grocery bags on the floor. The grocery bags complete with items she really should refrigerate—

"Staci?" Anna's voice from the door. "I'll clear this up. Just go, they're waiting to leave."

"Okay. Thanks." Eyes, throat, thick with tears, she stumbled to the flashing ambulance clutching her purse against her chest, scrambling into the back where Michael monitored Gran. The doors were shut and within seconds they were moving.

"Hey." The compassion in Michael's voice made her look up. "Just breathe."

She nodded, willing the tears away, forcing her shaky breaths to steady, to deepen. *Lord, look after Gran. Keep her safe. Let her live.*

The prayer became her soundtrack as they veered around corners, bumped across railway tracks, and alternately sped and slowed through traffic. "Will she be okay?"

Michael's hazel eyes met hers. "I hope so."

But he couldn't give a guarantee. Was it any wonder? Gran was in her early eighties—to Staci's shame she didn't know what year exactly she'd been born. Old people, young people, no one was guaranteed to live forever. But to have Gran gone, before Staci had really taken the time to truly know her, she couldn't bear for that to happen. Not to someone else she loved. Not again.

A sob escaped, and Michael's gaze caught hers with a sympathetic smile. "Hey, please don't worry. We'll do our best. The doctors at the hospital are really good."

She nodded, appreciation for his kindness curling warmth around her heart. *Thank You, God, for sympathetic medics, for Anna's willingness to tend to my mess.* She breathed in reassurance. Then frowned. Anna could be trusted, couldn't she?

The ambulance slowed, veering into the emergency drive, or so the small back window revealed. A tiny thought insisted that when Gran was settled, Staci would have to write down all her impressions; she'd never traveled in an ambulance before. Who knew but that it might prove good color for a story one day.

She blinked. Seriously?

Shaking her head at herself, Staci scrambled out of the way as the doors opened and Gran was wheeled out. She clutched the bags and followed, the doors to emergency flapping wide, the sense of urgency hitting her heart.

"Excuse me, miss, you can't go in there." A nurse with dark blonde hair held up a hand.

"But she's my grandmother. She's had a heart attack. I have her things—"

"Please, come and sit down for a few minutes. You'll be of more help out here than in there."

The patronizing tone wrinkled Staci's nose, but she obeyed, nonetheless. She still clutched Gran's bag and her own purse. The waiting room held the familiar disinfectant smell, and the usual suspects: a tired looking fern, torn and dog-eared magazines, and drooping patients, or waiting relatives of patients, consisting of a mother and baby and a small boy playing on a tablet, an elderly man with a handlebar mustache, and a grizzled man whose face and clothes looked as gray as the floor.

"Is there anyone you should call?"

What? Oh. The nurse was talking to her again. Staci glanced at her phone. Should she call someone? Who? Gran had no relatives apart from Staci. Should she call someone from church? The black screen looked up at her accusingly. Her shoulders slumped. "I… I can't. My phone has no charge."

She bit her trembling lip, hunching further into the uncomfortable seat, placing her head in her hands. Who would she call anyway? It wasn't like she had a list of Gran's contacts plugged into her phone, so calling anyone was pretty much out of the question. Oh why had she been so focused on her fictional world that she ignored the real one? Liquid seeped from her eyes. She was such a failure of a granddaughter, such a failure of a daughter, such a failure—

"Miss?"

A deeper voice stole past her recriminations, forcing her head up. And her jaw to sag.

Mr. Coffee stood eyeing her, an expression not unsympathetic on his face. She wiped her nose with her sleeve—classy—and tried to swallow the enormous boulder in her throat. Couldn't. So stared at him mutely.

"Is there something I can help with?"

The tenderness in his voice renewed the moisture in her eyes. Still she couldn't speak.

"Her phone hasn't got a charge," the little boy piped up.

Mr. Coffee smiled, and twin fans of tiny lines creased beside his eyes. "That's no reason to be upset now, is it?"

Her heart thudded. Stupid heart, she grumbled. Why it had to suddenly wake up and pay attention when Gran was—when Gran was possibly dying! Breath caught on a whimper.

Mr. Coffee's expression grew serious, and he drew near. It was only then she noticed the medical ID swinging from his neck. Dr. James Wells. "*You're* Jenny's son?"

"You know my mom?"

"She taught me English."

He nodded, lowered to his haunches. "And you are?"

"Staci."

Humor kicked at the corner of his mouth. "What? Not Pumpkin Spice?"

"Not today." And after her last encounter with that particular drink, probably not ever again.

His eyes grew kindly, his voice soft as he said, "And what brings you here today?"

Throat tight, she managed to squeak out, "Gran."

"Your grandmother?"

Staci nodded, hating that she was acting like a preschooler, but unable to do anything about it. "She… she had a funny turn, and I came home and found her slumped on the floor, and I…" She could feel the panic rising and stopped, forcing herself to drag in a slow breath. "I had to call the ambulance," she continued in a voice that sounded steadier and more like hers.

"Her name?"

"Rose Everton."

His head snapped up. "Mrs. Everton, from church?"

She nodded.

"Wait—did you have dinner with my parents the other day?"

What did that have to do with anything? "Yes."

"Man. I wish—" A mix of emotions flickered across his face, then he drew out his phone. "Mind if I call my mom? I'm sure she'd be more than happy to come sit with you."

"Oh, but I couldn't impose."

His expression turned wry. "Mom knows all too well the fun of waiting in hospitals."

"Dr. Wells?" the nurse called. "You're being paged."

He pushed upright, eyes still on Staci. "So I'll call her?"

"Yes, please," she whispered.

He nodded, turned to go, before swinging back once more. "I'll keep your grandma in my prayers."

Tears pricked anew, and all she could do was nod, as he offered a small smile and finally strode away.

Breath escaped shakily, and she hunched over again and closed her eyes, willing herself to be unnoticed. *Lord, be with Gran. Keep her safe. Let her live.*

She cracked open an eye. Dr. Wells studied her from the nurse's station, his brow furrowed. No wonder. How pathetic she must look! She summoned a smile of reassurance and he nodded and disappeared through the emergency doors. The blonde nurse eyed Staci with an expression she couldn't quite read, so she lowered her head and pretended interest in the contents of her bag.

"Jeff Watson," the nurse called.

The grizzled man hefted from his seat and padded to the nursing station where they began a low-voiced conversation.

"This game is boring," the little boy said. A clatter suggested he'd tossed the tablet to one side. "I wanna go home."

Staci glanced up as the mother remonstrated with her son.

The baby began a mewling noise, the mother sighing as she unbuttoned her blouse. Beside her, the little boy began hitting the spare chair with his feet. *Ker-thump. Ker-thump.*

"Simon, please stop," the mother said wearily.

Ker-thump. Ker-thump.

The elderly gentleman with the broad expanse of moustache frowned up from his newspaper.

"Simon." The woman's voice held a sharper edge.

Ker-thump. Ker-thump.

"Back in my day," the elderly man growled, "children knew to obey their parents."

Staci eyed him with a frown. Like any mother needed a reminder of her inadequacies.

He met her narrowed gaze for a moment then returned his attention to the boy's mother, who was valiantly ignoring him as she concentrated on the baby at her breast. From this angle, Staci could tell by the reddened tips of her ears that she was embarrassed.

"These days there is no respect, no discipline," he grumbled again. "I don't know what the world is coming to."

Ker-thump. Ker-thump.

The noise was irritating Staci's nerves.

"Simon," the mother said wearily, reaching out to hold his knee, "Stop it now. You're annoying the other people here."

Staci offered a smile she hoped proved she wasn't annoyed, as the elderly man said, "He certainly is."

Right. Staci slipped from her seat and moved to crouch in front of the little boy. From this close position he couldn't kick his legs anymore. "Hello."

He eyed her with big blue eyes, his gaze swinging to his mom as if to ask permission to talk to a stranger. His mother nodded, her half-smile at Staci seeming to hold a measure of relief. "Hi."

"My name is Staci. Is your name Simon?"

He nodded shyly.

"I wanted to thank you for before."

"For what?"

"For telling the doctor about my phone. It's a naughty phone, and its batteries don't seem to want to last very long."

He nodded, eyeing her curiously. "Your eyes are red."

Wonderful. "I was upset before."

"Your nose is red, too."

No wonder Dr. Coffee had been looking at her weirdly. "I think it's to match my hair."

He laughed, a delightful little-boy chuckle that squeezed tenderness in her chest. Motherhood was not something she dared think about too often; there was little point without a boyfriend one could consider husband material. She might be all about encouraging other women to fantasize about their perfect romantic life, but she knew the difference between reality and fiction.

"Simon, don't bother the nice lady."

"He's not bothering me," Staci assured, smiling at his mother who now patted the baby on her shoulder. She nodded to the tiny child wrapped in yellow blankets. "How old?"

"Three months."

"Oh, congratulations. Boy or girl?"

"Jordan is a girl. *I* wanted a brother," Simon complained.

"I'm sure Jordan will enjoy having a brother to play with when she's older."

Simon's pout said he didn't believe Staci, so she tried again. "What was the game you were playing—?"

"Angelina Brusselhorst?"

"Finally." The woman sighed and shifted. "Come on, Simon. Bring your things. We can go see Daddy now." Her gaze shifted to Staci. "Thanks for entertaining him."

"I hope everything is okay."

The young mother's lips moved into a smile, but her eyes

held no joy. "I hope so, too. David had a relapse, and I..." she broke off, eyes shimmering.

Staci laid a hand on her arm. "I'll be praying for you."

"Thanks," she muttered, carefully grasping her baby and clutching Simon's shirt as if he might run away.

Staci watched them move to the nurse's station, sorrow panging within. How challenging that must be, to care for a sick husband – relapse suggested he'd been very ill – whilst being responsible for young children. And here she was bemoaning the possible loss of her grandmother who had lived many years, many *good* years.

She resumed her seat, then noted Simon had neglected to collect his electronic device. She hurried to the nurse's station and held it to the blonde nurse on duty. "The little boy, Simon, left this just now."

"Thanks." The blonde eyed her curiously. "Do you have children?"

"No."

"Oh." Shuffle of medical papers.

"Why?"

"It's just you were very good with him."

Staci shrugged. Probably left-over skills from her long-ago days teaching Sunday school.

The nurse leaned forward. "Poor Angelina has her hands full with two youngsters and a sick husband."

Uncomfortable at the topic of conversation—did this nurse talk about all the patients this way?—Staci nodded to the device. "She'll probably appreciate that tablet being returned to keep Simon distracted."

The friendliness stiffened into offense as the nurse nodded curtly and walked away.

Staci pursed her lips. Well, she wouldn't expect any favors from that nurse anytime soon. She resumed her seat and her prayers for Gran—and added some for Angelina's family also.

After what seemed an age, the entry doors swooshed open and a familiar face walked in, wide eyes scanning the room then alighting on Staci with relief. "Oh, you're still here! You poor darling." Jenny Wells encased Staci in a hug that smelled of roses and pulled back, worry in her eyes. "Jem called me and told me your plight. Poor Rose. How is she? Have you heard anything?"

"No." Staci nodded to the nurse on duty, and said in a quieter voice, "I've asked several times but she's told me nothing. I don't think she likes me very much."

Jenny squinted. "Oh, but Larissa is a sweetie. Let me see what I can do. I taught her English too."

Mrs. Wells moved to the nursing station, Staci trailing in her wake like a lost pup.

"Larissa, hello, how are you?"

"Oh, hi, Mrs. Wells." Larissa's face brightened. Did all ex-teachers command such kindly interest and respect? Somehow Staci didn't think so.

"I don't know if you've had the chance to meet my friend Anastacia here, but she's very worried about her grandmother, and would really appreciate any updates you might have about her condition."

"Sure, Mrs. Wells. Let me see what I can find out." Larissa flung a smile in Jenny's direction, but nothing for Staci, and exited through the doors.

Jenny turned to Staci and raised her brows. "It seems you were right. I wonder what the problem is?"

Larissa returned, cutting off further speculation, and flicked Staci a look. "The doctor says you can go on through now."

"Thank you." Staci tried to inject as much warmth as she could into those two words, but Larissa's lack of response seemed to suggest it hadn't worked.

"Only family, I'm afraid, Mrs. Wells," Larissa said, a note of apology in her voice.

"No problem. I'll be waiting here for you, Staci. And praying."

"Thanks Jenny." Staci's eyes filled with tears. How kind she was.

Larissa led the way through a corridor to a broad white room filled with gleaming equipment, the likes of which she'd be hard pressed to identify their functions let alone the correct name. There was a reason she wrote historical novels. Another room held curtained cubicles, and it was to one of these she was led, where a white-coated person bent over a clipboard.

"Oh, Gran!" Staci hurried to her side, holding her hand which was taped with an intravenous drip. Another lead plugged into a heart monitor, whose steady pulse suggested Gran's heart was working as it ought. Gran's color nearly matched the bed linen, her closed eyes and relaxed repose revealing a hundred sunken little lines. Staci's eyes blurred. How old Gran looked. How frail she seemed. She pressed a kiss to her brow.

"How is she?" She finally glanced up at the doctor. "Oh!"

Dr. Coffee's lips curved, as if he was amused by her surprise. "Rose is doing well but needs to rest for a while. We're still waiting to run tests to see how much damage has been sustained to her heart."

"When will you know?"

"It's hard to say. We're not especially busy today, so maybe by tonight, maybe tomorrow."

She nodded, chewing her bottom lip as she studied her grandmother again and gently squeezed her hand. *Please Lord, heal her.*

"Rose seems strong, so we'll hope and pray she makes a swift recovery." He cleared his throat. "Did my mom come?"

"Yes, thank you." She met his dark green eyes again. "I really appreciate it. She's very kind." *As are you.* She blinked, dropped her gaze.

"Is your phone still dead?"

The abrupt change of subject threw her off balance. "Y-yes."

"I imagine you have some calls you'd like to make. I have a phone charger nearby. Want to see if it works?"

"That'd be great, thank you."

"No problem."

He nodded, drew the curtains aside and strode away. She turned back to Gran, stroking her pale freckled arm tenderly. It was like the skin had been leached of all strength, pooling to either side of her bones. Staci bowed her head, praying once more, conscious the emotions of the past hour could not be kept back much longer. A tear slid past her gated eyelids, then another, then another, dripping past her nose, sliding down the length of her chin to plop on the heavy white sheets.

A touch on her shoulder startled her, her eyes snapping open to once again encounter the compassionate gaze of James Wells. Staci wiped her damp cheeks, swiped at her nose.

"I can't lose her." Her voice sounded scratchy, wispy thin. "She's... she's all I've got."

"She'll be okay."

She shook her head. "You don't know that, not for certain, anyway."

"Nothing in life is certain, though, is it?" he said gently. "But I do know your grandmother follows Jesus so her future is certain, regardless of what happens here."

She swallowed. How did he know these things? She must have looked confused, because he smiled and said, "Your grandmother was one of those who wrote to me when I was away."

Away where? She placed a hand on her head. This all felt so confusing.

"Here." He held out a small black and green charger and lead. "Will this fit your phone?"

She drew out her phone, with its Jane Austen-inspired leather case, and fitted the lead. "Yes, thank you."

"Pretty." She glanced up at him. He tapped the phone case. "I haven't seen one like that before."

"I had it custom designed by a friend."

"Very nice." His eyes melded with hers again, his voice trailed away. The green depths held a magnetic quality, one that seemed to compel her gaze and caused a funny tightening in her chest. Then he glanced at his watch. "I should go. Nurse Wilson knows to keep you informed."

"Can I stay a while longer?"

"For a bit."

"Um, and your phone charger?"

"Keep it for as long as you need." His half-smile caused another peculiar tumbling sensation within. "You know where I live."

She would ignore that… bordering-on-unprofessional-sounding comment. Wait—he lived with his parents? "So, are you Gran's doctor?"

"For now. I'm scheduled for this shift, so I guess I'm the lucky one to have caught you."

She forced a smile, thanked him once more, and turned her burning face back to the bed, her stupid senses straining as his footsteps moved away. For a moment there it almost sounded like he was trying to flirt with her. But that was crazy. Probably just her hyper-romantic brain seeking what didn't exist. Besides, she was no judge of men. She'd misread them too many times before and knew she didn't understand them at all. Her lips twisted. Which was rather ironic, really, for someone who made a living pretending that she did.

Gran. She needed to focus on Gran. Not handsome, coffee-stealing doctors. Not even if they were someone who made her heartbeat hiccup, and someone her old English teacher had wanted her to meet. Speaking of…

Jenny! She needed to let her know. She'd been waiting out there for ages and must be wondering what was happening.

Staci placed the bags on the floor and kissed Gran's brow again, then rushed out to where a middle-aged nurse—presumably Nurse Wilson—monitored another patient. "Um, I'm Staci Everton, and that's my grandmother—"

"I know who you are, Miss Everton." Nurse Wilson smiled. "I've enjoyed reading your books."

"Oh! Well, thanks." This was awkward. "I, um, just need to go outside to speak to someone for a moment. Is that okay? My stuff—Gran's stuff—is still there, so..."

"I'll keep an eye on things. Most of our patients in emergency aren't exactly inclined to run off with people's possessions," she added drily.

Staci winced. Of course they weren't. "Thank you." She hastened back through the corridor, pushing open the great wide plastic flaps that led into the waiting room. "Jenny—oh!"

James was there, talking quietly to his mom, apparently filling her in on what had been happening. So he hadn't needed to get to another appointment? He'd just wanted to leave her? Proof she could never read a real man's intentions like she could write a fictional man's motives. But—stupid her —what did that matter right now? "Hi Jenny. Um, I guess the doctor here," she gestured to the man beside her, "might have filled you in, but I just wanted to let you know what was happening."

"Oh, sweetie, you didn't have to worry. I told you I'm perfectly content waiting here as long as necessary." She held up a Kate Morton hardcover. "See? Perfectly happy."

"But we don't know how long that will be," James said. "How about if you go home and I drop Miss Everton home when my shift is done." He glanced at her, his expression unreadable. "That is, if you are willing?"

"Oh, but I don't want to put anyone out."

"You wouldn't be putting me out at all. And that way Mom can be free to do what she needs to do with the rest of her day."

Staci certainly didn't want to appear eager for his company. "Are you sure?"

"Yeah. Now," he glanced at his watch again, "I really need to fly." He kissed his mom's cheek. "See you later." He turned to Staci. "I'll catch you in a few hours."

"Okay."

He exited, and Staci noticed as Larissa watched him leave. Larissa turned, their eyes met, and awkwardness quickly returned Staci's attention to Mrs. Wells. "Thanks again, Jenny. I really appreciate your support."

"Like I said, it was no problem. I'm happy things seem to be working out."

"I hope so." Her voice was shaky. "It's just Gran seems so old…"

Jenny grasped her hand. "I'll be praying for you. And Rose, of course."

"Thanks."

Jenny wrapped her in a swift hug, then called a farewell to Larissa and exited.

Staci moved back to the doors into Emergency, when Larissa's voice halted her. "Are you Dr. Wells' girlfriend?"

"No." What was this, junior high? "I've never really met him before." Encountered him, sure, a few times. But officially met him? Not until today.

"But you know Mrs. Wells."

"She taught me English."

"Me too." The blonde eyed her.

Staci tried out a smile. "She was my favorite teacher."

"Mine too. She always seemed to care." Larissa's brow puckered, and she seemed to draw closer. "Hey, I remember you. You were a couple of years ahead of me."

Ah, the blessings of a small town. Would she never escape people who remembered her way back when?

"Oh! Weren't you the girl whose parents died in—oh, sorry."

Pain stabbed. Staci's lips pressed together. Why was it that even so many years on she could still not hear a stranger's sympathy without stiffening up and wanting to flee? Would she ever learn to offer a gracious response? Oh well. Not something to worry about changing today. "I'm going to see my grandmother now."

And she pushed open the doors back to her grandmother, her wonderful, too-frail, aged grandmother, willing her head to remain high, and praying that her tears would stay away.

iona held her head high. They would not see her cry. Nobody would ever suspect how their words cut and flayed her soul like a soldier's whip scourged a prisoner's back. She was in her rightful place, in her father's house, and nobody could make her leave, nobody could bend her will to anything but what she desired. She was a royal princess, granddaughter of a famous queen—

Staci's nose wrinkled and paused the tapping on her phone. Was Fiona the granddaughter of a famous queen? Such was the problem with trying to write by the seat of her pants; her story bent and twisted as the words popped into her head, sometimes painting her into corners she could barely escape from. She had learned to trust her instincts, trust the flow, and knew story-telling ran in her veins, but not for the first time wondered about those who plotted and planned their stories to the nth degree, sometimes taking months to really get to know their characters. Whenever she tried to do that she felt the breath of creativity flee, and she was left with plodding words, words without the spark that ignited the scenes and turned them into page turners. And taking months to truly get to know her characters would mean she'd have written far fewer books in these past years. Then where would she be? Exactly. At least five years behind on her current career trajectory.

She glanced at Gran, still resting comfortably. She had been moved to the ICU ward an hour ago, her belongings now neatly stored away. Staci hadn't left her side, except once for a bathroom break and to grab a coffee from the cafeteria. The coffee she'd been forced to immediately dribble back into the cup, foul as it was. Why was it that in a place that tried to offer comfort they offered torture through their caffeine? She shuddered and returned her attention to her screen.

Was Fiona the granddaughter of a famous queen? If only Staci had her computer, and her notes, instead of tapping out her scene on the notes app on her phone, maybe she could find out more about Fiona's past, and see her way into her future. She frowned. Sighed.

"Hi."

Staci jumped. "Oh, it's you again."

"I seem to have an alarming effect on you." Dr. Wells—sans white coat—grinned, and this time she noticed a dimple in his left cheek.

Oh, yes, alarming all right. She told her pulse to behave.

"How is Rose doing?"

"There hasn't been much change. The nurses say she's doing fine."

"That's what we want to hear." He moved to the end of the bed, flipped through the folder holding Gran's details, before moving closer to the bed. "Hi, Rose."

Her eyes remained closed, her breathing unchanged. He checked her vitals, then glanced back at Staci. "She seems to be doing okay."

"She hasn't stirred at all."

"It's her body's way of coping. The heart attack has taken a toll, and she's been given sedating drugs to reduce the demand on her heart. But remember, she's in good hands here."

She drew in a breath, his words bringing ease to her own heart.

His head tilted. "Are you happy to leave now?"

"Yes." If she went, she could finish cleaning the mess sure to still be on the floor and grab her computer before driving back. Oh, and let Penny out, poor thing. "If you're sure you don't mind."

"Not a problem at all."

He waited as she collected her bag, gave Gran another kiss, and told the nurse on duty she'd be back soon.

"See you, Mildred."

At his attention, the gray-permed nurse twinkled like a little girl. Staci also couldn't help but observe just how festive he looked in his dark green jacket and red scarf, colors that drew attention to his face, and somehow made his eyes seem all the greener.

"Shall we?" His gaze seemed intense, and she was conscious of breath constricting in her lungs. This wasn't a ballroom scene for Cinderella or one of her imaginary heroines. He was simply being a—surprisingly—nice guy and helping her from some sense of Christian charity. Besides, she reminded herself sharply, he had a girlfriend, as his presence in church last Sunday with the blonde beauty attested. Even if the blonde wasn't someone his parents seemed to know about. Although how they could not know when they'd been cozying up in church seemed beyond her...

Staci shook away the thoughts and continued to speak sternly to herself as they walked through the corridors and eventually attained the waiting room.

"Bye Larissa," he called.

Larissa seemed struck dumb—either by his notice of her or

the fact he was walking out with Staci—so Staci offered her a weak wave and hoped her lack of smile conveyed her being by his side was nothing more than a chivalrous gesture. Which it *was*.

They headed outside, the bite of wind rushing through Staci's too-thin sweater. It felt like an age since she'd been outside, and in all the rush of the ambulance she hadn't remembered to bring a thick jacket or scarf.

"Here." He unwrapped his red scarf and handed it to her.

When she protested he murmured, "What kind of doctor would I be to let you get sick on my watch?"

On his watch. She shivered again, spoke sternly to herself at her nonsense, and gingerly wrapped the scarf around her neck. It smelled of spiced oranges, and some other subtle yet delectable masculine scent.

Tall trees guarded the parking lot, what few leaves remained were shriveled and brown among drifts of snow. "Careful," he said, holding out an arm. "It's slippery here."

She picked her way carefully across the iced path, wondering if he had a different vehicle from the other day. He was a doctor, so of course he'd drive something nice, like an Audi, or Mercedes. Didn't doctors have a reputation to uphold?

But no. He beeped open the Ford truck again, then helped her in, his large warm hand holding her small cold one. Again, a frisson of… something, like expectation, trembled awareness within. Which was stupid! He had a girlfriend. She didn't need a boyfriend. She just needed Gran to get better and to finish writing her book.

He got in, turned the ignition, and the large vehicle rumbled to life. He flicked a few dials and heated air propelled to her face. After a few seconds, he said, "Warmer now?"

"Yes." Was this an implied request for his scarf back? She gently unwound it.

James glanced across, one eyebrow raised. "The heat worked that fast?"

"I don't want to forget." Awkwardness weighted her smile. "Sometimes I have to do things straight away or else I get distracted and they don't get done. And I imagine you'll need your scarf later on."

He shrugged, his attention now back on the road.

She settled back in her seat, remembering the last time she'd been driven by him, wondering about the strangeness of it all. She peeked across. He certainly had a few of the heroic qualities she tended to use for her characters: a rugged jaw, the beginnings of a five o'clock shadow, the broad shoulders that suggested he worked out. But there was nothing that screamed mirrored gyms and Lycra about this man; she bet he got those muscles from felling trees rather than lifting weights and admiring his form in the mirror. In fact, for someone as attractive as he was, there seemed little of the arrogant jerk about him. Granted, he hadn't appeared his Oprah-approved best self on that first encounter at the coffee shop, but since then, she'd witnessed kindness, concern, and an appealing kind of chivalry that she really didn't know what to do with. Arrogant jerk she could put into his place, but kind Christian man made her edgy and tense. She doubted she could shut him up with a few well-chosen words. Rather, she hoped she could not.

Staci stifled a groan and turned to gaze out the passenger window. This was ridiculous! He was simply driving her home. He was being nice. Being kind. That was all. He had a *girlfriend*. She should get these silly feelings back in their box where they belonged.

But that was really hard when his scent seemed to waft alluringly between them, when she felt the weight of his gaze on her, when the space between them seemed to thicken with things unsaid. She should break this tension and talk; she was supposed to be good with words. But none would come.

They passed the architect's office, the medical clinic. She saw his name posted once again. Suddenly the words were there. "I thought you worked at the clinic."

"I do."

"And yet here you are, not working there."

"I'm covering for Dr. Strauss who's taken leave for six months."

"Dr. Strauss." A memory pinged. "Isn't he the one who used to deliver babies? I think I remember him coming to the school and talking about, er—" Why was she blushing like a pre-teen girl? Surely a romance novelist could say the words "sex ed."

"That's him." He glanced across as they waited at a stop sign. "You went to Muskoka Shores High."

"That's where your mom taught me."

His eyes narrowed, as if he was trying to remember. And failing. "You must've been a few years behind me."

"I was a year behind Jeff."

Jeff Wells. The athletic, slightly serious boy whom she'd once wondered if he'd make a good boyfriend. Jeff, who was now married and had moved away.

Another shrug. "School seems like a lifetime again."

"Thank God," she muttered.

She felt his questioning gaze on her skin, but she said nothing. Like she wanted to explain how school had been one tortuous day after another.

As the truck turned into Gran's street, the tension riding in her chest climbed higher. So much to do, so little time. She'd need to release and feed Penny, who'd doubtless be *thrilled* to see her and not Gran, clean up the mess from before, grab a quick shower—she'd accidentally worn her smelly armpit t-shirt and wanted to get changed as soon as possible—and collect her stuff before heading back to the hospital.

He pulled up outside the Changs. "No, it's the next one."

A soft chuckle escaped him.

"What?"

"You seem to change houses quite a lot."

"No, I don't." She caught his raised brow. "Oh."

Heat scampered across her cheeks as she remembered where she'd directed him on their previous journey. He must think she was extremely odd, but "A girl needs to be careful when it comes to strange men."

"Strange, huh?"

Had she truly said that aloud? "Uh, I meant unfamiliar."

"Some would say strange works, too."

She appreciated his self-deprecation, but could think of no reply, as the panic from earlier resurfaced. So much to do. Who should she call? Where to begin? A groan escaped.

James glanced swiftly at her, then steered the truck to the curb outside Gran's house. "You okay?"

"Yes." Noting the doubt in his eyes, she added, "Just not wanting to deal with the mess inside."

He offered a sympathetic smile and she unclasped her seatbelt and got out. The bitter cold caused her breath to hitch.

She scrabbled for her key from her bag—something organized Staci should have done while back in the car—feeling heat flush her cheeks as he saw how messy it was. Heaven forbid he saw the items needed for sanitary protection! Although, being a doctor he probably knew about such things… "Ugh!"

"Can't find your keys?"

"They're in here somewhere," she said, still searching frantically.

"Want me to take a look?"

"No! Thank you," she added in a voice she hoped would assuage the panic-stricken note of earlier.

"Sometimes when we're stressed it can be hard to see—"

"Voilà!" She held the keys up triumphantly.

"Want me to come in? You know, just to check everything's okay."

"Um, okay. But only if you want to. I don't want to interrupt you if you're supposed to be somewhere else."

"I wouldn't offer otherwise."

"Well, thank you." His kindness did deserve a cup of tea at least. "I'd appreciate it."

She turned the key, and a small barking bundle of white energy rushed from the door. "Penny! Penny, come back!"

"I'll get the dog, you get inside," he said, waving her indoors. "Go."

Biting her lip, she watched as he hurried after the speedy demon, then turned to survey the damage. Someone—she presumed Anna Morely—had put away the groceries, but the smashed African violet still awaited attention, albeit now on a newspaper on the counter. Thank goodness it had been placed there, otherwise Penny would have tracked dirt all through Gran's spotless house. How had Penny escaped from the laundry? Had she clawed a hole through the door? Had Penny managed to trash all the rooms? If she'd gotten into Staci's room...

She hurried to the spare room, dismay filling her chest at the partially opened door. "Oh no!"

Paper was strewn everywhere. Ripped up papers. Dog-foot-printed papers. Together with a tornado-like frenzy of trailing clothes as if Penny had ripped through Staci's suitcase with abandon, it was enough to make her want to scream. Or cry. Why, oh why, hadn't she thought to put her clothes away in the drawers as Gran suggested? She could only hope the little pest hadn't...

Apparently she had. Evidence sat mounded on Staci's favorite shirt. The one she'd hoped to change into.

"I can't believe it!" A creak behind her made her spin, to see Dr. Coffee holding the white-furred monster who was wearing a sly doggy grin. "I thought you were supposed to be toilet trained!"

"I am," Dr. Coffee said mildly.

Her gaze lifted to meet his, the spurt of humor fading as he glanced around her room. "Someone's been busy."

She snatched a floral bra from the floor, stuffed it behind the bed. "Someone is in a lot of trouble."

His gaze had fallen to the torn manuscript. "Maybe you could turn those papers into kitty litter, as obviously someone here needs a bit more training."

"I need to turn those papers into a story, thank you, though how I'm going to do that now, when I can't even find—" At the sound of her wobbly voice she pressed her lips together, willing herself not to cry. It was enough that he'd seen her upset too many times today already. She wasn't a weak woman; she was supposed to be tougher than this.

"Where do you want the little terrorist?" Penny whined in his arms. He glanced down at the dog. "No, don't you start complaining. You've been very naughty. No, don't try to give me big eyes, I'm not buying. You should try apologizing to Miss Staci here, and we'll see if she wants to forgive you." He lifted the white bundle of fluff to eye level, before saying in a lower voice. "But I have to warn you, she's not a pushover, so you'll need to try very hard to make it up to her."

His words pricked unexpected moisture at the back of her eyes, as if he'd prodded her soul. To hide the emotion, she bent to pick up the rest of her clothes, except for the shirt with the unlovely pile of Penny's conquest. Ugh. Nausea clutched at her throat.

"Uh, where do you want her?"

"In a land far, far away," she muttered.

"I'm not sure they'd want her."

His humor shaved the edge off her frustration. "Penny has a box in the laundry. It's the second room down the hall."

"Got it. Come with me, you little rascal."

Clothes away, Staci stared at the mess of papers, half ripped, half chewed, her work now all out of order. She shook her head. How had today turned so bad? It seemed an age ago that she'd been wanting a moment to clear her head and go to the store and somehow find her story rhythm again. Now it seemed as though she'd never find it.

But she could never really do anything with the aroma of doggy deposit demanding attention. Screwing up her face, she carefully slid her hands under the shirt and lifted, praying not to gag. Princess Fiona—wait, did that make her sound too much like someone from *Shrek?*—would never have had to deal with such indignities. No heroine should.

"Here, let me." Warm hands slid under hers, gently lifting the burden as if carrying a pillowed ring. "Keeping the shirt or throwing it?"

She sighed. "I suppose it should be thrown."

"Probably not something you'd enjoy wearing again."

Staci shuddered, he gave a sympathetic smile, and left once again.

God bless him.

She turned back to the paper trail of destruction that now constituted her room, surveying it with hands on hips. Where to begin? She bent to pick up a paper, frowned. Collected another. Knees buckling, she sank onto the floor, collecting paper, trying to collate them as best she could: ideas, snatches of dialogue, rough scenes. She gritted her teeth. Stupid dog. Stupid dog!

"Hey."

She stilled, keeping her back to the door in her crouched position.

"Anything I can do?"

She shook her head. Tried to speak. Couldn't. Tried again. "Thank you." Her voice sounded like a strangled cat. "You've done so much to help already." She dared peek up, somehow found a smile. "I should let you go so you can get on with whatever else you were doing."

He leaned against the door frame and crossed his arms. "I don't think so."

Her brows shot up. "No?"

"It's my doctorly opinion that you might need a cup of hot tea, sweetened of course, for the shock." One eyebrow pushed up. "Unless of course you have some pumpkin spice coffee lying around somewhere."

"No to the pumpkin spice, yes please to the tea." A nice cup of hot tea sounded like heaven.

"Glad to hear it."

"I beg your pardon?"

"No to the pumpkin spice. It's not really something anyone should ever drink, is it?"

A chuckle escaped. "I went back and had another one, well," she eyed him, "actually it was my *first* one"—he looked suitably chagrined—"and decided I didn't need to be that adventurous again."

"Some adventures are best avoided," he agreed.

"Especially when they'd simply be better kept for a pie."

"A woman after my own heart."

He smiled at her, and a peculiar fluttery sensation crossed her stomach. She glanced down at the papers. "Uh, Gran has some English Breakfast teabags in the container near the kettle. I can get them in a moment."

"I've got it. You have plenty to do there, it seems."

"Gran uses an electric kettle. Do you know how to use one of them?"

His lips twitched. "I should be able to figure it out."

"It's just not everybody does," she said lamely.

"Honey, I've been living with Brits and Aussies in Africa for the past five years. Believe me, I understand how to make a good cup of tea."

Her shock at the endearment subsided under the weight of the new information just shared. He'd been working in Africa?

But before she could ask details, he'd moved away, and from the sounds that soon came from the kitchen she figured he had things under control in the tea-making department.

Unlike her. She studied the bedroom. The room looked slightly less like a bombsite, but she had her doubts she'd ever have things in pre-Penny order again. She sorted the rest of the papers as best she could, stacking them into neatish piles, until her room looked more like when she'd left this morning.

"Tea's up," he called from the kitchen.

Staci staggered unsteadily to her feet, wincing at the pins and needles in her foot.

She made it to the kitchen table, where her tea awaited in one of Gran's silver-rimmed china teacups, along with a plate of Gran's special biscuits—they were always biscuits, never cookies—and her guest.

"I thought you'd like the fancy cup." He had an earthenware mug in front of him.

"Thanks." Surprise at his thoughtfulness filled her heart as she sank into the seat opposite his.

"Get it sorted?"

"As best I could." She lifted her cup, sipped a welcome sweet mouthful, and eyed him over the teacup rim. "This is good."

"Told you I could make tea," he said smugly.

"You said you lived in Africa?"

"Yeah."

She waited, but when he said nothing further, said, "Come on. You can't say things like that and not explain more."

He leaned back in the dining chair and eyed his mug, then her. "I was working in Tanzania for a while."

"As a doctor?"

"Yes. I work at a medical mission in a remote village in the north." He shrugged. "I thought you knew."

"Because of your parents?"

He nodded.

"They only said you'd moved away. They never mentioned where." She sipped her tea. "So you're a missionary doctor?"

"Yeah."

"Telling people the good news as you stitch them up?"

"Yep."

Her storytelling heart prickled with interest. "I don't think I've ever met a missionary before."

"Probably because most of us are in the field."

"Probably." She took another sip—it really was good tea— and nibbled at the edge of the biscuit. "Do you enjoy it?"

His eyes lit, and she didn't need his many words to know how much he loved his job. She watched his animated features as he explained about the mission, the visits to remote villages, the lives his team had touched.

"That sounds fascinating."

"It keeps me busy."

"I've never been to Africa." Or anywhere involving a plane, really.

"Not many North Americans have." He shrugged.

"But you're here."

"On furlough." He tilted his coffee mug and returned it to the table. "The organization I work for insists I take an extended break every five years. It allows time for further study, to take care of family matters, personal stuff, etcetera."

"And you'll return there soon?"

"Maybe. Maybe not." His eyes met hers then glanced away.

Her heartbeat mounted. How foolish to read something of interest into that look. He was a nice guy—proved by his job. A nice guy. That was *all*.

She drained the rest of her tea, reveling in the pleasure of warm sweetness trickling down her throat. "That cup of tea was about the best thing that's happened today."

"Easy to please."

"Not exactly."

"Shame." He leaned back in his chair, his large frame contrasting with its usual petite occupant. Gran.

Shame washed over her at how quickly she'd forgotten her grandmother's plight. "Um, how long do you think Gran will be in the hospital?"

"It's hard to say. People respond to such episodes differently." His expression softened. "Today has been tough, hasn't it?"

She nodded. "I just want to know she'll be okay."

"Of course you do."

The tenderness of his words elicited a curl of warmth toward him. Truly, he had proved most thoughtful and considerate. Was this the product of his doctor training in bedside manner or something else?

Bedside manner. She blushed and ducked her head. For a romance author, she was pretty hopeless at this romance stuff.

"What's that look for?"

"Nothing for you to worry about." She pushed back her chair and stood. She would conquer this stupid, inappropriate attraction. She *had* to. "I think I should get back to the hospital."

"You sure? I can understand that you wish to see your grandmother, but she'll likely be resting for quite some time."

"But if she wakes, and I'm not there—"

"Then the nurses will do their job and reassure her that you're getting the rest you need. It's been a pretty big day, I'm sure."

"It has." As if to emphasize that, she yawned.

His smile peeked out, as if he found her amusing like a playful kitten.

"I... I would like to see Gran tonight, even if it's only for a few moments."

"Just don't overdo things," he advised. "You'll need to keep well rested if you're going to care for her when she's released. No point getting run down before that begins."

Another weight to add to her deflating spirits, one she hated herself for. How could she ever finish this book and care for Gran? Would caring for Gran mean she'd be stuck here again? She loved Gran, she wanted to help her as much as she could but didn't want to be marooned here. She wanted big city lights, fancy shops, international cuisine at the press of a button. Not Smallville. Not Muskoka Shores. She sighed.

He—fortunately—must have misinterpreted her rogue sigh. "Hey, you'll have help. Rose has lots of friends. You're not in this alone."

But she was! Gran was her only relative. Her one link to the past. She couldn't lose her, couldn't lose that. Oh, how selfish was she to think only of her career when Gran's life hung in the balance! A sob rippled past her chest. "Excuse me."

Staci rushed to her room, stuffed her computer into her laptop bag, grabbed the pile of papers, a pen, her handbag, jacket, and a scarf. She needed out, right now. Needed away from his disconcerting presence. She couldn't think straight around him.

When she returned he was standing at the sink, filling the cups with water. "I just thought—"

"Thanks, but I need to go." He was too thoughtful, too kind. "I do appreciate all your help today."

His head inclined, his eyes holding a dark edge of worry. "Remember not to push it. I know you care for Rose but getting worn out yourself will not help her at all."

"I know, I know," she said, all but shoving him toward the door. "I'll be careful, doctor."

He nodded, eyes still worried, then murmured goodbye and left.

Leaving her feeling like she'd been immeasurably rude,

incredibly ungrateful, yet also a mite relieved that his handsome presence would not distract her anymore.

JAMES GRIPPED the steering wheel as he drove home, mind ticking over the past hours. So many questions finally answered —Pumpkin Spice had a name: Miss Anastacia / Annie / Staci Everton, Mom's dinner guest and gold-star student, or so she'd murmured before Staci had entered the waiting room. Of course, the pleasure at finally learning this had been tempered by the circumstances of her grandmother's ill-health. Not exactly the way one wanted to commend oneself, by being the principal caregiver of one's only remaining relative.

He steered around the corner, a yellow haze of headlights cutting through the night. What was he doing, wondering about her? It wasn't like there could ever be any future there. For a moment he'd dared to wonder as he'd shared about Africa to her round-eyed attention that maybe such a future was possible. Her interest, her compassion, coupled with a sense of sympathetic understanding made him dare to hope—

But no. His future was too uncertain. Pursuing a relationship when he still did not know where he'd be living in six months' time was scarcely a wise use of time, and unfair to any girl. Besides, even if he knew the future, what could he offer? That he'd been sidelined from the mission due to panic attacks and depression? That he drove his dead brother's old truck because it reminded him of John? That he had little in the way of savings because he gave it all to the mission? Some kind of catch he was. Not.

He pulled up outside his parents'. He didn't even have a house to call his own, too busy paying off student loans to save toward the future.

The outside sensor light came on, his signal to go in. But he didn't want to move, didn't want to explain. Didn't want to pretend that he didn't like her.

Not when every sense remembered her, like she was imprinted on his brain, and everything inside him longed to help her, and do all he could to help ease some of her pain.

What a hopeless, tangled mess this was.

"God help me," he muttered.

CHAPTER 10

*F*iona's *finger tapped wearily at the tambour. How much longer must she wait? The last news had come hours ago, and still she sat, or paced, or prayed.*

Staci frowned. Would her readers resent the inclusion of a religious practice? But earlier times had often seen more overt examples of piety; it would be historically correct.

Perhaps if she could only be good enough then her world might finally be put right.

Staci stared at what she'd just typed. Is that truly what she thought? She glanced up from the screen to where Gran lay, her body motionless except for the slight rise and fall of her chest as air was pumped in. Staci stretched, rolling her shoulders to work the kinks from her neck and back after a torturous night's sleep in the chair. She'd barely slept, worry for Gran keeping pace with the urgency to finish this story. She had less than two weeks before this was due; she was running out of time.

But the story *was* slowly being written, even though at times it felt like it was being dragged from her, inch by blessed inch, the writerly equivalent of having her fingernails pulled. Thank goodness. Not that she'd been too good yesterday with Dr.

Coffee. She was sure her rude, dismissive actions had given him a right royal distaste of her.

She shook her head, eyes staring unseeingly at the screen, as his kindness twisted guilt again. Who did that, deal with a virtual stranger so patiently, then deal with a stupid dog—even deal with dog mess for goodness sake!—and still proved considerate when she had all but bundled him from the house? Maybe he was a masochist. Maybe he was a glutton for punishment. Maybe he was—

"Here you are."

She flinched, clutching at her computer as papers fell to the ground.

"Sorry." Dr. Coffee smiled his warm smile at her. "Didn't mean to cause another paper crisis." He bent down to collect a sheet, glanced at the lines, then at her as she nearly snatched it from his hand.

"Thanks," she muttered. Heaven forbid he saw her writing. What would Dr. Good and Kind say if he knew she'd written for Flame's Passion Defiant line?

"Why is it that you constantly seem surrounded by so much paper?" he asked. "Don't you like trees?"

"Actually, I quite like trees."

"Really?"

"Yes. Have you ever been forest bathing?"

His eyes widened. "Somehow I don't think you're talking about skinny dipping in a mountain stream."

She fought a smile. "It's a Japanese thing where stressed out workers are encouraged to spend time in the woods and be refreshed among nature."

"That sounds interesting."

"It works, too. I tried it among the redwoods in California."

"Really?"

"Really." When on a weekend's break from university. Best stress relief ever.

"Miss Everton, I must admit that sometimes you say the most surprising things."

What did he mean? Was he mocking her? But that look in his eyes didn't suggest such a thing. Oh, why did this man jumble her thoughts and emotions so much? Her gaze untangled from his, and she turned to the figure lying in the bed. "Any news on how Gran is doing?"

"That's why I'm here." He flicked open the charts and was perusing them when the nurse came in. "Ah, Nurse Wilson. How's the patient?"

"No change." The middle-aged nurse eyed Staci with something like a frown. "Have you been here all night, young lady?"

Staci kept her gaze averted from the doctor. "I got some rest."

"Tsk, tsk. You need to make sure you rest properly," Nurse Wilson continued. "Your grandmother will need you well when she gets ready to go home."

A snicker made Staci shoot the doctor a sour look. Were they all in on this together? "I wanted to be here for Gran," she maintained.

"So she hasn't stirred at all?"

"Only once, Doctor, and only briefly."

"She'll improve with an easing of the drugs today." He issued some instructions, then turned to Staci once more. "If—when—she does wake, just talk to her quietly. Sometimes in situations like these people can get a little agitated and confused when they realize they've undergone such an experience, and it's best to keep them calm, let them know they're in good hands, and so on. I'm sure you being here will provide Rose with that reassurance."

She nodded, slumping back in her seat, hiding a yawn with her hand.

"I'll be back to check on her later," he murmured to Nurse Wilson, before nodding to Staci. "Miss Everton."

"Dr. Wells."

She watched his white-coated-self walk away, then turned back to the bed, but not before noticing the nurse give her an assessing look. Staci ignored her, and moved closer to Gran, picking up her hand and caressing it. "Hey, Gran, I'm here. Feel free to wake up soon."

"There are no guarantees for when she'll wake up, but you keep on talking to her and we'll hope for the best."

"And pray."

Nurse Wilson looked startled. "Well, yes, that too."

Staci swallowed a smile. Was it any wonder the nurse who'd admitted she enjoyed Staci's racy novels was taken aback by her mention of prayer?

Soon she left, and Staci was left alone again, save for Gran, and the accompanying beeps and sighs of modern medical technology. She gave Gran's hand another stroke, then returned to her laptop and was soon lost in Fiona's world again.

The door slowly opened. Fiona's heart beat increased its pace. Who was there? What should she do? Friend or foe? Oh—

"Excuse me?" A graying head popped around the door. "Anastacia?"

"Oh, Jenny! Hello." Staci waved her inside. "This is a nice surprise."

"I was in the neighborhood, and thought I'd drop by. It can get a little lonely waiting here on one's own. Well, that was my experience, anyway. And when Jem mentioned you were here again—"

"He mentioned me?"

"Oh, just last night, when he finally got in. He thought you might spend the night here." Her smile, reminiscent of her son's, flashed. "He was right, huh?"

Staci shrugged. "I just wanted to be here in case Gran wakes up."

"Of course you did, hon. Did you get some sleep?"

"A bit."

"Have you had something to eat? I know the cafeteria food isn't all that great, so I brought you some muffins and fruit, just in case."

"Oh, you didn't have to do that," Staci said, touched. Was this what mothering felt like? It had been so long since her own mother had passed, she barely recognized the feeling. She met Jenny's gaze and smiled. "But I'm so glad you did."

Jenny beamed. "I just knew that was what I was meant to do today. Now, would you like a cup of coffee? I brought some in a thermos as well. I know it's not as fancy as some of those flavors you can get at The Coffee Blend, but Jem assures me it's good."

Staci straightened in her seat, accepting the blueberry muffin with murmured thanks. "Um, coffee would be great, thank you." She took a bite. Blueberry tartness sang through the sugar and butter melting in her mouth. "Oh, my goodness, Mrs. Wells. Did you make these? They're *so* good."

Jenny wore a proud smile. "I like to think my muffins can hold their own at the Spring Fair."

"The Spring Fair?" Was this a new town tradition, or another she'd forgotten?

"It's probably a more grandiose title for what it really is. But Muskoka Shores does like to celebrate the end of winter with a fair in early May. We hold it just before Mother's Day, which is a wonderful time for people to buy gifts and such for their…"

Her voice trailed away, and she looked at Staci apologetically. "I'm sorry. I should not have mentioned Mother's Day."

"It doesn't matter. It was a long time ago." No wonder people hadn't gone out of their way to mention such things to her.

"Anyway, you look like you were rather busy when I came in. Is that another novel?"

"It's the one I need to submit by Christmas," she admitted.

"Ah, and here you are being distracted by your poor grandmother's illness and all manner of things." Jenny eyed Staci thoughtfully. "Would it help if I stayed with her for a while? You could go home, have a shower, then spend some more time working."

Her heart leapt at the idea. But, "I couldn't ask you to do that."

"Oh, don't be silly, dear. I know, better than anyone, how hard it can be to rest in a hospital. In some ways you should be glad your grandmother is not yet awake. It can be mighty hard to get to sleep with IV drips and buzzers and all the noises all the time."

How well Staci knew that, stifling another yawn.

"Go. I'll be the friendly face Rose needs when she wakes up. And if she doesn't wake, then we'll be trusting God that He's continuing to restore her body to full health, and when you do return she'll be sure to be happy to see you. And you'll be able to focus on her without the distraction of looming deadlines."

"Are you sure, Mrs. Wells?"

"Really sure. Now, go." Jenny pulled up a chair and drew out her knitting. "I'll be quite happy sitting here talking to Rose. We have a lot to catch up on." Her eyes twinkled. "Even if she can only listen, I'm sure she'll be interested in what I have to say."

Staci didn't doubt that but couldn't help wondering how much of what Jenny would share would pertain to her. She tamped down the thoughts. Really, she was acting almost as self-centered as Davis Scott, thinking every conversation needed to pertain to herself. Rose was Jenny's friend and Jenny would have far more interesting things to share than whether James was interested in Staci. Ugh. Was this the curse of the romance writer, seeking romance wherever she went, even if it was entirely in her imagination? Although James *had* mentioned Staci to his mother a few times, and must have shown something of his concern for Jenny to be here checking on Staci's welfare…

Oh, enough! She was being *ridiculous*. He had a girlfriend. Didn't he?

She collected her papers, stuffing them with her laptop into her computer bag, retrieving the various items that constituted time spent in hospital. A water bottle. Her scarf. Her down-filled jacket. Her phone.

"Oh! This battery charger belongs to James—I mean, Dr. Wells. He lent me his yesterday. Should I give it to you?"

Jenny waved it away. "You keep it. I'm sure if Jem needs it he'll come find you."

Why did that feel like a set-up? She winced at her thoughts. She obviously *really* needed sleep. "Okay, then. Thanks so much, Jenny. You'll let me know if Gran wakes?"

"Absolutely. Now go, write that story."

"Yes, ma'am." Staci managed a mock salute and, with a last press of lips to Gran's brow and smiled thanks to Jenny, hurried away.

Her shoes echoed down the hall, her arms filled with bags and equipment. She wondered if she'd meet Dr. Coffee and was strangely disappointed when she reached her car without encountering him. She did manage to see Larissa and offer her a half-smile which was met with a lift of fingers probably meant to constitute a wave. No matter. Staci had to get home, had to get changed, had to—had to check on Penny! Oh no! What if the dog had escaped again? Staci had secured the laundry door properly, hadn't she? Or had that been Dr. Coffee? The past twenty-four hours were beginning to blur; she couldn't be sure of anything anymore.

Balancing her bundles carefully, she beeped open her car and carefully stowed her items, annoyed at herself for thinking how much easier it had been to have Dr. Coffee's assistance the previous time. She was an independent woman for goodness sake! She didn't need a man to help her.

But some small part of her—a part twenty-first century

feminist Staci would deny—still liked the feeling of being looked after, the feeling of protection, of belonging. Like the feeling that Jenny had brought with her, with her baking and motherly concern. Her eyes pricked. It had been way too long since she'd felt that way.

"Stop feeling sorry for yourself," she muttered, and started the car.

The drive home took only minutes, minutes in which she could appreciate last night's dump of snow and the Christmas decorations neighbors had begun putting up, cheery lights that seemed to warm her heart—and the frigid air—by several degrees. She pulled in, grabbed her bag and laptop essentials, and made her way inside. Sure enough, Penny's yelping penetrated the walls. Great. Didn't the dog know how to use the doggy flap in the laundry door? She'd have to deal with her later.

She filled the kettle and switched it on, propped a teabag in her cup and waited, gazing at the sink where the two cups from yesterday still taunted. Had she been rude to James today? She pressed at the dull pain centering her forehead, the boiling water reaching a crescendo. It was so hard to juggle her work, her responsibilities, her friendships, let alone try to forge new ones. Is that what he was? A friend? She tried the word on. He certainly seemed interesting, but could she really be friends with a man with a girlfriend? That seemed weird; she bet the girlfriend wouldn't be too happy. Or maybe she was more secure than Staci had ever been. She looked the sort who should be, all tanned Barbie curves and hair. With her Celtic coloring, Staci had always felt she looked and acted different, even before her parents' accident had cemented the fact.

When the teabag had bled the water to a satisfactory brown, she added milk, then moved to the sink, gazing out the window. The trees seemed to have lost more leaves; she could see more of the neighbor's house today. She sipped her tea. Time was passing. She really should get started on her book, but for a few moments she just wanted to stand here, to be still.

A cloud passed over the sun, dimming the sky. She placed her cup down, felt her shoulders sag as weight seemed to swarm over her. She was so weary. And the dog still barked for attention. Her book still needed to be written. Gran.

But Gran *was* at least being cared for by medical staff and friends. And Gran did have friends, people willing to put away groceries and help with other things. Such was the benefit of a small town. People might know each other's business, but it meant they knew when to care. Staci had a few friends in Chicago, but how many would know when to offer assistance, or even would think to offer? Her life of takeout and isolation barely accommodated that.

Her eyes lifted to the windowsill, where yesterday's African violet was now potted. Had Dr. Coffee done that? Her heart snagged. Maybe God was helping her more than she knew, enveloping her with kindness she did not deserve. Kindness she could not afford to indulge in, she told herself firmly. She had a story to write, then a Smallville to leave. Her future was not here.

Dragging in a deep breath, she pushed away from the counter, and moved reluctant feet to where eager paws scratched at the laundry door. "Penny? Are you in there?"

The way the yelping escalated said her voice had been registered. Her heart caught anew. No wonder Penny was excited. She probably expected to see Gran, her faithful companion for this however many years. Was that why she'd gotten frustrated before? Poor thing.

Staci opened the door and Penny rushed out, barking madly, pawing at Staci's jeans-clad legs before rushing to Gran's room. "Sorry, Penny. Gran is still away."

But Penny paid no heed, sniffing around corners and clawing at the furnishings as if she expected Gran to suddenly appear. Staci watched her for a moment, then sighed. She really couldn't let Gran's house get trashed from the enthusiasm of a ten-year-old puppy.

"Hey, Penny. Do you want something to eat?" Staci moved to the refrigerator where Gran kept the special dog food normally fed to Penny on Sundays. Today counted as special enough. She spooned some out into a bone-shaped bowl and placed it on the floor, which Penny fell on ravenously. Oh. Hadn't she left food enough in the laundry? She peeked inside. Nope. The dog dispenser food bowl looked like it had been topped up yesterday; the water looked like the same. Dr. Coffee again? Staci owed him, big time.

Apart from that, the room looked surprisingly okay, although—her nose wrinkled—it seemed Penny preferred to do her business inside rather than outdoors. A quick search revealed the offending item, and she carefully wrapped it in newspaper and took it outside then flung it into the far corner of the garden. She supposed she should be grateful that the little wretch at least knew to use the doggy door for other matters.

Back inside, she quickly washed her hands then moved to her room. But Penny barred her way, her yelps demanding attention. Staci's irritation surged, then waned. Poor thing. It must be hard to be unable to communicate with anyone who understood doggy language. She crouched down, stroking Penny on her head, and spoke softly. "You poor thing. I'm sorry I haven't been very nice to you. You must be missing Gran as much as I am."

Penny's head tilted to one side, then she uttered a short bark, as if in agreement.

Staci smiled what felt like her first smile that day. "So if you'll forgive me for not understanding, then I'll forgive you for wrecking my papers and ruining my favorite shirt. Deal?"

Another bark.

"Okay then." Before she could stand, Penny lunged forward,

licking Staci's face with the eagerness of a two-year-old child with an ice-cream. "Penny!" Her laughter sounded rusty. "Come on, girl."

Staci picked her up, feeling the heat of the little body press against her, as the barks softened to an ecstatic canine version of a purr. Staci rubbed Penny's head slowly, the little body quivering with delight. Why, all Penny wanted was to feel comforted, to feel loved. Her eyes blurred. How well she knew that feeling.

She stood, and a new wave of tiredness hit her. She forced her eyes open. She really should get back to her laptop, but there was no way she could write while holding Penny, and she sensed the dog would be reluctant to give up this cuddle anytime soon. She stumbled to the lounge room, spying the calendar on Gran's wall. She really should check if Gran had any appointments that would need to be cancelled, but right now, all she wanted to do was sleep. Sleep, with the comfort of a drowsy dog in her arms. Feeling like someone loved her, feeling a sense of rightness, of assurance in this world. A few minutes wouldn't hurt. So she lay down on the floral lounge, stretched out, and closed her eyes to rest.

❧

"James, do you mind?"

He did, but sensed Brandi wouldn't stop until he agreed. "Sure, we can do a car swap. I can be there in an hour."

They ended the call, and he stared at his phone as a text from his mom pinged for attention. *At the hospital with Rose, sent Annie home. Please check on her as soon as able. Tx*

Annie? Who on earth was—oh, Anastacia.

Aversion at his mom's request to see an unknown person soon changed to anticipation. See Staci he'd gladly do, her humor meshed with his, her whirlwind energy intrigued him.

He pressed the buzzer for his next patient, and the remaining consultations made the time fly—or maybe that was simply his impatience to see Staci. Glad for the chance to finish early, he drove John's beat up Ford downtown to the bookstore where Brandi had requested him to come.

"Oh, thanks so much," Brandi said, a smile lighting her face. "We've got some large displays we need to move, and they won't fit in my car, so yours is the only vehicle large enough to carry them."

He nodded, although he had his doubts. "What's the display?"

"Oh, you should come and look." She grabbed his arm and led him inside, but there were no sparks, no nothing between them. Not like there was with—

"Look." Brandi pointed to the front window where a Christmas display of Santa's sleigh packed with books held pride of place.

"It looks good as it is," he said. "What needs to change?"

"I thought we could have some reindeer. And more snow. What do you think?"

He picked up a book from a nearby display, a historical romance, judging from the picture of pirates and sailing ship on the front, then placed it back. "I think you don't really need to change a thing." And that this had been a waste of time.

"Oh, but you're here now. Won't you help me?"

He bit back the words of impatience hovering on his tongue and nodded his acquiescence. He had nothing else to do, except visit Staci, and if he left that visit a little longer then maybe he could see if she were free for dinner…

"Let's get this happening then. I've got things to do a little later."

"Thank you." She smiled up at him, and for a moment he could see why John had fallen for her. Brandi was attractive, and obviously enjoyed her books, and so was not unintelligent.

She and John had been a couple since high school, which made her almost part of the family. He just hoped others didn't see them together and assume other things.

The next two hours were spent lugging bulky polystyrene reindeers from a storage shed on the town outskirts to the bookstore, his truck making the trip a few times.

He studied the display, offering advice when requested, as Brandi and her assistant rearranged things. He glanced at his watch. "I really need to go now."

"Oh. Well, thank you again for your help, James."

"You're welcome." He moved back outside and turned the ignition, only to discover the extra trips had used up his extra gas. He smacked the steering wheel and made his way back inside.

"Brandi, I need to borrow your car. Mine's run out of gas."

"Oh, well, can you give me a moment? It's nearly closing time, and then I can drop you back."

He was tempted to say her assistant could do it but refrained as it might have sounded churlish. After a few minutes waiting they finally headed home, but his dad was out and not answering his phone, and Mom was still at the hospital. He grabbed a gas can and made his way back to the car. "Sorry. Seems I'll need you to drive me back after all."

"No problem."

But ten minutes later, after purchasing gas and carefully pouring it in, he discovered his truck still refused to go. Exasperation bit. He pushed it down. Africa had provided many opportunities to practice patience; he should be better at this by now.

"Looks like I'll need to wait until Dad can come and check things over."

"Oh, but you don't want to wait in the cold, do you?"

Not particularly.

"And didn't you say you had an appointment? I can drive you there if you like."

Yeah. Okay, this could be awkward. "It was something Mom asked me to do, to check on one of her former students," he felt it necessary to say.

"Of course. Do you know the way?"

"Yeah."

Glad she didn't ask him why he knew such a random thing, he directed the way to Rose's house. When he arrived it was very still, save for an insistent yapping inside, that suddenly stopped.

He knocked on the door. "Hello?"

A glance back at the Volkswagen revealed Brandi watched him, her forehead pleated.

He knocked again. "Hello? Staci?"

"Maybe she's gone out," Brandi called.

Maybe. But something insisted he remain.

He pounded on the door again and called out more loudly. "Staci?"

CHAPTER 11

*L**ord Markworth drew her close, his lips descending to hers, eliciting a shiver of delight. Oh, how wonderful to know she had his approval, and that the Queen had deigned to sanction this union with her blessing. She drew back, resting her head against his chest, and heard the loud thump, thump of his heart.*

Staci sighed, her lips curling in a smile. She really should write this down. Even if it wasn't in the correct sequence, she needed to grasp scenes while they floated by in her subconscious. And this scene could be *so* romantic…

A thump sounded. She opened an eye. Penny was gone. The thumping noise came again. "Penny?" What had the silly dog got into now? She hoped it wasn't—

"My room!" She pushed upright on the couch, squinting. No lights were on, and it was much darker now. How long had she slept? She could barely see. She swung her legs to the side and stumbled up, when her knee banged into the coffee table. Sharp pain splintered through her leg. "Ow!" She grabbed her knee, pressing against the pain. "Penny!"

Where was the dratted dog? Her brain felt woozy, the dimness making shapes seem unfamiliar as she stumbled through the kitchen to her room. The thud came again, one that matched the thudding pain between her eyes. She groaned, a sound that seemed loud enough to finally attract Penny's attention as she bounded toward her. Then, somehow between Penny's bounding and Staci's drowsiness, she stumbled, and her ankle turned to one side. Pain ricocheted up her leg, magnifying a hundred times as her ankle twisted—the wretched ankle that had been twisted too many times before. She gasped, a noise that sounded more like a scream, and collapsed onto Gran's tiled kitchen floor. Her head cracked hard, and she lay there, eyes closed, as the throbbing in her brain escalated to something technicolor.

Seconds later, she was being licked, her face pushed by a rough tongue. She coughed but couldn't move her arm for the sheer pain. Was it broken? How could she write? How would she ever finish the story?

Panic rose. Forget the story: would she ever be discovered? What if Gran never woke again, and it took years for them to discover Staci's remains on the cold tiled floor? Would she ever be remembered? Forget the NYT list; she just wanted to be alive!

Gradually she became aware of muffled shouts, and that thudding sound again. She closed her eyes, willed herself to roll and push upright with her good arm. She gasped as the movement jerked more pain. In the gloom she could see her right wrist—her main writing wrist—hang as limply as her ankle surely did. A ripple of hysteria escaped. She was never this clumsy. Never. What had just happened in the past three minutes?

Penny's ears pricked, and she ceased her pawing at Staci to go whine by the front door. Was someone there? Not that Staci dared move. Nausea heaved, begging release.

"Hello?"

She closed her eyes again, willing the queasiness to abate.

What, she was dreaming aloud now? The characters in her head were speaking with deep, mellifluous tones…

Wait. She pried her eyes open. *Was* someone at the door? This wasn't a dream? Penny's pawing hadn't ceased.

A thud came again, then another, then a loud cracking sound and Gran's door was flung open. "Staci?"

Lights came on, and she caught a glimpse of dark hair and concern before she closed her eyes against the brighter light and turned her head to release her stomach's contents. Gross. She tried lifting her hand to wipe the residue from her mouth, gasping once more at the pain.

"Staci? Oh, you're here."

For a blessed few minutes, she felt herself being cared for as a child. Her mouth was wiped with a cool washcloth, an arm wrapped around her shoulders, helping her to a sitting position. She inhaled the faintest scent of bergamot. A scent worthy of a hero…

"What happened?"

She couldn't speak; her mouth felt like slurry.

"There's blood on her head." A fainter sound, higher-pitched. "Was she attacked?"

"Were you attacked?" the deeper voice asked.

Though unutterable weariness threatened to claim her, she forced her eyes open again, to meet Dr. Coffee's gaze. He was so close now, she could see the individual hairs bristling his chin, and could smell the mint on his breath. Which meant he could no doubt smell the vomit on hers. Her vision blurred, her head lolled.

"Staci?" She felt herself being clasped in warm arms, being picked up from the floor. Pain quivered up her arm. She bit her lip to stop the moan. Vaguely heard the deep voice mention the hospital. Police.

"I don't think she's been attacked," the feminine voice said.

"Only by a dog," Staci finally managed to mumble.

She was hefted closer to the lean body of hero-worthy aroma. "What did you say?"

"A dog. Penny." It was so nice being cradled here. "Tried… tried to lick me to death."

A rumble of something that sounded like amusement rolled across his chest, then she was placed gently back on the couch she'd lain on before, her back and shoulders sinking into the soft cushions.

"Staci."

She forced herself to not think about the pain, but to concentrate on the masculine lips speaking her name. The firm-looking lips. The lips she'd seen pulled into wryness and humor. Her head tipped closer. What would those lips feel like—?

"Staci?" Vertical lines marked James's brow, emphasizing the frown in his voice. "Are you feeling dizzy?"

"Yeah."

"Headache?"

"Big time."

"Blurred vision?"

Was that one handsome face or two? "Yes."

"You cracked your head pretty hard on the floor. I think you'd best come in for observation."

"No." She pushed his arm away. "Don't want to. Too much to do here."

"I'm afraid that will have to wait for a while longer. You need to be checked out properly."

"Haven't you checked me out?" A hysteria-laden giggle pushed out. "That's what your mom says anyway." Wait. Had she? Or had Staci only wanted him to? So confusing…

She heard soft laughter in the background and turned to see the Barbie doll from church. Why was she laughing? She tried to frown, but the movement only caused her senses to swim. "I don't feel too good." She pressed her fingers against her mouth.

"Get a bucket," he called to his girlfriend.

Staci vaguely heard her flustered arguments in the background but was more conscious of trying to keep her dignity as the too warm, too gentle hand softly stroked her back, and the lovely voice spoke soothingly.

"You have a lovely voice," she mumbled.

"Do I? Well, you have lovely hair."

As if to emphasize his comment, he gently gathered her hair dangling across her face and swept it behind her ears. Her skin trembled as his fingers brushed gently across her neck. She groaned. How could she notice things like that at such a time?

"Staci?" His face lowered to meet hers, worry shading his eyes. "Can you hold on a moment longer?"

For what? Oh, the bucket, which Barbie had finally found and had placed before her, along with a murmured complaint about an overly friendly Penny. Staci pushed it away, tilted her head back against the pillows. "I'll be fine. Just need to rest." She closed her eyes, tried to focus on her breathing. Maybe if she rested long enough, Dr. Coffee and his perfect girlfriend would go away, and she could wake up and pretend this had been a nightmare.

"You do need to rest, which is why you should come to the hospital."

"Don't want to rest there. Too tired."

Another soft chuckle, and she felt her wrist being gently grasped. She hissed out a protest as her eyes flew open.

"Did you hurt this when you fell?"

"Yes," she whispered. His dark green eyes held golden specks. Drops of gold. Drops of warm gold. Delicious gold. Could you eat gold? Not that she wanted to eat… *Focus.* Focus! She dragged her attention away, trying to focus on what he was saying. But a girl could get lost in his eyes. Eyes perfect for a hero…

"…other injuries?"

What? Oh, her injuries. "Ankle," she said, raising a foot, then wincing.

He pulled away, checking over her ankle with careful, prodding fingers, eliciting another whimper as he found the site of painful tenderness. "Is this the same one you twisted before?"

"Yes. I have a gift."

"Seems you do." He glanced up and looked beyond Staci's shoulder. "Can you check the bathroom cabinets to see if there's a medical kit? I need long bandages."

"Rice," Staci mumbled, as the sound of departure suggested he was being obeyed.

"What was that?" He peered closer, "Did you say something?"

He had such pretty eyes. A pretty color, like— "The sea."

"*Si?*" He pushed closer, so all she would have to do would be to lean in and she would know what his lips tasted like. "Do you speak Spanish now?"

"What?" She had dim memories of learning Spanish for a year or so in high school. "I'm an English major."

"Never mind," he muttered, glancing as the blonde reentered Staci's vision. "Must be why Mom loves her so."

Jenny loved her? The thought swelled her heart, pushed the ever-near emotion into her eyes, to mass inside her throat. She knew Gran loved her, but to think someone else in this world cared for Staci...

"Staci, I'm going to wrap your ankle now. We'll need some ice, too."

"Rice," Staci murmured again.

He chuckled. "That's right. You'll need to rest, ice, compress and elevate that ankle for a good while. You've hurt it a few times before, haven't you?"

The nausea had subsided enough she thought she could risk a nod. Bad mistake. Thank God the bucket was within grasp, as she made full use of it, retching her way to complete humiliation. Oh well. She'd just need to ensure none of her heroines ever acted with such lack of decorum. Although, Dr. Coffee had totally nailed the sympathetic hero part.

A cold, damp washcloth was handed to her, and she gingerly wiped her mouth. It felt weird performing the action with her left hand.

"Better now?"

"Much," she croaked.

"Poor thing. Let's get you to the hospital—"

"And see Gran?"

"And we'll see how your grandmother is doing after we get you fixed up."

"Okay." It was nice to have someone look after her. He made her feel… at ease, like she could exhale.

He wrapped an arm around Staci to prop her upright and she snuggled closer. Then caught the look on the other woman's face, and almost died of mortification. She pulled away, heat pulsing past the fingers covering her cheeks. What the heck was she doing? Acting like a… like a hussy, like someone she was *not*, like one of her evil characters who always ended up unhappy and alone at the end after trying to steal the heroine's suitor. She was *so* not going to behave like that person.

"Sorry." Maybe her actions would be overlooked due to her lightheaded confusion. She hoped so, anyway.

"Brandi, can you grab some clothes for Miss Everton?" Seriously, Barbie's name was Brandi? And what was with the professional 'Miss Everton' now? "I'm going to help her into the car. I'm afraid I'll need to drive her to the hospital."

Brandi's "sure" didn't sound too delighted, but Staci didn't care. It was enough to hold her balance as she was gently boosted to a standing position, Dr. Coffee's arm supporting her shoulders as she drag-hopped her way to the door. "Oh!"

"What is it?"

"I need my bag."

"Let me get you out to the car, then I'll grab it."

"Thank you."

He really was proving to be something of a hero, someone

with the capacity to match Fiona's heroics. She stifled a moan as the chill of late afternoon darkness rushed at her. How was she ever expected to manage the icy path?

A muttered, "Excuse me," and a swoop of arms holding her soon solved that problem. Her body stiffened as she fought the temptation to snuggle again, tried to look cool and not like Clumsy Vomit Woman who'd succumbed to the alluring scent of Tough He-man Doctor. She wasn't that kind of female, all helpless and needy. Although she *did* feel pretty helpless right now…

He reached a muscled bicep past her nose to open the Volkswagen's passenger door—he had to be muscled, right, or else how could he hold her?—and gently placed her inside. "There you go."

"Thanks." It was a relief her weight—and breath—hadn't made him keel over and die.

His hands braced either side of the car door frame. "Anything else you need, apart from your bag?"

Penny's yelping hammered through her mind. "Penny. Gran's dog."

"Got it." He nodded, then gently closed the door, leaving her to lean back against the headrest and close her eyes. But not before catching the disgruntled expression on Barbie's—no, Brandi's—face as she exited Gran's house, with a rattan enviro bag of clothing-like lumps and a package of something that looked like frozen peas.

Staci was tired. So tired she didn't bother opening her eyes as the car door released and cold air suggested Brandi stood there waiting. "Here you go."

She wrenched ajar her eyelids enough to manage to hold the cold pack handed to her and offer a thanks and a smile she hoped looked like a non-boyfriend-stealer. A minute later, Dr. Coffee was back, her handbag was stowed at her feet, Gran's door was closed and the squirming pile of puppy was given to the unhappy camper in the back seat. "I called Dad to ask him to come fix the door. He should be here shortly. We'll drop Penny at Mom's so you don't have to worry about her anymore." He got in the driver's seat, glanced in the rear vision mirror. "You don't mind staying at Mom's to explain, do you, Brandi?"

"Nope." But judging from her facial expression in the mirror, Staci thought she kind of did.

"Thanks," he said.

Staci echoed her thanks weakly, then turned to look outside. Twinkling lights decorated house after house, lawn after lawn. The dusky light suggested she'd been asleep for several hours now. She glanced at the clock. At least four hours. So much for her little rest.

The car turned into the Wells' drive, and he parked, unlocked the front door, then guided Brandi and Penny inside. "Bye," Staci whispered, before biting her lip. She hoped Jenny and Mitch were up to the challenge of Penny's delightful companionship. Brandi, well, she hoped she wouldn't hold Staci's clumsiness against her.

James returned, noticed Staci watching him, and his lips pulled to one side. He dragged open the car door, rubbing his hands against the cold. "Well, this day hasn't exactly gone as expected."

"Sorry to be such a burden."

"I don't mind."

"I think Brandi did." The words escaped before she could stop them. Honestly, why couldn't she remember to filter?

"You think?" He turned to her, one arm almost touching her shoulder as he turned his head and reversed before his eyes touched hers once more. "I didn't notice anything."

"Probably because you're a man." For crying out loud, where was this coming from? "Ignore me," she mumbled.

"I'll do my best."

She peeked across, met the amusement in his eyes and felt her shoulders relax. "I'm sorry. I don't mean to be so rude."

"Oh, you were being rude, were you? I just thought it part of your special brand of charm."

She bit her lip. She deserved that.

He steered the car around the corner.

"Where is your truck?" she asked.

"This is Brandi's. Mine is at her store."

Oh. Her heart drooped.

"How is your vision now?" His manner had reverted back to professional medical practitioner. "Any more headaches? Nausea?"

"My head still feels like a chainsaw is slicing through it."

"I'm not surprised. You'll likely end up with a nasty bump."

"Another thing to add to my special charm," she mumbled.

His chuckle caught her by surprise, and she felt herself relax again. Maybe humor and regret and enough distance could prove an effective buffer against this disconcerting attraction.

Within minutes they were once again at the hospital, though he parked in the staff parking lot. "Your new home away from home."

"Awesome," she muttered, her mind flicking back to her judgy comment about Davis from weeks ago. Although if said with sarcasm, surely one teenager-like 'awesome' could be overlooked, couldn't it?

"I'm glad you're excited."

She shot him a sour look he ignored as he opened her door, concentrating on helping her move.

"Want me to carry you again?"

Her pulse leapt. But no, she could be mature, instead of the man-stalker scary woman of vomit and injured limbs. "I should be fine."

He eyed the path and then her doubtfully. "I don't think it's worth risking. Come on. Let me have you."

She gulped and allowed herself the pleasure of being carried once more. His coat couldn't hide the muscled strength she'd noticed before, nor completely disguise the scent she found enticing. She forced herself to relax, to not give rise to comments about excessive wriggling—which might give rise to suggestions of improper snuggling.

The automatic doors swooshed open, then the second set permitted entry to the emergency room waiting room, where, once again, Larissa was on duty. "Hey, Larissa."

Larissa's eyes bulged. "What happened?"

"Clumsy girl here," Staci said with a weak wave.

"Okay," Larissa said, dragging a wheelchair from behind the desk. "Put her in here."

Dr. Coffee slowly lowered Staci into the seat and looked deep into her eyes. "You'll be fine."

The intensity of his stare, his kindness, his assurance, swelled the ever-lurking pressure of emotion once again. She blinked it away, nodded, found a smile. "Thanks again."

She thought she felt his hand caress the back of her head, but she couldn't be sure, not with the way he snapped back into professional mode, issuing instructions and orders like a boss. She couldn't help but wonder what Larissa thought of it all.

Two hours later, she was tucked up in white cotton in a ward shared with a skinny teenage girl and a woman in her sixties. A sign attached to the wall above her bed declared that Staci should be checked every hour for concussion. Really, it seemed a little overkill for her to be here, but maybe this was another benefit of a small town, lacking the drive-by shootings and such that made city hospitals too busy for such things. And she *was* grateful, even if it meant she'd need to stay a while longer, ankle wrapped as her swollen wrist waited for an x-ray. The drugs to ease her pain seeped into her bloodstream, and she felt her eyes drift closed. And wondered if Dr. Coffee thought of her in any good way at all.

THE KITCHEN WAS SHADOWED, the day's long hours stretching across his heart and wearied brain. Brandi had gone home, Penny had finally settled in a basket in the corner, his dad had fixed both Rose's front door and James's truck, but still the whirr of the past few hours refused to go away.

"James?" His mom touched his shoulder. "What's bothering you?"

He exhaled, lifted his gaze from where he'd propped his head, elbows against his knees as he sat at the table. "What would have happened if I hadn't arrived then?"

"You mean with Staci?"

The scene from earlier continued to track across his mind. "She was so helpless." So fragile. And yet still somehow had maintained a sense of humor.

"She'll be okay," his mom assured.

Her gaze continued, as steady as any time when she'd had something to say he wasn't sure he wanted to hear. "What is it, Mom?"

"Do you care about her?"

"You want me to." He posed this as half question, half statement, and was unsurprised when she nodded.

"Staci is smart, believes as we do, is funny, successful and understands loss. I think you'd make a good match."

The more time he spent in Staci's company the more he thought that too. "You could say the same about Brandi," he pointed out.

"Well, Brandi is a lovely girl, but I don't think she'd be right for you."

He agreed, but still felt a perverse need to be contrary. "Regardless, it's not as simple as that."

"Why not?"

"I can't think about a girlfriend. Not when I'm returning to Africa."

"Are you?" his mother asked gently. "Have you received the letter from the board?"

"Not yet."

"Do you mean to say you want to return to Africa?"

"Maybe. I don't know anymore. I know there is still good I can do overseas, but…"

"But not if your heart isn't in it anymore." She stroked the back of his head, like she used to do when he and his brothers were young boys. He found the motion soothing. "There is good you can do here, too," she reminded him.

"I know. But the need there is so much greater."

"And the need won't lessen just because you serve, or not." A beat. "And how can you serve well, if you need strengthening yourself?"

He nodded, aware of the truth of that statement. He knew himself to often wear a coat of affable good-humor, but still the loneliness burned, the depression hovered at the corners of his soul. Since his return to Muskoka Shores he'd felt the brittle edges of his heart start to ease, to find hope. The letter might say he could return to his duties in Africa, but faced with the unrelenting nature of pain and death, would that indeed be wise?

"You need someone who makes you smile, someone who lifts your heart, someone who understands the value and grit of life."

"And you think Staci does?"

"Yes."

The confidence in his mother's answer bolstered his wearied emotions, whilst sparking him to recall something else. He glanced up at her. "Did you tell Staci I'd checked her out?"

"What? No. Of course not."

He chuckled. "She was a little spacey." His mind flicked back to earlier. She'd said she liked his voice. He remembered the way she'd almost cuddled into him. Almost as if she liked him.

Despite her occasional rebuffs, and blunt comments others might construe as rude, part of him wondered if maybe she really did like him.

And maybe if these feelings he'd suppressed could be encouraged to live a little too.

CHAPTER 12

Fiona felt herself being scooped up, pressed tight against James's beating heart. "I won't lose you," he murmured in her ear. "We have not gone through so much only for it to end like this."

"But I cannot come with you to your kingdom. I have matters to attend to here in Rubitania."

"You can still see to them with me when we're in Scotland. It will be different to what you're used to, but it will still be most enjoyable, I assure you."

She smelled his scent of bergamot, leather, and moss, and felt her defenses crumble. "I don't know."

"I do."

Something about his supreme confidence niggled. Why must things be done to suit his pleasure, his purposes? Wasn't her life and responsibilities of equal importance?

But such things drained away, as his mouth descended to meet hers, their lips touching in a holy embrace that soon turned to fervor. Her hands clutched at his shirt, then crept upwards to wind around his neck, as his hands caressed her cheeks, her jaw, her hair.

She dragged her lips away, desperate for breath, then eyed him between half closed lids, her chest rising with fervor. "I love—"

"Good morning!"

The overly bright voice flung her eyes open, heat filling her cheeks. Thank God there was no dream-reading medical instrument in this hospital, although judging from the look the nurse was giving her she might have some idea what had filled her thoughts.

"And how are you feeling today, Miss Everton?" Nurse Wilson checked her charts. "Any headaches? Blurred vision?"

"I feel much better."

"It's a good thing Dr. Wells was able to attend to you so promptly."

"Um, yes." Was that speculation in her eyes?

Nurse Wilson nodded. "Very fortunate indeed that he was on the scene."

"Yes, I'm very thankful."

Staci didn't hear the rest of the comments, struck by the earlier words. She *was* very thankful for Dr. Wells, and for poor disgruntled Brandi, but most of all she was thankful that God had somehow led them to her. How had they known she needed help?

"…will be in shortly, so best eat it all up, then the doctor can talk about when to release you."

"Okay." Anticipation filled her. She really needed to thank James Wells properly, and only hoped he'd chosen to overlook her latest bout of rudeness when he visited today. The eagerness rode high as she wrangled her right wrist's stiff splint to eat her basic breakfast: cornflakes, weak tea, and toast. It continued as she was greeted by a different nurse, who gave her the welcome news that Gran had woken up, had spoken for a few minutes, before drifting back to sleep. Thank God!

But when the white-coated doctor came in an hour later, it

was not Dr. Wells at all. This doctor was female, spectacled, and in her fifties. "Hello, I'm Dr. Hines."

"Um, hi."

"I understand you've had a mild concussion, and a few other sprains and things."

"Yes." This disappointment crashing against her chest was stupid. Stupid! She wouldn't ask. She wouldn't! "Um, I thought Dr. Wells would see me."

"Oh no. He's at the clinic today." She smiled gently. "Besides, we don't tend to think it is good for doctors to treat their friends."

"Oh, but I'm not…" Her voice drifted away as the smile being offered her suggested hospital gossip implied otherwise.

"Now, I see from your charts you've had some breakfast, yes? No more headaches, blurred vision?"

"No."

"And while we ascertained that your ankle was sprained rather badly, you're still waiting on the x-ray to see if your wrist is broken, yes?"

"Yep."

"We'll get that checked out as soon as possible. I'm sure it must be painful. Do you need more medication?"

Staci nodded as Dr. Hines glanced up from where she was taking notes.

"I imagine you would be eager to return home soon."

Home. A funny kind of twinge streaked across her chest. Imagine if she'd really been at home in Chicago and this had happened. She could go days without real human contact. Even her editors and agent knew when she was on deadline she might ignore emails for days. Imagine if she hadn't been found, hadn't been helped, hadn't had a strong, muscled someone to help her down the elevator and into the hospital. She shivered. Yesterday's thoughts about her skeletal remains being found suddenly didn't seem so funny after all.

"Miss Everton?"

"Yes?"

"I think I lost you for a moment there." Dr. Hines's brown eyes twinkled kindly. "I said you must be looking forward to going home."

Staci nodded. Except she wasn't. She didn't want to return to big city anonymity, to big city unconcern. Something within longed for connection, with people who truly did care, with family, and friends. Even if the particular 'friend' Dr. Hines spoke of simply thought Staci a clumsy, vomit-prone woman, and possessed a girlfriend on the side. She might not want a connection with him, but this sense of finding assurance, finding a home, tantalized.

A few more instructions, which Staci promised to obey, then she was given into the charge of a nurse, who promised to take her to x-ray. She gritted her teeth. She had no desire to know how much all this was going to cost. Would an author's medical insurance cover this much care?

Two hours later, having learned her wrist was definitely broken, Staci was finally wheeled back to the elevator, with the promise her arm would be cast this afternoon. "We'll get you seen by a specialist soon. In the meantime, to avoid pain you'll need to keep it as still as possible, which means no eating, or trying to dress yourself, or driving."

Or writing.

Panic clambered up her throat. "But what am I going to do?" Her voice was definitely too high-pitched to not be mistaken for Hysterical Woman. She dropped it a notch. "Gran is still here in the hospital somewhere—I haven't even seen her yet today—and there's nobody at home to help me."

The nurse gave her a sympathy-laden smile. "I'm sure we'll figure something out. We have social workers who help with such things."

But she didn't want some stranger telling her what to do!

And her book—how on earth would it get finished now? She'd have to tell Max and Bronwyn she'd need an extension. She groaned.

"I know this is not to your liking, but these things are sent to test us."

What did that even mean? Test what, exactly? Her patience? Her fortitude? Was it a test sent by God, or did people mean some vague universal entity to help humans develop to be their best self? Or was that getting just a little too Oprah?

Wrist splinted for stabilization, she clutched the hospital gown to prevent gaping as she was wheeled inside the elevator. The nurse punched the button for upstairs—the hospital was so small it only had two floors—and Staci lowered her gaze to her lap. She had no desire for anyone to recognize today's indignity.

"Hold the elevator!" a male voice called.

Against Staci's silent protest the nurse blocked the closing door with her arm. The older man entered the small space, his gray dress pants rather formal for the usual visitor's attire.

Staci glanced up. Met the dark eyes of the church minister whose name she couldn't remember. They widened with surprise. "I know you." His brow wrinkled for a moment then cleared. "Rose's granddaughter, ah, Anastacia, right?"

"In the flesh." She cringed. Reminding pastors of flesh was probably not what one was supposed to do.

Fortunately, he smiled. "I was here to see your grandmother, but it appears you have been in the wars, also. What's happened?"

"Just me being clumsy. I tripped and managed to sprain my ankle and break my wrist at the same time. Apparently, I like to be efficient."

"I'm very sorry to hear it."

She gave him a smile she hoped appeared brave, but probably just looked pathetic.

The elevator door pinged open and the pastor exited first,

allowing room for the wheelchair to be maneuvered to the corridor.

He remained standing, eyes filled with concern. "So, what will you do now?"

"Good question. One we were just discussing now," Staci said, glancing at the nurse.

"Miss Everton was staying with her grandmother, and with no nearby family—"

"No other family," Staci corrected.

"—she's at something of a loss as to how to manage her recovery. I told her the hospital social worker will have some solutions, so we'll just have to wait until then."

Something of Staci's apprehension must have flickered in her face, for the pastor caught her eyes again and gave a slow nod. "I'll pray for a good solution, too."

"Thank you."

"Well, I suppose I should leave you now, if I'm going to see Rose."

"Oh, please, would you mind if I came too?" Staci asked. "I haven't seen her yet today, and I was told she had woken earlier."

"Be more than happy to," he said, glancing at the nurse. "Would you mind if I push Miss Everton?"

"Please. I'm afraid we're a bit busy today, so that would be most helpful."

"Thanks," Staci said.

"Remember, keep your arm still," the nurse cautioned.

"Yes, ma'am," Staci promised. Any slight movement only reminded her of the importance of obeying this medical instruction at least. No way did she want to run the risk of long-term injury to the wrist of her writing hand.

The pastor wheeled her to the room at the end, a different one from yesterday's ICU. Gran's room was filled with light, pouring in from the two windows facing either wall, light that spilled onto the three beds positioned to capture the views, two of which were occupied, one by a woman Staci loved more than life.

"Gran!"

The figure in the far bed turned, smiled. Well, smiled as best she could with an oxygen tube up her nose. "Annie. And Pastor McPherson. How wonderful to see you both."

Staci's eyes filled. How wonderful to see Gran looking so well. Remarkably well, considering her appearance on the last visit.

A crease crossed Gran's features. "But Annie, whatever are you doing in a wheelchair?"

"I had a little accident." She gestured to her bound foot. "I sprained my ankle again, the one that always gives me trouble, then managed to break my wrist. They've been waiting for the swelling to go down before putting on a cast."

"Oh, precious girl! However did that happen?"

"It was just a dumb accident at home. I tripped, that's all."

Gran's features softened with relief, before tightening once more. "But what does that mean for your writing?"

"An excellent question."

"You're a writer?" Pastor McPherson asked.

"She writes historical romances, but not the sort you or Angela probably read."

"Oh?" He looked at Staci inquiringly.

"I write for the secular market."

"Oh, I don't mind some secular fiction," he confided. "And I know that Angela enjoys Jodi Picoult's books, though I'm not sure they're quite my cup of tea."

"To be honest, I'm not sure that Anastacia's books would be your cup of tea either," Gran said, "but never mind."

Awkward vibes abounded. It was definitely time to change the subject. "It's so good to see you looking so much better,

Gran. You had us worried. You took the longest time to wake up."

"So the doctor tells me. But I feel better, like I've had a really good, long sleep."

"Praise the Lord," said the pastor.

Amen, Staci echoed silently.

"Did they say what the problem was?" Pastor McPherson asked Gran.

"Oh, just a little heart trouble," she said, dismissing his concern with a waved hand. "I've been told they want to keep me here a little while longer, until I get my strength back." Gran's face pinched into apprehension. "But staying here a tad longer doesn't faze me. I'm far more concerned about what will happen for you, Annie dearest. If your wrist is broken, how ever will you take care of yourself?"

The million-dollar question. "I'll be fine. I can get takeout. I can shower with my wrist in a plastic bag. I'm not the first person who's had to cope with such things."

"But your writing."

"I'll just have to ask for an extended deadline. I can dictate, and I'm not completely useless with my left hand."

"Yes, but—"

"I'll be fine, Gran. There's nothing for you to worry about, I promise."

The dear wrinkled face eased a fraction. "If you're sure."

She wasn't, but there was no way she'd add to Gran's concerns for the day.

"If you don't mind me adding my two cents' worth," Pastor McPherson said, "I agree with Anastacia here. The hospital has someone who deals with situations like these, and I'm sure there's something we can do at the church to help you both in these unfortunate circumstances. Some casseroles perhaps, and cleaning."

"Oh, that would be very kind," Gran said with a relieved smile.

Staci nodded, unwilling to express her reluctance at the sense of obligation this would put her under. She appreciated the thought, but she could feel the ties of indebtedness slowly winding around her, suffocating any sense of freedom.

"Now, if neither of you are opposed, this sounds like something we should pray about," the pastor continued.

"Why should we object? We'd appreciate your prayers, wouldn't we, Annie, dear?"

"Yes," she mumbled.

The pastor bowed his head, as if unaware of the room's other occupant who'd watched them during a very entertaining few minutes and prayed for both Staci and Gran.

"Amen," they echoed.

"Now," he said, eyes twinkling, "I feel certain a solution will present itself, young lady, and soon."

It would need to. "Thank you."

"Ah, I'm afraid, Mrs. Everton, that I will have to ask your visitors to leave," a nurse carrying an official looking clipboard said, nodding at Pastor McPherson. "We can't have too much excitement for you." She eyed Staci and the wheelchair with raised brows. "Although it looks like one of your visitors has had an interesting time of late."

"This is my dear granddaughter, Anastacia," Gran said. "She's staying here, too."

"Hopefully for not too long," Staci murmured.

"Well, it might be best if you said goodbye now, and headed back to your room. I'm sure I don't need to tell you the way to the exit, reverend?"

"Indeed you do not," he said, far more graciously than Staci would have replied.

She eyed the rude nurse with her own upraised brows, but

the nurse seemed impervious, turning away to fiddle with something next to Gran's bed.

Staci rose carefully to press a kiss to Gran's brow, trying not to wince at the jolt of pain as she accidentally bumped her right arm. "I'll come back as soon as I can," she promised.

"I'll look forward to it, dear," Gran said, patting her good wrist tenderly. "You'll be in my prayers."

"And you're in mine, too," Staci whispered, heart catching at the sudden glow in Gran's expression.

"Thank you, dear."

Staci straightened, and carefully resumed her seated position. "I suppose I should go." She glanced up at the pastor. "Is it okay—?"

"Of course. Just point me in the right direction," he said, before smiling at Gran. "I'll be praying for you, Rose. And you too, Nurse Kaminsky," he added, his cheekiness earning him an eye-roll for the ages.

They were met at Staci's room by another nurse who relieved Staci from the pastor's charge and helped her into bed. "I'm not an invalid," she grumbled.

"But neither are you to be traipsing about willy-nilly."

"I was only seeing my grandmother." She motioned to the pastor. "Pastor McPherson has been most helpful."

"You need to rest and not get carried away with things."

Staci was forced to wave goodbye to the pastor, who promised to think about how to help her situation, and the nurse resumed her spiel. "Now, I've been told the medical assessment team will be here in a jiffy to discuss your release, so you just relax and someone will be by shortly."

"Thanks," Staci murmured.

But relaxing was so hard. What was she to do? They didn't seriously expect her to lie here staring at the ceiling doing nothing?

She drew in a breath, slowly released. That's right. She

would have to trust God to give direction. But it wasn't likely He would send a message over the intercom, was it? She reached across for her phone, and then spent long painstaking minutes trying to type out an email to Max and Bronwyn requesting an extension for her submission, then scrolled through her social media feeds. Funny how much she hadn't missed this in recent days. No dopamine-inducing highs at instant likes meant she'd had more time to ground herself, to consider what really mattered. And her world had boiled down to wanting likes from one person. A face flashed through her mind. Okay, maybe two.

Staci gave an eye-roll she reckoned Nurse Kaminsky would have been jealous of. Seriously? She wanted James to like her? Still? She had to be the vainest, most pathetic kind of fool. Hadn't he made his non-interest perfectly plain by his non-attendance today?

But he had work at the clinic today, a tiny voice whispered.

So what, she told Pathetic Self. It didn't matter, because she was definitely *not* interested in a missionary doctor from goodness knows where. Where exactly in Africa was Tanzania, anyway?

Thanking God for the marvels of modern technology—and the fact she had sufficient internet capability—Staci spent the next few minutes flicking through her phone to learn that Tanzania bordered the Indian Ocean to the east, and was sandwiched between Kenya, Zaire, and half a dozen other countries. Its former name, Tanganyika, hinted at its old German roots, which led to a search of other historical aspects, like the mystical city of Zanzibar. Her lips pushed to one side. You could try to take the novel out of the novelist, but the historical research skills would never be completely lost.

She was busy finding out what she could about the mission in Tanzania's north when a cleared throat snared her attention. "Oh!"

"Hi," Jenny Wells stood smiling at her. "I hope I'm not interrupting anything."

"Oh no," Staci said, hiding the phone under the bedclothes. Heaven forbid Jenny discover Staci was Googling her son's former work environment. "It's nothing important."

"Which is why it took me a good two minutes to get your attention."

"Sorry." Staci offered an apologetic smile. "And sorry about all the drama yesterday. I understand you've been forced into looking after Penny. I hope she's been behaving."

"Oh, she's been fine. And don't worry about it at all. Mitch has enjoyed trying to teach that little girl some manners. Well, I don't know if enjoy is quite the right word, but it's definitely been entertaining to watch them."

Staci chuckled. "I can imagine."

"And from what my son says it seems that you scarcely had any choice in the matter. He was most insistent that you not have any of this to worry about."

"That was kind of him."

"He is a kind boy," his mom said fondly. "Although I don't think he'd take too kindly to me referring to him as such."

Probably not, thought Staci, though she could see him patiently putting up with his doting parent without complaint.

"I'm here to see how you are going, and to ask you a small favor."

"Well, I'm doing better than yesterday," Staci admitted.

"How is your arm?"

Staci held up the stiff splint. "My wrist is broken but should get a cast soon."

"You poor thing."

Jenny's sympathy stabbed behind Staci's eyes. "Thank you again for staying here with Gran." She smiled sheepishly. "I certainly didn't plan to add to all the drama with my little clumsy moment yesterday afternoon."

"I don't think these are things anyone ever plans for, are they?"

"Still, I think my debt to the Wells family is ever increasing. I feel like saying thanks is all I'm ever saying to you, Mitch, and, um, James."

"We're happy to help."

"I'm glad, but I still feel like I've burdened you with all this unnecessary bother. I'm sure you're all so busy. I hate to think I've been keeping anyone from their duties."

"Now, now, my dear, don't think such things. Mitch and I are retired, and as for James, well, I know he can be a tad over-responsible at times, but don't for one minute think he hasn't the wherewithal to request assistance if given a task he has little liking for."

Staci eyed her but said nothing. Did Jenny's cryptic comment and little smile mean James had liked helping her? Why?

"Um," Jenny's disconcerting smile meant Staci had to change the subject, fast. "You mentioned you had a favor?" Whatever it was she'd do it. She owed them so much already.

"Well, you might think this a little peculiar, but I was at home this morning catching up on some ironing, when I felt a little prompting to see if you have a plan of recuperation for when you're released. Obviously with poor Rose being here and unlikely to be released for some time, it will be hard for you to manage at home for a little while yet, so I was hoping you might consider coming to stay with me."

Staci almost choked. "That's the favor? You want me to stay with you?"

"With us, naturally. Mitch and James would be delighted to have another female to fuss over."

Her cheeks warmed. "I couldn't, I don't need—want—any fuss..."

"Oh, but it would be good for them, James especially. I don't think you know just how much that boy wants a wife, and it would do him good to be encouraged to spend time with a smart, attractive Christian girl like you."

"Mrs. Wells, Jenny, I *really* don't think James will appreciate you saying this. Thank you for the offer, but I cannot accept."

"Can't you?" Jenny said, almost wistfully.

"No. I'm sorry, but no."

"Please?"

Staci stared at her. "Why? Don't you think James will be upset when he finds out what his mother has done?"

"Then don't tell him."

"But he would have to know, sooner or later. I couldn't very well just show up without explanation. Besides, what about Brandi?" Staci persisted. "You can hardly think she'll take too well to having another girl on her territory."

Jenny's brow pleated. "What does Brandi have to do with anything?"

A finger of doubt stole across her heart. "She's James's girlfriend, isn't she?"

"Brandi?" Jenny looked shocked. "No."

"Yes," Staci insisted.

"No. He couldn't. They *wouldn't*. She's not his type at all."

Sorely tempted to ask just what exactly his type was, Staci pressed her lips together instead, and forced herself to meet Jenny's gaze evenly and give a tiny nod.

"I don't believe it," Jenny said, real worry in her eyes.

Yes, but not believing things didn't mean they weren't true. Staci kept that thought to herself. "Well, you should ask him. I'm just not convinced either of them would be thrilled at the thought of my staying with you."

"But you have to do something. How are you going to manage by yourself?"

Great question. "The hospital is apparently sending someone to talk to me about possible arrangements."

"Oh, but you don't want them. Can you imagine a stranger dressing you, taking care of you?"

"It might be less embarrassing than someone I know," Staci said wryly.

"But could they help you with writing your story?"

Probably not, but it didn't change what needed to be said. "Jenny, thank you, but I must decline your kind offer."

"Oh." Jenny's deflating features suddenly perked up again, as she excused herself to go visit Rose. "I need to see her before visiting hours close for lunch."

"Of course," Staci said. "Thanks again for visiting. And for your kind offer. I do appreciate it, you know."

"I know," Jenny said, with a wave.

She departed, and Staci was suddenly struck by the possible subject of Jenny's upcoming conversation with Gran. Would she be so underhanded as to make the same request to Rose, knowing Staci would be hard pressed to refuse Gran's request? Or was such a thing mere foolishness and fancy?

Before she could wonder too much more about this, the door opened and a lanyard-wearing woman in her late twenties drew near. "Hi, Staci, my name is Deanna Parker. I'm the medical outpatient's assessment team."

Staci shifted irritably. Why did strangers assume they had a right to use a patient's first name in some guise of false friendliness? And didn't these people know the word 'team' implied more than one person, usually three or more? Were such attitudes a sign she was getting old? But honestly, some people had no clue. "Hi."

Ms. Parker went on to talk about Staci's medical discharge, then possible at-home care options, none of which held much appeal. Again the scent of money wafted through the air. How much would all of this cost? She posed the question to the woman, unsurprised when she was met with a great deal of hmming and hedging.

"I'm afraid, Miss Everton," so Staci was Miss Everton now, "that I cannot say precisely."

"Then I suspect I will not need such services. As soon as my wrist is dealt with I plan to leave and return home."

Ms. Parker looked up from her clipboard. "Have you thought about how you'll manage, given your injuries?"

Not yet.

"Would you like to speak to a case manager or social worker?"

"No thanks. I will manage on my own." Somehow. Maybe she could get someone to help her. Surely she had one friend from Chicago who would like to spend some time in a sleepy village like Muskoka Shores.

"Are you sure?" The hospital worker's tone was laced with doubt.

"Yes!" She gritted out a smile to compensate for her raised voice.

"Now, now, Miss Everton, there is no need to get upset."

Heat crossed her chest at Ms. Parker's patronizing tone. Honestly, the woman was younger than Staci. She swallowed her first reaction with an effort. "I am not getting upset," she said, clutching at her last dregs of patience. "I know you're just doing your job, but I really would prefer you to leave now."

"Miss Everton, I'm simply concerned for you, and want to know once you're discharged that you'll have someone looking after you who has sufficient skill."

"Would a doctor be considered to have sufficient skill?" a deep voice said from the doorway.

JAMES GLANCED AT THE PATIENT, then at the hospital officer. He'd learned in his short time here that Ms. Parker's reputation for meddlesomeness had put more than one nurse off-side. "You must excuse me, ladies, but your conversation could be heard halfway up the hall."

He caught the way Staci winced, and nodded sympathetically to her, then turned his attention to Ms. Parker fully. "I understand your concern, but you can be assured that Miss Everton will be cared for."

"But—"

He gave a small smile. "It's not as if she's without friends in the medical community."

Ms. Parker eyed him suspiciously. "Do you mean to say *you* will be caring for her?"

He swallowed the spike of irritation, willing his tone to evenness as he studied her. "Are you accusing me of unprofessionalism?"

Her cheeks pinked. "Well, no."

"I'm glad to hear it," he said softly. "I understand Miss Everton has received an offer from my mother to stay until she is feeling suitably able to return to her own premises. Isn't that right, Miss Everton?"

He turned to Staci and caught her panicked look. He smiled and nodded gently.

"Is this true, Miss Everton?" Ms. Parker demanded.

"Well, yes," Staci said slowly. "Mrs. Wells was just in here."

"And you've agreed to be in her care until the appropriate time?"

"I... I've agreed for her to help me, yes."

He smoothed his grin as Ms. Parker turned with an expression bordering on suspicion, gazing back blandly. "Now, is that all, Ms. Parker?"

"Well, yes."

"Good. Then you can release Miss Everton to the rest she needs."

He ignored the bristling Staci, pretending interest in his folder as they waited for Ms. Parker to finish her discontented mutterings and finally depart. Then he turned to Staci, one eyebrow aloft. "Was there something you wished to say to me?"

"Yes, yes, there very well is," she sputtered. "I don't know what possessed you to say all that—"

He held up a finger for silence. "I don't think you should talk in such a loud voice." He gestured to the partially opened high windows facing the corridor. "Sound tends to travel remarkably well here."

"Maybe," she continued in a loud whisper, "you could consider whether I actually want to be included in your schemes."

"A scheme? Here I was just thinking I was offering Christian charity, being a Good Samaritan as it were, and instead I'm being accused of having ulterior motives." He grinned and lifted his eyebrows. "I wonder what ulterior motives you think I have."

She sucked in a breath, then exhaled loudly. "Have you always been this cocky?"

"What, you're accusing me of being cocky now? Miss Everton, Staci, please, I thought we were becoming friends."

She huffed out another breath. "I don't understand you at all."

"The feeling is becoming mutual."

She eyed him narrowly. Then shook her head. "I suppose I should thank you for saving me from Ms. Parker's clutches."

"Yes, I think you should."

She gave a sudden chuckle then demanded, "Have you spoken to your mother at all?"

"About what?"

"About my staying with you?"

Heaven forbid Ms. Parker hear this part of their conversation. "I rather believe that you would be staying with my parents, at whose house I merely reside for a while."

"I'd rather stay at my Gran's house. Not that I don't appreciate your mother's offer, but I hate feeling like I'm constantly inconveniencing them."

"Perhaps that can be arranged."

"Really?"

"If you agree to my mother checking in on you regularly, that is."

"That would be far more preferable."

"Indeed." He continued to watch her, enjoying the sight of the indignant red curls that spilled across the pillow. "I suppose I should go speak with Mom—"

"About what?" a familiar voice said from the door. "About how we're going to convince my star student to stay with us so we can care for her while she recuperates?"

"I doubt she'll need too much convincing to agree to being cared for by you," he murmured.

"Don't tell me you managed to convince her?"

"Rather I think it was the hospital's outpatient adviser who did."

"Well, I don't care who did, I'm just thankful you are," Jenny said, with a fond glance at Staci.

Staci bit her lip. "Jenny, just to be clear, I said to James that I'd actually prefer to stay at Gran's. Not because I don't appreciate your very kind offer, but because I hate feeling like I'm putting you to so much trouble when I've already done that so many times already."

"Oh, but it's no trouble at all."

Ms. Parker returned, and, spying his mom, spoke to her most seriously about patient care while Staci glowered at him. He fought the amusement, fought for his expression to appear neutral, so that any thought of unethical behavior would be banished from the air.

"Miss Everton?" he asked. "Do you have a headache?"

"No."

"Ah, I just wondered, because you looked rather in pain."

"Thank you, Doctor, but I'm sure I'll be well enough very soon, probably as soon as the rest of my fate has been quite decided."

"Oh, we are keeping you from your rest, aren't we?" his mom said, worriedly. "I'm sorry it's taken a while, but look, as Ms. Parker should know by now, we have things under control."

"Well, thank you, Mrs. Wells. It's good to know our patients will be with someone responsible," Ms. Parker said, with a side-long look at James that made him wonder if she doubted his responsibilities. Or his professional interest in these matters.

And made him wonder just what was being whispered around the hospital about these matters at all.

CHAPTER 13

A few hours later, her wrist now freshly cast, she was being driven home by James—again. Why it should prove to be in his company, and not his mother's, she couldn't fathom. It was enough to make her think—

But no. She wouldn't go there. He had a *girlfriend*. And she was into creating relationships, not wrecking them.

She glanced across, noted his profile, the small bump in his nose that suggested it had been broken once upon a time. He met her gaze as they waited at a stop sign. "You okay?"

"Yes." She shrugged, then winced as her wrist protested the movement. "As well as anyone with a broken wrist can be, I suppose."

"I'm sorry."

The tenderness in his eyes, the authenticity he projected, swelled fresh gratitude within. "I... I do appreciate all you've done for me. Your parents have been so kind, offering to have me stay, but I really couldn't impose on them any longer."

"I understand." The truck moved forward again. "It can be hard to lose a sense of independence."

Like he must have, moving back from Africa to live with his

parents. "Why are you staying with them, and not just in your own place?"

"They're my parents. I love them."

Her heart melted into sweetness, like ice-cream on a hot summer's day. When was the last time she'd heard any adult express such sentiment, let alone a very attractive young man?

"Besides, we have to make the most of what time we've got. You never know…" His voice trailed away, a cloud shading his features.

Sympathy coiled in her chest, followed by a stab of fear. Was something wrong?

Houses flashed past. He glanced across again. "What have I said now?"

She swallowed. "Is… is your mom sick again?"

"No. She's healthier than she's been for a long time. Why?"

"You just talked about making the most of what time we have, and I thought—"

"You thought someone was dying, right?"

"Well, you're a doctor, and looked concerned, and I've got a pretty good imagination, so…"

"So the only conclusion to draw is that Mom is sick again?" He pulled the vehicle to the curb but kept the engine running.

"What are you doing?"

"I'm going to test this imagination of yours." He turned to face her more fully. "Let's see if you can guess what I'm thinking."

He eyed her intently, his gaze flickering to her lips and back, and she found herself holding her breath. Surely he wasn't thinking what she was thinking?

"I think you'd be better off driving me home," she whispered.

"You sure?"

She nodded. Either that, or she'd find herself in lots of trouble. Best to get his thoughts traveling in a different direction. "I, um, I hope your mom wasn't too offended when I said I wanted to stay at Gran's rather than her home."

"I think she understood."

"It just would have proved awkward," she added softly. Fighting the sense of obligation, fighting this attraction swirling between them. And she so wasn't that girl. She *wasn't*. Best to remind him of where his interest should be. "And I don't think Brandi would have liked it."

"Probably not," he agreed mildly.

"Really?" She turned to look at him squarely. "That's all you have to say?"

He shrugged. "Brandi is a bit odd at times, a little proprietary."

She choked. "You don't think being a girlfriend gives her the right to that?"

Pain washed over his face. "Not anymore."

She barely heard his words, so focused she had been on his features. "Wait." She hated the flicker of excitement and tempered her voice down to disinterest. "Have you two broken up?"

"What?"

"You and Brandi. I thought you were going out."

"No." He half-smiled, then reached across and gently tugged at a loose lock of hair. "Maybe you should work on curbing that imagination of yours."

Not the first time she'd wondered that. "So, she's not your girlfriend?"

"Never has been, never will be."

"Why not?" she felt to ask, partly from surprise, partly from a muted sense of indignation for the worldwide sisterhood, partly from a secret, shameful sense to hear him say Brandi wasn't his type at all and he much preferred sarcasm-prone bookish types with a propensity for discounted designer shoes.

He looked away, and she hurried to add, "She's so pretty, and perky, like a real-life Barbie doll. What man doesn't want that?"

"This one."

"But why?" She hoped she'd kept the eagerness from her voice.

He finally glanced back at her. "Because she was the fiancée of my brother who was killed."

Oh. Oh no. "I'm so sorry, James. I didn't know."

"Evidently." His wry smile took away some of the sting of humiliation.

"It's just she seemed a little physically affectionate with you," she felt compelled to say.

"She's always been that way."

"You've known her long?"

"Long enough." He raised a brow. "Anything else you'd like to know?"

A hundred things begged to burst from her lips. "Nope."

He seemed to be amused by her denial, his smile flickering once more. "I suppose we best get you home."

"I suppose." Suddenly the thought held little appeal. How exactly was she going to cope these next few weeks? Maybe she should have been more gracious in defeat and allowed herself to be persuaded to stay at the Wells'.

"Unless you feel it necessary to get a coffee."

"Do you think it's necessary?"

"I do."

She glanced at him and found his intense gaze on her. She shivered.

His frown instantly appeared. "Are you cold?" He fiddled with a dial and heat renewed blasting in her direction.

"N-no, I'm fine." Her voice held too much squeak to be convincing. From the way he stared at her, she could almost think he was interested.

"I'm thinking you'd warm up even more with a cup of pumpkin spice something," he suggested. "I know I would."

"Pumpkin spice?"

"Well, maybe not that. But I'd like something."

Judging from the way his gaze flickered to her lips again, she suspected she knew what he meant. Her pulse skyrocketed. She swallowed, aiming for casual as she shifted to face the windshield. "Well, far be it for me to get in the way of Dr. Coffee's desire."

A snort of laughter came beside her, and she swung her head, hearing the echo of her words. Had she really said such a thing aloud?

"Dr. Coffee, huh?"

Judging from the heat radiating from her skin the car heater could turn off about now.

Another chuckle escaped him, then he steered the car to Main Street, and she kept her gaze focused outside. The less she spoke, the less she looked at him, the better. The stores had their various window displays lit to charming effect in the dim mid-afternoon light. The storefronts evoked a pull of interest she rarely experienced in Chicago. Sure, the city held pretty window displays too, but here such things seemed so much more personal, the physical representations of so many hopes and plans, small business owners who'd invested their lives into making their dreams come true. Something she could truly understand.

He found a spot right out front of The Coffee Blend and cruised into a parking bay like one of the enchanted, and not a mere mortal like herself, forever destined to spend long minutes searching for a parking space to no avail.

"What can I get you?" he asked, killing the engine, before motioning to her foot. "I'll grab us a couple to go. I don't think you should try out that ankle on these icy pavements."

"A vanilla latte would be nice."

"No pumpkin spice?"

"That ship has sailed—right to the bottom of the sea."

He grinned. "Nice to see we have some things in common."

He shut the door, leaving her to the truck's warmth and her own thoughts. What exactly did they have in common? A taste for caffeine, a weird sense of humor, varying degrees of faith. Muskoka Shores High. A fondness for his parents. That was about it.

She thought back to previous guys she'd dated and realized proximity and similar work had scarcely proved enough for any relationship to last beyond a handful of dates. What mattered more, similar careers or similar values? Not that she wanted to jump the gun, but James had seemed a little bit interested. Would things be different this time?

This time? Staci shook her head at herself. She was being ridiculous. Entertaining thoughts of a relationship with an Africa-based doctor was ridiculous. Foolish. Stupid. She would write her book, and then leave. She had no time for a relationship, let alone staying here in the past hoping for some kind of miracle for her future. And she had no desire whatsoever to *ever* live in Africa.

Rolling her eyes at her ridiculousness, she studied the storefronts. Squinted. So that was *Brandi's* bookshop one door down? She wondered if they'd ever stocked her books. As if. But maybe she should visit...

Her phone pinged, and she carefully fished it from her handbag. A new email. Bronwyn. She quickly flicked it open to see her agent's assurance that *of course* Flame would be okay with extending, so not to worry but concentrate on getting better ASAP.

A knot in her chest unloosed. Thank goodness. She hoped she could have something submitted on time, but these past few days had really slowed things down.

Movement at the side caught her attention, and she realized

James's charmed status meant he'd been served already. He knocked on the window and she powered it down, letting in a blast of cold air and her coffee which he handed to her.

"That was fast."

"What can I say? They like me."

Of course they did. "Doesn't everybody?" she muttered.

"Apparently the jury is still out on that one," he said, with an upraised brow, before motioning for her to raise the window, which she did as he hurried to the driver's seat. "I may have mentioned it was an emergency."

"But it wasn't."

"I beg to disagree. The way you were snapping at me earlier made me think you were feeling very caffeine deprived."

"I wasn't snapping!"

"Oh, just your usual self?"

Probably. When had she become such a cranky pants? "Thank you for the coffee," she murmured, before taking a sip. The creamy deliciousness trickled down her throat, hitting her bloodstream like magic. Oh, this was good.

She glanced across, saw him smooth away a smile. "Did I moan?"

"Yep."

"It's good coffee."

"That it is." He placed his cup in the cupholder and started the ignition. "Time to go, m'lady."

Indeed it was. Then, maybe when she was home she could find a way of curbing both her stupid imagination and this stupid attraction. She sipped the hot beverage all the way home, admiring the town decorations, including the giant tree in the town square that was festooned with lights and baubles.

"See the big tree? They're doing a lighting ceremony tomorrow night."

Small town North America, she thought, before instantly

recalling seeing the Rockefeller tree lit in New York City on TV. Okay, maybe it was all North America.

"Want to go?"

She choked on her coffee. "Um, maybe? It depends on how work goes."

"What do you do again?"

"I'm a writer." Surely his mother had told him.

"A journalist?"

Apparently she hadn't. "I write books."

"Ah, that's why you're always surrounded by so much paper."

"That's why."

"What sort of books?"

"Come on. Didn't your mom tell you?" Judging from the blank stare she guessed not. "I write fiction. Historical romances, actually."

"Really?" He shot her another look, one she couldn't quite decipher. "That must demand good research skills."

"Yep."

Thank goodness they had once again pulled onto Gran's street. It was kind of embarrassing to realize just how much of a nonentity she was to him. She bet a million dollars he'd never Googled her. Not that he needed to, or that she even really wanted him to. If he did, he might find all the racy covers that search engines associated with her name.

He turned into Gran's drive and killed the engine. "Here we are."

"Well, thanks again." All she ever seemed to do was say thank you. "I really appreciate all you've done."

"You don't think I'm gonna let you go inside by yourself, do you?"

Well...

"Come on. How are you going to manage?"

"I'll manage. I'm used to taking care of myself."

"But why take care of yourself when somebody wants to take care of you?"

His concern made her heart glow. But no, she was an independent twenty-first century woman, who certainly didn't need a man to look after her. Even if his words did fit the bill as appropriate fare for one of her heroes, something one of her leading ladies would no doubt swoon over. But she wasn't one of them, and this wasn't her imagination. She had to keep her head screwed on straight and not get swept away.

But no sooner had that thought crossed her mind when the passenger door was opened and, somehow between his murmured offer and her stunned acceptance, she was once again picked up and carried to the front door. Talk about being swept away.

"Keys?"

"Uh, yeah." She tugged them from her purse. "Here." She held them up, and he bent a little so she could fit them to the lock. Then she was inside, safely deposited on the living room's sofa, thanking God James didn't seem to have broken out in a sweat or be rubbing his back at having lifted her.

"There you go." He studied her, arms crossed. "Do you have a plan for dinner?"

She needed to figure out a plan for using the toilet. Dinner could wait. "Um, sure."

He waited, eyebrow aloft, but it wasn't like she needed to tell him everything. And she certainly wasn't going to hint that he needed to be involved in her dinner plans.

"You know that my mom will be asking as soon as I get home," he explained.

Oh. Misread that one. Again. "I'm sure Gran has some leftovers somewhere." Even if by now they'd likely be past their best-by date.

"Is there anything else I can do? I imagine you're eager to get back to your computer. Want me to fetch that from the car?"

He'd said fetch! A girl had to love a guy who used such words, didn't she? Well, maybe not love. Or maybe…

A minute later he returned, carrying her stuff from the car, handing her the zipped leather bag containing her computer. "Want me to get that out?"

"Yes, please," she said meekly.

"Uh, how do you plan to use it with only one hand?"

Another excellent question. How was she going to do lots of things with only one hand? "I have a dictation app I can use."

"Does that work well?"

"Most of the time. Sometimes I need to change a few words, but most of the time it's fairly accurate."

He nodded, then eyed her seriously once more. "You're sure there is nothing you need? Bathroom?"

No way was she going to admit to that. She'd figure it out on her own if it killed her. "I'm fine," she lied. What she really needed was for him to leave so she could start figuring out how to manage this, this, well, whatever *this thing* between them was. "Once again, I'm in your debt."

"Then maybe I'll have to collect."

"I beg your pardon?"

"Your debt. I might have to call it in."

"That's hardly a gentlemanly action."

"I'm hardly a gentleman." He gave her a wolfish grin that did funny things to her stomach.

And made her more determined than ever to encourage his departure. "Please say hi to your mom for me. And thank her again for looking after Penny for us."

"Will do. Now, make sure you take it easy. Don't move unnecessarily."

"Yes, sir."

He smiled crookedly again. "See you later."

She nodded. "Bye."

She lifted her—left—hand in farewell and waited as he

closed the door and she heard the vehicle start. Thank goodness. She propelled herself up to stand, eyeing the distance between the couch and the bathroom, then began a slow limp down the hall. It wasn't as if she was completely helpless. She could get there, even if it took ten times longer than normal.

Once inside the bathroom she managed the basics, even washing her hand, when a knock came at the door.

She limped to the hall from where she could see the front door. Was he back already?

Confirmation came at the sound of his voice through the door. "Hey, Staci, I just remembered…"

Before she could reach the front door it opened, and his head popped in. "Hey, sorry if this seems intrusive, but it was unlocked, and—hey, where—oh, there you are." He frowned, moving forward to offer his arm, which she, twenty-first-century woman though she might be, did not hesitate to accept. "Moving already?"

"You didn't really expect me to advertise my bathroom needs to you, did you?"

"I might have known that you'd be stubborn."

"Should've picked it," she agreed, relieved as he helped her reach the sofa and ease into its comfort.

A smile poked out. "That's it, then. I'm calling in my debt."

"What?"

"Dinner. Tomorrow night. Before the tree lighting."

"What if I already have plans?"

"Cancel them." He looked suddenly unsure. "*Do* you have plans?"

"Only with you, apparently."

"Great." Pleasure lit his features. "I'll be here after my day at the clinic tomorrow."

"Okay, then."

"Okay, then," he echoed, smiling at her again. "Don't forget to take it easy."

"Yes, Doctor."

"Good. See you then."

The door closed, and she collapsed back into her seat, thinking about the day, thinking about James. Excitement bubbled away. Yes, she had a million things to do, but he—clever, handsome, interesting James Wells—wanted to spend time with her.

Maybe Christmas miracles happened in Muskoka Shores after all.

CHAPTER 14

Fiona glanced at the carriage, eyeing the carefully sculpted chest—

What? Staci tapped the delete button, then carefully typed in *carved crest.*

—adorning the side panel...

How had she thought this would be easy? Foolish, foolish girl. It seemed her dictation app had forgotten her voice and was going rogue with its selection of words it thought appropriate, adding in extra nonsensical words here and there, just to add to the confusion.

Would she ever get this done?

Six hours, and she'd only written fifteen pages. Of course, that might have had something to do with the many and varied interruptions she'd sustained, and the way basic tasks took ten times longer to complete. But if she didn't pick up her pace she'd certainly be late, and though Bronwyn had said a late submission would be fine, Staci didn't feel truly comfortable until she finally heard it confirmed from Max.

She glanced at the clock. Almost five. When could she reasonably expect James to come? He'd said after work. But

181

what time did his work finish? And did dinner mean pizza ordered in or something else? Pizza would prove immeasurably easier than a restaurant that demanded the use of a knife and fork. What should she wear? She'd managed a sponge bath of sorts this morning, enough so that she didn't smell—she hoped. She was wearing the easiest, stretchiest clothes she could find, ones that didn't demand much lifting or tugging, but they weren't exactly stylish. Surely that wouldn't matter if they were just staying in?

But wait, hadn't he said something about a tree lighting? Would today's rain still mean that went ahead? If so, she'd need to wear far more snow-appropriate clothes. And with all the zips and fasteners such clothes demanded, should she have accepted his mother's kind offer to come help her from before? She'd thanked Jenny but turned her down.

Her email pinged, and against her better judgement—why hadn't she quit it before?—she opened it.

Hey Staci,

I'm so sorry to hear about your accident. Everyone here wishes you a speedy recovery. Unfortunately, Flame can't extend your deadline. We've had some issues with our spring schedule which don't allow any other delays, so I'm afraid we'll need to see Fiona's manuscript on the 24th as previously agreed in your contract.

Wish it was better news. Happy writing,

Max.

What? After all she had done for Flame? He could not be serious! Could he? Her chest grew tight. How could they treat her like this? She carefully stabbed out a savage reply then deleted it, character by character. No, this was what agents were for. They earned their fifteen percent by intervening in such moments. She stabbed in Bronwyn's phone number, waited as it rang to voicemail.

"Hi, this is Bronwyn, please leave a message."

"Bronwyn, I've just forwarded you the email Max sent me.

Can you believe they want to keep the 24th as originally planned? Please sort this out. I'm too tired and angry to do it now – oh, and look, it's the end of their work day. How convenient of them to send something like this just when they know I can't respond. Please sort this out as soon—"

The phone beeped, signaling the end of message capability, and she threw it at the sofa, where it bounced off onto the carpet.

Her breath, her fingers trembled. She hoped Bronwyn could do a miracle, but Flame had proved pretty inflexible in the past. She'd heard stories of how they had leashed certain authors considered recalcitrant, not offering further contracts, even when the authors had been with them for years. She worked to get her breathing under control. Is that how they'd treat Staci if she made more of a fuss?

A knock came at the door. Oh no! Was James here already? And she, this shaking, near-blubbering mess? "It's unlocked," she called, then instantly hoped it wasn't a psycho killer. Had she even locked it last night? Maybe she was the one going crazy…

The door pushed open, revealing James. His hair and shoulders were wet. "Hey, it's only me." He chuckled, closing the door behind him. "You look relieved. Did you think I was some weirdo coming to get you?"

"You wouldn't be too far wrong," she admitted. "Blame my overactive imagination."

He moved to stand in front of the electric heater which she'd turned to the second highest level of heat. "Muskoka Shores isn't exactly prone to weirdo killers. Or any other killers, to my knowledge."

"Good to know."

"In fact, the only murder I'm aware of happened years ago, when a woman poisoned her husband's coffee."

She felt her eyes widen. "Really?"

He nodded. "My dad was classmates with poor Ron. Ron

wasn't a fan of bitter coffee and was prone to telling his wife—and anyone who'd listen—all the things she did wrong."

"Sounds like he was right to be concerned, then." She gestured to the seat opposite, and he sat. "Is this why you're a little fussy about your coffee?"

His chuckle was warm, like melted caramel. "I don't expect Suzy to poison me if I complain, if that's what you mean."

"She doesn't really strike me as the kind of person to do that."

"Yeah. It wouldn't exactly be—"

"—good for business," she finished with him.

They smiled at each other, that funny sense of connection swirling between them once more. She glanced down, pleating her emerald-green shirt between her left fingers.

"So, are you an expert on killers, then?"

His face sobered as he obeyed her hand gesture to take a seat. "I've had experiences I wouldn't want to see inflicted on those I care about."

Her heart grabbed at his "those I care about" comment, her mind pouncing on his mention of experiences. She decided to go with mind. "What experiences? Here, or in Africa?"

"I've been in a compound where tribal men tried to set a house alight."

She gasped. "Really?"

He nodded, settling back on the sofa as if he'd just mentioned the weather forecast. "I have friends who have had church members stoned because they refused to deny they were Christians."

How could he be so calm about this? "I thought that was only something that happened back in Bible times. You mean people really threw rocks at them?"

"And killed them."

Breath caught in her chest. "How awful!"

He dipped his chin.

"That must have been so difficult to deal with."

He nodded, glanced away. In the ensuing silence she waited, sensing he still had more to say.

"I... I didn't deal with it very well." His eyes touched hers again. "I was told by the mission board I needed to come home."

"Because?" she asked quietly.

"I started having nightmares, and the lack of sleep affected my decisions. For a doctor I got kinda sick."

Her heart grew soft in sympathy. The dear man. The dear, sweet, caring man. "I'm so sorry."

"Yeah, me too."

"Does... does the hospital and clinic know what happened?"

"Dr. Hollis and others who need to know do." He shot her a quick look. "Are you worried about my care of you?"

She gazed at him steadily, ignoring the edge to his voice. "I think your level of care of me is just fine."

After a long moment, his gaze disentangled from hers, and he drew in a shaky breath, rubbed a hand over his face. "I don't know why I'm telling you all this."

"I'm glad you have. Thank you for trusting me."

"I hope I can." He bit his lip, brow pleating.

"Oh, you can." She was a safety deposit box full of secrets, most of which were hers because she'd never been brave enough to share. But after his confession, she suspected this man, this courageous man, might actually understand. "I... I think you've been incredibly courageous working over there. I think you're very kind, and very generous." *And very wonderful,* she added silently.

"You don't think I was weak, reacting like that to such things?"

Her throat grew tight, forcing her to swallow. "I think you responded as any compassionate individual might, when faced with violence and cruelty. And it's not something to be ashamed of, not at all."

His shoulders slumped, as if in relief. "People can be ignorant and cruel. The world isn't always a pretty place."

Which was why she wanted to add something of beauty with her novels of escape—with a guaranteed happily ever after.

"Thank you for telling me. I… I'm happy to listen anytime you want to talk."

"You mean that?"

"Of course."

His expression softened. "Thanks. I don't want to bore you. I'm afraid I'm prone to saddling my high horse at times."

"Aren't we all?"

He offered another rueful-tipped smile, and she felt the tension ease a mite.

Her phone buzzed, and she shifted forward, but he beat her to pick it up. "Yours, I believe?"

"Thanks." No way was she going to tell him why it was on the floor. She glanced at the caller ID. The tension renewed. "I'm going to have to take this. It's my agent."

"No problem."

He moved to the kitchen to give her a modicum of privacy and she pressed the green button to answer the call. "Bronwyn?"

"Oh, Staci. I'm so glad I got hold of you! I've just got off the phone with Max and I'm terribly sorry, but he refuses to budge. I don't know what's going on, but I've heard whispers that there are going to be some changes at Flame, so maybe that's got something to do with it."

Really? What kind of whispers? No, she needed to stay focused. "But that isn't fair. I don't understand. How can they treat me like this when I've only ever met their deadlines, and never been late once? How on earth am I ever going to get this written in time?"

She glanced up to see James looking at her, a frown in his eyes. She sucked in a breath, looked away. *God, help me stay calm.*

"Look, I know this seems unfair. I will call tomorrow and

speak to Bryan and demand an explanation. He's a managing editor who owes me more than one favor. In the meantime, I suggest you do your utmost to get something ready even if it's not your most polished work. Better to hand something in than nothing."

It was clear that Bronwyn didn't like her chances. "I appreciate that," Staci managed. "I don't mean to sound hysterical. But these last few days have been pretty challenging, and this was the icing on the cake."

"I'll do my best," Bronwyn reiterated, then ended the call.

Staci sighed, the breath feeling like it leached from her toes as she placed the phone on the coffee table.

"Something's wrong?" James murmured.

"My book is due soon and my publishers are not willing to negotiate a delayed submission. You'd think a busted wrist would be a sufficient excuse, but no."

His lips pressed together, and she remembered their previous discussion, so she pasted on a smile.

"First world problems, hey?"

"You don't have to have someone trying to kill you to need help, Staci."

She glanced away. How could he talk like that when all she dealt with was fictional romance, a genre long decried as fluffy and lacking any real depth? She so needed to change the subject. Before she could, he spoke again.

"So, tell me about your day."

Staci gestured to the phone. "I think you now probably have a fairly good idea."

"How far through your book are you?"

"About three quarters. I've never been this close to the deadline before, and obviously did not count on all the drama I've had since being here."

"Drama is never convenient."

"No. It can be useful though."

"For story ideas?"

"Sometimes," she admitted. "Although it's not always easy for contemporary situations to translate into historical contexts. I find it useful in other ways, though."

He looked interested, so she explained, "I try to journal my emotions. I find that helps in channeling my feelings so they live on the page and not in my heart."

There was a beat or two of quiet, then he said, "I journal too."

That made six things they now had in common. Or was it seven?

"I've never thought about it in regard to being a cathartic experience though."

"You should try it sometime, Doctor." Her heart smiled at his expression. "So, how was your day?"

"Good. Well, good enough, all things considered. The only thing of interest to report is that I managed to see Rose during my lunch break. She's doing well."

"She sounded well when I spoke to her earlier."

"I hope it won't be long until we can see her released."

"I'm sure she's looking forward to that."

"And you? You didn't mention before how you are feeling physically."

"I'm okay."

He studied her with another of those deep looks that made her wonder what he really saw. A look that made her nervous, made her want to speak and pierce this bubble of supposition her imagination was only too eager to run wild with. "So, yesterday someone mentioned something about dinner."

"Someone did, didn't he? What do you feel like eating?"

"Anything I don't have to cook myself."

"My sentiments exactly." He rubbed a hand through his hair. "But judging from your earlier phone call, I can't imagine you want to spend too long away from your computer."

"You imagine correctly."

"Would you rather wait until it's done? I don't want to interrupt you, especially now I know you've got deadlines."

She fought the insecurity his words evoked. His look of concern suggested it wasn't an excuse to get out of things. Instead, he was being thoughtful, considerate. Something she wasn't used to. "My deadline is not until Christmas Eve, and I don't think I can afford to wait to eat until then."

His smile poked out as she'd hoped.

"You need to eat, so do I. I'm very happy to do something, provided it doesn't take too long." She winced. "Sorry, that makes me sound so ungracious, doesn't it?"

"No. Just a woman who speaks honestly and tries to honor her commitments. I like that."

The approbation in his eyes begged her to duck her head, but she studied him instead, enjoying the unfamiliar feeling that a man of character approved of her. Even if he might not for much longer, once he knew the sorts of books she'd written in the past. Something she'd best confess to, especially if this dance around flirtation had any hopes of blossoming into something real. But did she really want real? What future could they have? He'd be heading back to Africa one day, wouldn't he?

"So, given your wrist injury, I suppose it needs to be easy to eat one handed, and quick." His lips turned wry. "I'd had hopes of showing you the Christmas tree lighting, but it doesn't seem like that's on the menu."

"I wish I could." She gestured to her leg. "I've managed to hobble around okay, so if there was a way to see it that'd still be good. I just don't want you to need a chiropractor after all your carrying."

"I don't mind," he said, his gaze and tone firm and deep.

Again that spark flared between them. She should probably turn down the gas heater.

She swallowed. "Would you think it terribly rude of me if I suggested we order in pizza?"

"Not rude at all." Relief eased over his features. "I was thinking the same."

"Then let's order delivery. What time is the tree lighting?"

"Oh, didn't I mention it? Today's rain means it's been postponed until tomorrow." His lips lifted. "So if you're not busy tomorrow night…?"

She held his gaze. "I'm not busy tomorrow night."

He grinned. "Then maybe we'll need to do something like this again."

She echoed his smile. "Maybe."

GLADNESS SWELLED HIS HEART, threatening to bust out on his face. How nice to have something to look forward to, to have someone to look forward to, at the end of a tiring day. Today had been wearying, with meetings, patients, and the incessant ice-tinged rain. But all that drained away as he'd entered Rose's house, and had seen Staci's relieved face, and somehow their conversation had quickly grown serious and he'd finally shared about his past.

He'd sensed her deep compassion, something her quick wits and easy repartee had cloaked. It had seemed like he'd handed her a piece of his heart and she'd held it gently, like a treasure, her words wiping off some of the pain and grime as if she saw something more.

He liked her. He trusted her. Could he trust her for the future?

"So, pizza." She eyed him. "Have you got a preference?"

They spent a few minutes discussing pizza options.

"Let me guess. You're a man who likes olives and anchovies."

"What makes you say that?"

"You seem like the kind of guy who is up for anything."

"I do, do I?"

"Let's just say anyone who chooses to live in Africa isn't exactly going for tame."

He chuckled. "I don't know if it equates to a liking for olives and anchovies but I'll take it. I'm glad you don't think I'm boring, anyway."

"Boring? Hardly."

The corner of his mouth twitched. "My turn now. I'd say you're a woman who likes cheese and chicken."

"How did you know?"

"Years of observation."

"You can tell a person's pizza preference from what they look like?"

"Sometimes." He smirked.

He caught the way she seemed torn between a smile and offense. "So what about me screams cheese and chicken?"

"Doesn't exactly scream, but I can tell you like the finer things."

She frowned. "Are you calling me prissy?"

"Not at all. But," he nodded to her Kate Spade bag, "it's not exactly Target."

"I tend to be more Target than designer," she confessed. "I just like to have nice things to remind me of the goals I've achieved."

He nodded, they ordered, and settled down to wait.

"So, I bet you don't get the chance for much pizza in Tanzania."

"Not too often. I have to make it from scratch."

"Dough included?"

"Yeah. I don't suppose it would ever meet any true Italian standard, or even any mediocre standard, but it works."

"One of the best things about Chicago is its deep-dish pizza. I'd miss that if I lived somewhere else."

That led to a discussion of their favourite foods, and places they had lived, or visited, which led to laughter. "You can't say that about London. They make the best pies there."

"Have you been?"

"Well, no," she admitted. "I've just done a lot of research."

"Do you travel much for your research?"

"Not as much as I'd like." She bit her lip. "I mostly travel via the great world wide web."

"You should try and get out there." He proceeded to tell her about some of London's more interesting haunts, places he'd visited after college. Her wistful expression made him wonder what she wasn't saying and be thankful when the doorbell chimed and he could be distracted with paying for the pizza.

He closed the door, and the next minute was taken with finding plates, napkins, and glasses of water.

He helped Staci hobble to the dining table where they sat, then he offered to say grace, and they ate. Great gobs of cheesy goodness trailed between the pizza slice and her lips, her lips which he was growing increasingly interested in knowing more about.

James blinked, ducked his head, and concentrated on ensuring every strand of stringy cheese made it inside. "This is good, huh?"

She swallowed, sipped her water. "Not bad for a small town."

"Pizza snob."

"Coffee snob."

"Yep," they said at the same time, then laughed.

This was so not how he had thought about their date. But its very casualness, its very ordinariness, made him feel comfortable and at ease.

He eyed her curiously. "So, are you okay now? You seemed a little pensive before."

"Did you say pensive?"

"I said pensive," he confirmed, watching the light in her face fade at the word.

She glanced away, the moment of ease trailing away like a piece of thinning mozzarella.

"I know I shouldn't ask, and I'm not trying to pry, honest, but if ever you want to talk, well, I'm here."

"Thanks," she whispered. "You're very sweet."

Sweet? Not what he'd been shooting for, but then this date had become so much more than what he'd expected. And if it helped them know each other better, then maybe this Christmas season would be better than he had thought.

CHAPTER 15

Lord James Markworth eyed her, his disconcerting gaze prickling her skin. She wasn't used to being the object of a man's attention for so long. It made her feel a little... warm. A little nervous. And a great deal uneasy. What if he wanted more than she could give? What if he demanded her heart? Could she trust him? Would he cope with the secrets of her soul?

Staci eyed James as he shared about his day, conscious that since last night's brave sharing she'd felt a prompting to do the same. That awareness had lodged in the back of her mind throughout the day, even as she'd painstakingly typed, and her ideas had flowed, and anticipation built, along with questions about where this friendship was heading.

Tonight he had arrived with Chinese takeout consisting of chicken-and-cashews, and beef-and-broccoli, which she ate so she could pretend she was healthy. It led to more shared stories about his travels abroad, the food he'd eaten, the places he'd seen, that had left her envious, wishing she didn't have this phobia about planes. But she did. So she hadn't traveled. So she'd have to deal with it as best she could.

He glanced around the room. "Hey, you don't have a Christmas tree up yet."

"Gran was waiting for the time to go together and pick one out. I guess that won't be happening now."

"It still could. Maybe some time this week we could see if there's any for sale at the tree lot. It might've been a few years, but I remember the last time I was home for the holidays that they usually fresh cut trees available after tree lighting night. Does Rose have decorations somewhere?"

"Probably in the garage."

"Mind if I take a look?"

"Be my guest." She gestured to the door that led to the garage. "I'll man the fort here. Well, woman it, anyway."

James grinned and went to explore the contents of Rose's garage, while she cleaned up as best she could. He brought out a large plastic tub labeled 'decorations', and after lifting the lid, and sorting out the Thanksgiving decorations from the Christmas décor, they looked at Gran's dusty and dilapidated collection. A few baubles, a few homemade crafted items, some tinsel that had seen better days.

But the collection of decorations, meager as it was, pricked tears in Staci's eyes. She lifted out a glass bauble filled with a wintry London scene.

"I remember this," she whispered. "Mom and Dad bought it just before they were due home. It was one of the few things that survived…" The lump enlarged in her throat, forbidding further speech, as memories flooded in.

Her excitement about that last Christmas, the thought her parents would finally arrive and they'd be reunited at last. She hadn't thought she would miss them as much as she had—what teenager did?—and had mumbled goodbye with rolled eyes and protests at being left with Gran and Granddad. "Why can't I come too?" she'd whined to Dad.

"Because this is a work trip."

"That you're taking Mom on."

"Because it's our twentieth wedding anniversary and we wanted to make the most of it. Your mom and I will miss you, but it won't be forever."

"But I still don't understand. It's not fair. I could stay home, it's not as if I'm five. I don't need to stay with Gran. I'll miss school, and my friends. You're being completely unreasonable!"

Those mild words had escalated to something ugly, and it had been with stiff hugs and sighs that they had finally departed. And now they were coming home. And she would give them the biggest hugs ever and whisper a sorry against her mom's hair.

She'd listened in as they spoke with Gran and Granddad on the phone and had managed a few words as they talked to Staci about the fun sights and foods they'd experienced. "Anastacia, when you're older you have to try the pies, they have these delicious steak and kidney pies that are to die for."

To die for…. Her wobbling lips pressed together.

"Staci?" A touch on her shoulder banished the memories. "What is it?"

She shook her head. James might be willing to reveal his pain, but if she shared, she might spill all her heart, and there would be nothing left to scoop up and keep life beating.

He nodded to the box of Christmas décor. "We should probably get a smaller tree, seeing that your grandmother doesn't have too many decorations."

"Probably," she mumbled, glad he'd taken the not-so-subtle hint and moved the conversation to safer ground.

"I know I said this yesterday, but if you ever want to talk, well, I'm here."

"Thanks," she rasped.

In the silence that followed she thought about his offer. She'd never shared what happened with anyone. Not really. A school counselor, a psychologist, both knew parts of her story, but the only one who really knew was Gran, and even then it was because she'd forced her way into Staci's bedroom one night when Staci had been overwhelmed with pain and tears. Refusing to take no for an answer, Gran had held Staci in her arms as she'd poured out her heart in whimpered bursts and heavy sobs, until she'd gone limp, when she'd finally succumbed to Gran's whispered prayers for God's mercy and slept. Then Staci became a wall, no one in, nothing out. Her only escape was in schoolwork, running, and spinning dreams of happily-ever-afters, dreams she eventually started writing down, even though she knew those dreams could not come true.

But how to explain this, even to this man with whom she felt an unsettling connection, was a step too far, a step too hard right now.

One day, though. Maybe.

He cleared his throat, drawing her attention back to him. "Have you had enough?"

"Of the meal, or the inquisition?"

His lips curled to one side. "I'm guessing you're done with both, right?"

"Right."

"Then if you're still feeling up to it, do you want to go to the tree lighting ceremony now?"

"Okay." Anything to get away from the memories, away from the pain. "That'd be nice."

He cleared up the remains of their meal, placed the plates and glasses in the dishwasher, while she hobbled to her bedroom to retrieve a thick coat, gloves, and scarf. Not that she needed both gloves. She dumped them on the table, then hobbled back for her hat, boots, and purse. But sitting on her bed trying to pull boots on one-handed was impossible.

A tap came at the open door. "Can I help?"

She nodded, ducking her head, hating the feeling of indebtedness again. She studied him, admiring his dark curly hair as he helped put on her boot. What a kind man he was. How patient he was with her. She bet everywhere he worked he was admired by both staff and patients. Especially those of the female variety. She'd seen the way Larissa had acted.

He zipped the boot up, then attended to her other foot, working slowly, checking often that it wasn't hurting as he carefully drew the boot over the swollen ankle.

"There. Can I help you with your jacket?"

She rose unsteadily, feeling his breath brush her skin as he helped ease her into its warmth, leaving one sleeve dangling free, her right arm in its sling next to her chest. Then he gently tugged the zipper up, snapped the buttons closed, an action that necessitated his lifting her hair at the nape.

"You have really pretty hair," he murmured.

"Thank you," she whispered.

His nearness was intoxicating, his fingers brushing her skin, sending chills up her spine. Waves of awareness simmered between them, something she recognized in his dark eyes as he adjusted her scarf around her neck, his fingers trailing down the emerald-green length to the fuzzy pom pom at the end.

"We really should go," he said.

He remained standing so close she'd only need to lean a tiny bit forward to know what his lips tasted like. She swayed forward, then pulled back, breaking the connection. "We really should."

Before she got carried away into something that could never be.

Muskoka Shores was awash with lights, the twinkling spots of color pooling on fresh fallen snow. She snuggled into her coat, glad for its protective layers as James carefully negotiated the snowy streets. She peeked across at his side-lit profile.

The earlier moment had passed, a fact she was grateful for. For really, how could she entertain the idea of romance with someone guaranteed to leave the country? She couldn't. And someone like her could hardly be the right kind of person he was seeking forever with. He needed someone who didn't freak out about planes, who would enjoy things like camping, who'd be comfortable with roughing it (whatever that meant). He definitely didn't need someone who preferred fiction over reality, who liked designer shoes, and wrote frivolous romances the content of which would not be missionary approved. No. She'd best guard herself from allowing this to go any further. In fact, she'd best ensure this date proved to be their last.

But all thoughts of relationship ending ceased when they gained the town square. The tall fir tree pointed to the heavens, reminding people as it had for centuries, about the truth of the origins of Christmas. The tree was surrounded by a group of townspeople, all dressed warmly, their breath releasing puffs of white clouds in the air.

She pressed her face against the truck's cold window, but it kept fogging from her breath, forcing her to wipe it clear. "Do you think we could get out to see it?"

"You're sure you can manage?" James asked.

"Yes." Maybe. She hoped so, anyway.

He opened her door, and she gingerly stepped out, holding onto his arm. The ground was slippery beneath her boots, making her grip all the more tight. They slowly made their way to join the crowd, his arm around her back, something which caused more than a few raised brows as various people noticed their approach.

James nodded and greeted a few of them, but his focus was on Staci, his requests for assurance she was okay causing a warm glow within. He pointed out the mayor and his boss Dr. Hollis, but she scarcely noticed, distracted by the speculation she could see as his mom and dad eyed them, before a broad grin filled Jenny's face.

"Staci!" Jenny hurried toward them. "Jem mentioned you might be here. Oh, I'm so glad. I'm sure it's been awhile since you've seen the tree lit here."

"It has." That was easier than admitting she'd never seen it lit in person before. She'd had no heart for such things in Muskoka Shores, and neither LA's balmy December nor Chicago's frigid one encouraged such things.

There was a murmur from the stage area, then the voices around them hushed, the mayor explaining about the tradition of lighting trees, harking back to candles in earlier times. Staci could have given him a few more stories about the beginnings of such traditions – she'd researched such things for her Christmas medieval novel – but on the whole it was entertaining, and mostly true.

He moved to a specially lit button and began the countdown.

Staci glanced up at James. "I get the feeling this is supposed to be a little like New Year's Eve in Times Square."

"Only if there's a kiss involved," he said, his gaze sweeping to her lips and back.

She gulped. He *was* teasing. Wasn't he?

"Three, two, one!"

The tree before them lit in a rainbow of bright colors, all topped off with a gleaming star, a silent reminder of the original Christmas star that led wise men to worship a king.

Staci's breath constricted as the crowd erupted in cheers. How lovely it was! Almost enough to make her believe Christmas miracles could still occur today.

Then she felt the arm around her shoulders nudge her closer, felt James's body move to align with hers. In the darkness she saw his face illuminated by the tree, bend slowly down to hers. There was a moment of anticipation, then his lips slowly brushed hers.

Fire and magic and reverence and starlit possibilities sang between them. Ohhh…

She opened her eyes, saw him staring at her, a stunned expression on his face, like she was some kind of angel. "Happy New Year, Staci," he murmured, just loud enough to be heard above the crowd.

She blinked. "But it's not even Christmas yet."

"It isn't?"

"No."

"Are you sure?"

She shook her head. She couldn't be sure about anything right now.

"I must have got carried away," he murmured. "Sure felt like a new year to me."

"Yes," she whispered. It had felt exactly like the start of a new year, where the horizon of hopes and dreams awaited, a moment when anything was possible. If he ever felt like getting carried away again, she'd be totally up for that. Forget whatever silly thoughts she'd had earlier about severing their connection before it had even had a chance to truly start.

"Hey, you two." Mitch Wells lumbered into her line of vision. He wore a smile—or was it a smirk? "Want to join us for hot chocolate at Suzy's?"

James turned to Staci, brows lifted in a question.

"Oh, don't be silly, Mitch," Jenny said, slapping him gently on the arm. "I'm sure they'd much rather spend time getting to know each other than be with us two."

Thank God it was dark and they couldn't see Staci's flush. "I don't mind—"

"She's being polite," James interrupted. "She's on deadline, so we'll need to get back soon. Besides, we really need to get to the tree lot. Rose needs a tree before she comes home, and we were going to surprise her with one."

They were? Staci eyed him with raised eyebrows, before turning to his parents. "Um, yeah," she agreed lamely.

"Okay, okay." His father held up his hands. "I believe you. Though millions wouldn't," he added, with an expression that definitely counted as a smirk.

"I didn't realize Rose was heading home so soon. How wonderful! Well, we'll see you when we see you." Jenny patted Staci on the shoulder and gave James a quick hug.

"Catch you at home," James said.

Staci said her goodbyes then he escorted her back to the vehicle, and she was helped inside the truck again. Staci felt her body stiffen. Would he explain his actions earlier? Should she press him? What should she say? "So, about that kiss…" Or "What did you really mean about a new year?" Or "Are you suggesting we have a relationship?"

She couldn't. She might be a liberated woman, but the romantic within didn't want such a clinical response. Surely such a thoughtful man as James would mention something about what had just happened?

But when he got in he said nothing about their kiss, only saying the tree lot wasn't far away, and if she'd like he could pick a tree for her tonight. "But if you prefer to get home and get writing, we could do it tomorrow. Which do you prefer?"

"Oh!" She suppressed her desire for answers to the questions she *really* cared about. "I'm happy to do it tonight. Happy for you to choose one." She'd managed the earlier excursion okay. And it had been years since she'd picked out a tree before. The last time had been with her dad…

Emotion throbbed within, and she drew in a sharp breath.

He glanced across. "You okay?"

"Yes."

"Sure?"

His sensitivity squeezed her heart. "I'll be fine."

She backed up her words with a big smile, which he seemed

to take at face value, and concentrated on his driving once more, permitting her to silently exhale. And let the doubts in once again.

What was she doing? She couldn't let this kind and gorgeous man think she was going to stick around. She wasn't Smallville, no matter how prettily Muskoka Shores was packaged. It wasn't fair to him, was it? And now a kiss had been involved—and he didn't seem the Casanova-kind to treat a first kiss as a regular event—everything was more complicated. Held more potential for hurt. For pain. For loss. She bit her lip. Loss sure to be hers as soon as she told him about the subject content of her books.

"You doing okay?"

Such solicitude! Oh, Fiona could only *wish* her suitor was so thoughtful. "Yes." She studied him, driving to their destination, a small smile on his face. "You seem to be enjoying this."

"It's different to the past few Christmases I've had, that's for sure."

Of course. His time in Africa would likely mean past Christmases had been *very* different. "I'd love to know what you did for Christmas in recent years."

So he told her of sunny skies, church services that lasted for hours, tribal singing, roasted pork, fruit-topped pavlovas from Aussie colleagues, days that melded into long sunsets and nights filled with big stars.

"Sounds like you enjoyed your time there."

"Yes."

"Do you want to return?"

He pulled up in front of a tree lot, his gaze sliding to hers. "I've got some things still to sort out here," he said slowly. "But I was hoping to get back by Easter."

She nodded. Yet another reminder she should not get too attached. He was leaving, same as her.

"So, shall we see if we can find Rose's tree?"

The next half hour was spent carefully maneuvering around

the lot, James's arm around her shoulders, as they inspected, selected, then paid for the perfect spruce she was sure Gran would enjoy. She could only watch on in amusement as he wrestled the small tree into the back of his truck.

"I don't think it wants to leave." She laughed, as James got back into the vehicle, breathing hard.

"I didn't think I was that unfit, but that was heavier than I realized."

"And the pine needles were rather sharp," she said, leaning over to trace the cuts grazing his cheek.

The dark pools of his eyes connected with her, and his hand closed over hers, sending tingles down her spine. Her breathing hitched, her body tensed. But she couldn't do this, couldn't allow feelings to develop, so she pulled away, tugging her hand free. "We should go."

For a second he looked disappointed, before murmuring, "That's right. I should have remembered that you need to finish writing your book."

Of course! Her book. How could she have forgotten?

"But first…" He swung the truck back to Muskoka Shores's Main Street, slowing as they neared The Coffee Blend. "First, I think we deserve hot chocolate. You can count it as dessert, if you like, seeing we didn't have any earlier."

She agreed, allowing him to help her as he opened doors and ensured her safe passage inside the café. The warmth hit her like a tropical breeze. "Whew!" Off came the hat, she unwound her scarf, and tried to slide from her coat. To no avail.

"Want me to help?"

She agreed, and soon he was assisting her once more, the brush of his fingers on her skin eliciting fresh shivers, and releasing her to sit unfettered, in a booth underneath the picture of the lake cabin.

"What shall I get you?"

"Just a hot chocolate would be nice."

"With marshmallows or without?"

"What do you take me for?"

"With."

His grin curled her insides. Who needed hot chocolate with this warm sweetness inside? At her nod he moved to the counter, permitting her to study the picture on the wall as Christmas music played softly in the background. Where *had* she seen it before?

Maybe it was the memories stirred earlier, but a new memory suddenly resurfaced. Of course. It had been that last summer. The last summer she'd been happy here in Muskoka Shores. Dad had hired a little cabin on the shore, one that belonged to the friends of a friend, and Dad and Mom and Staci had spent a perfect two weeks swimming, fishing, boating, eating ice-cream and just being away from the bustle of the city in this town where her grandparents lived.

Of course she had protested being separated from her friends—what teen wouldn't?—but it hadn't taken long before she'd succumbed to the charm of the place, the unpretentious ease of a cottage of mismatched furnishings and a quiet locale. She'd read nearly a dozen books and relaxed for what felt like the first time since she'd started high school. With nobody who picked on her lack of dress sense. Nobody who giggled about her frizzy hair. Nobody with whom to play "let's pretend your words didn't hurt me." Nobody except those who had truly loved her.

Her eyes prickled with heat. Who had truly *loved* her…

James returned, settling into the seat across from her. "Hey, I hope you don't mind, I ordered some raisin toast as well. Suzy makes the best."

Her throat was clogged, she could only nod and duck her head.

"Staci?" His voice came whisper soft. "Are you okay?"

"I'm fine," she eventually croaked. "Just thinking."

His hands reached across the table to clasp her left fingers. "What about?"

She watched his thumb gently caress the back of her hand, the action soothing, mesmerizing, caring. Suddenly she didn't care about their separate futures, she only wanted to hold onto this moment, hold onto his care and concern. She knew no other man who had ever demonstrated such compassion, save her father, and Granddad.

"You don't have to tell me."

But suddenly she did, and in a low voice, her eyes fixed on the table lest she lose focus and be distracted by the kindness in his eyes, she pointed to the picture and told him of her recent discovery.

"I don't think I've ever been truly happy since then." Sure there had been moments when she'd felt momentarily uplifted, but underneath the deep discontent had continued, had pursued her. All the way back to Muskoka Shores.

Their hot chocolates were served, their buttered raisin toast, but she let it grow cold as she talked on. It was like a dyke had burst, and all her thoughts were tumbling out, and she had no reserves left with which to plug it.

"My parents died that year, in a plane crash on their return from England, and I was forced to stay here with Gran and Granddad. I hated Christmas. It was the first holiday without them, which is why I tend to hole up in my apartment and watch holiday movies, wishing I had a tiny taste of that happy ever after." She finally looked up, wiped her burning eyes. "I've never spoken like this to anybody."

He gently squeezed, then said gruffly, "The first Christmas after John was killed we were all together, and it was hard, being reminded of how things used to be, how the various traditions now had to be different. It helped though, knowing he was with God."

She nodded. "Mom and Dad believed too, but I guess I thought God didn't really love me since He took them away."

"Bad things happen," he said gently, "sometimes without explanation."

She dragged in a deep breath. "Maybe if I'd believed a little more it wouldn't have been so hard."

"Life can be filled with maybes and what ifs. We can live focused on regrets or focus on the now and what you feel like God wants for the future."

What did God want for her future?

"Drink your hot chocolate," he encouraged.

She obeyed, heart listening to a quieter voice within.

What did God want her to do?

To trust Him. Trust Him with her future, trust Him with her pain. Her gaze lifted to where James watched her carefully. And to trust *him*, she felt that still, small voice whisper.

But what if he hurt her?

But what if she hurt him? she felt that same voice say.

But he's a medical missionary to Africa, she argued.

And you could minister to the world.

She stifled a disbelieving chuckle, conscious James still studied her with concern. He might send her to have her head examined if she admitted to this internal dialogue. But he probably wouldn't, she thought, offering him a weak smile.

"Try the toast." He shifted the plate toward her.

She took a slice; the butter melded with the sugary cinnamon goodness so it was tasty, but chewier than she preferred.

"It's probably better warm."

She nodded, dropping her gaze, as her thoughts returned to before. How could she minister to the world?

With your writing, that small voice whispered. *Write to honor, not dishonor. Dignify marriage, and glorify sacrificial love, not self-*

ishness. Live that way, write that way, and be a good instrument of love in this world.

She closed her eyes, propped her head in her hands, her elbows on the table, seeing a future unfurl before her. She didn't need to live in Chicago—or any city, really—to write. She didn't need to live in North America, even. And learning sacrificial love meant not isolating herself anymore. Relationships were key. A relationship was key. And if fostering that relationship meant moving—meant flying on a plane—then she could do it. What had Mitch and Jenny said? Love meant living by faith, not living in fear. And surely living with love, living knowing she was loved by God, was of greater importance than bestseller lists and fame?

God, I really need Your help, she prayed.

The heaviness in her spirit, the knots and gnarled tangles of emotion weighing down her heart lifted, as a feeling of peace lapped the edges of her soul. Gone were the weeds of grief and confusion, the stew of stagnant pain, as this reminder of God's love washed them away. She exhaled. She felt lighter, cleaner, happier.

Her eyes opened. His intense look eased. "Okay?"

"Yes." She smiled. She was the most okay she'd been in a long while.

"How are you two doing over here?" Suzy asked.

"Fine, we're fine," James said.

"Really good," Staci murmured, reassuring her with a smile.

Suzy nodded, then motioned to the ceiling. "I suspect you might feel even better once you see what's up there."

A sprig of mistletoe beckoned them. Staci glanced at James. He met her gaze with a smile. "I wouldn't want to disappoint."

And he reached across and brushed her left hand with his lips.

"That's not a kiss!" Suzy exclaimed. "Come on."

"And I'm not going to spoil what should be treasured because of someone's demands."

Staci's heart swelled. This was the sort of gentleman she desired—honorably, of course.

Their hostess moved away in a mock huff, and James eyed Staci once again. "Sorry about that."

"I'm glad you said that," she confessed. "Not because, well, um…" her cheeks grew hot. "Well, you know."

He grinned. "I don't think I quite do."

She swatted his hand. "You know exactly what I mean."

"Not because you don't want me to kiss you, but because you agree that something special like that should be reserved for a time without spectators."

"Exactly," she agreed.

"So you wouldn't mind if we left now?"

And escape spectators? "Not at all."

He glanced at his watch and winced. "I'm sorry. I've kept you far longer than I intended. And you still have your story—"

"Forget the story." She almost had. "I'm so thankful to have had this time with you."

"Really?"

"Really." She nodded for emphasis.

They'd come for dessert, but she'd experienced something far sweeter. The renewal of hope and a sense of peace for the future.

"Dr. Wells, it's good to see you."

"Dr. Hines, hello."

She eyed James with a smile that made him wonder about his own. Of course his smile had scarcely left his face in recent days, his times with Staci merely cementing his emotions, their kiss last night a precursor to something more permanent. He hoped.

He tried to pull his smile back down into something professional—he didn't want to seem clown-like or Tom Cruise-couch-jumpy here at work. But he suspected he wasn't too successful, judging from the looks the staff gave him, with everyone from Dr. Hollis to the cleaners smirking as James strolled past. Still, it made a nice change from the fear and regrets that had left him feeling sad and edgy and had left his future in Africa up in the air.

Staci had trusted him. She'd opened up and shared the broken pieces of her heart with a vulnerability that made him admire her more. He'd known she was pretty special, had appreciated the blessings of brains and humor and passion, but the fact they shared this understanding of grief dared him to wonder if he'd found his forever girl. Would such a Christmas miracle be possible in Muskoka Shores?

He hurried into the hospital ward where his rounds began today.

"Hello, Doctor."

"Hello, Mrs. Everton. How are you today?"

"Not feeling quite as good as you, judging by that smile you're wearing."

"Ah. We'll have to see what we can do to boost your spirits."

She chuckled. "I'm not sure my granddaughter would approve."

"Mrs. Everton," he mock-frowned, "I hope you know hospital policy takes a very dim view of patients who try to flirt with their doctors."

"Is that what I'm doing?"

"*Is* that what you're doing?" he countered, his lips upturned. "Judging from such comments I think it must almost be time for you to go home."

"I wasn't sure my granddaughter's beau would appreciate

that." She peered at him. "I understand you've been having meals together."

They'd talked about him? Staci considered him her beau? His smile widened. "I think your granddaughter's beau would just like to see you happy and healthy at home."

She smiled up at him, and he caught an echo of Staci's grin. He blinked, aware of his distraction, and forced his attention to his purpose again.

They chatted about her medical prognosis and agreed she should look to return home within a week. "Now that it seems your heart condition has stabilized on this new medication, so long as you promise to rest and take it easy and agree to home visits from people such as yours truly, then I think you should be right. I'm sure Dr. Hines will agree."

"You are a good boy, aren't you?" She patted his hand.

"I try."

She nodded. "I hope you know that this particular grand-mother is very pleased with a certain young doctor." Her expression grew serious. "You've made Staci very happy. I hear it in her voice when she calls."

"She's very special."

"I'm so glad that you can see it. It's been a long time since anyone has made her feel like life can be worth living, and not just be found in the pages of a book."

He heard the faint warning. "I will do my best to not hurt her."

"I know you will, dear boy."

Her approbation swelled his chest, adding wings to his steps as he completed his rounds, as he engaged in consultations, even as he was called in to speak to the head of the hospital, Dr. Hollis.

"Ah, Dr. Wells. I wanted to check in with you and see how you are settling in." His boss peered at him over silver-framed glasses. "Although I don't need a medical degree to make that diagnosis. You seem much happier than when you first started."

How to answer without implying he had, in fact, been unhappy? "Certain personal circumstances have improved of late."

Dr. Hollis nodded. "I saw you last night at the tree lighting with a young lady. Anyone I know?"

"Staci Everton, sir. Rose Everton's granddaughter."

"Rose? Oh, Dorothy's friend from church. Well, I'm happy for you, son, but don't let it distract you, or impact your good work here, or that at the clinic."

"Of course not, sir. I'm well aware of what I owe you and will strive to honor your faith in me."

"Good, good. I think I speak for the rest of the hospital board in that we'd hope you might wish to stay, but we take a dim view on anything untoward, especially in how our staff conduct themselves. The hospital can't afford a scandal. Well, be off with you then."

James nodded, and escaped the office, exhaling. Dr. Hollis may have thrown James a lifeline, hiring him when the mission board had insisted he take leave, but he'd sensed the man's resolve. Perhaps James should be more guarded.

CHAPTER 16

Fiona smiled, the happiness pervading her chest still something she did not dare trust. It felt so long since she had known happiness, she barely knew what to do. Did she dare sing? Dance? Such things might be considered scandalous but might prove release to her soul. He loved her. Didn't he? Oh, how wonderful to feel this way...

Staci eyed her words, finger hovering over the delete key. Too schmaltzy? Maybe. But she'd leave it, for the moment at least. How could she not? Last night had proved the perfect inspiration for her words today, the writing flowing, her words shaping this story into something with heart, and soul, and passion.

She sighed, glanced at the clock. And James would soon be coming!

A press of the keyboard to save today's work, and she pushed away from the desk. Tugged at her shirt. Would he like this color? Not that a twenty-first-century liberated woman should really mind about such things—and she sensed that he wouldn't mind what she wore, anyway—but it was nice to have this happy glow of anticipation riding through her veins.

The phone rang. She snatched it up. "Hello?"

"Anastacia?"

"Gran? Oh, how are you?"

"Much better, thank you, dear. I wanted to call and see how you were doing. I've missed you."

"I've missed you, too." The snatched phone calls during her lunch breaks weren't nearly long enough. But Gran had insisted Staci work, had said she would not wish to be a burden on her granddaughter not completing her work on time.

"How is the story coming along?"

"It's nearly there. Just a few more chapters and it should be done by the end of the week. That should give me some more time to proofread and revise as necessary before the twenty-fourth."

"So you'll get it done?"

"It would appear so," Staci said. "Thank God."

"I do. I have been praying."

"I know you have, Gran. Thank you."

"Well, I'm very pleased to hear it. It will be good to know I'm not going to impinge upon your time too much."

"Oh, have they given you a discharge date?"

"Dr. Wells mentioned something about early next week."

"That's wonderful!"

"It will be good to get home," Gran admitted. "They keep telling me to rest, but it's something of a challenge when there are always so many people around. And the noise! I know you think Penny can be a little noisy, but that's nothing compared to here. But I shouldn't complain. The staff have been very kind, and I certainly haven't wanted for visitors."

"You certainly haven't," Staci said, smiling.

Every phone call she'd had with her grandmother this week had seen Gran interrupted by a friend or two from church, or one of the ladies from Gran's sewing circle, or one of her long-time neighbors. It seemed Staci had met—via video calls—more townsfolk visiting Gran's hospital bedside than she had walking up the street. Anna Morely and her grandmother, Dorothy; Anna's friends Jackie and Toni Wakefield; even the Thomas family whom she'd once falsely claimed to know. One such phone call had even led to an invitation to Staci from Serena and her friends, including Toni Wakefield, to join Serena's upcoming Christmas 'soiree'—a dinner party being held in the week before Christmas. Staci had demurred, not sure about her manuscript deadline, but had expressed hope she might be invited to a future event. A girl needed female friends, after all. Just like she needed to make the most of family.

"I can't wait for you to be here," Staci said to her grandmother.

"Well, we'll know a bit more come Monday morning. Just as long as my return won't be putting you out anymore."

"I'll be fine, Gran. Don't worry about a thing."

"And Penny?"

"Jenny and Mitch have been looking after her. I'm pretty sure Mitch thinks he can train her for you while you're away, but I don't know if either Penny or Jenny agree."

Gran chuckled, her laughter nestling in Staci's heart. How wonderful to hear her joy, when once upon a time Staci had wondered if Gran would ever wake again.

"And how is that handsome doctor son of theirs? I understand he's been keeping company with a certain granddaughter of mine."

"Oh, Gran, I meant to tell you, but it's all rather new. I didn't think anyone knew, except for Jenny and Mitch."

"Now you don't need to worry that the hospital rumor mill is working overtime. James came and spoke with me about you today."

"He did?" She swallowed. "That, um, sounds rather official."

"It's nothing to worry about. He was simply demonstrating his gentlemanly qualities."

But what did 'demonstrating his gentlemanly qualities' actually mean? It didn't sound like something heading to a proposal…

She slapped her forehead. Seriously? This wasn't the 1800s. This was all so new she shouldn't even be *thinking* about proposals.

"Well, it looks like my dinner has arrived, so I'd better go. Goodnight, dearest Annie."

"Goodnight, dearest Gran."

Staci pressed end on the call and replaced the phone in its position on top of the microwave. Surely James had to be serious about her if he wanted Gran's blessing? But what did that mean?

She sank into the dining chair, all thoughts of dinner having flown away. Her readers would never buy a successful happy-ever-after relationship based on mere weeks of interaction. How could it even work? James had said he hoped to return to Africa by Easter. That was less than four months away. Would he expect them to conduct a long-distance relationship? She'd vaguely expected things could progress while she lived in Chicago and he continued to work here, especially given the ability to visit on weekends. She could manage it. Trains would likely work, if she didn't feel up to driving. He could always fly to visit her.

Her heart jolted. What if this did get serious, and he wanted to get married and take her with him to Africa? Traveling by train certainly wouldn't work. She doubted even ships would. There really was only one way to travel to Africa, most likely in aircraft without the North American safety ratings she'd scorned. Could she do it? Even if she loved him?

She exhaled. This was stupid. This was another case of too much imagination. They hadn't mentioned the 'L' word! It was way too soon, way too new. But if he did, they'd need to have another honest discussion. For the memories of the past would not let her get into a plane.

"Stop it, brain!" The words echoed around the living room. "Just relax."

James was coming over, with dinner supplied by his mother, and a promise to put up the tree he'd wrestled off the truck last night and propped into a bucket of water in the garage. Her heart beat with anticipation. What else might tonight have in store?

She'd just turned on the oven when a knock came at the door. "It's open!" she called.

She limped over, twisted the handle, and admitted James, closing the door against the cold night air. "It's so cold out there."

"But warm in here." He held a casserole dish in mitted hands and smiled, as if seeing her was the bright spot of his day. "Hi, Staci."

"Hello, stranger," she said, her smile holding a new shyness since his kiss yesterday.

The mutual smiling continued a moment longer, and she wondered if she should limp closer and see if he wanted a hug, when she realized he still held the ceramic dish.

"Oh! Does that need to go in the oven?"

He glanced down, as if noticing it, then shrugged. "I don't know. Maybe?" He placed it on the kitchen counter and took off the glass lid.

A tantalizing sweet-savory smell scented the air. "Smells amazing."

"Apricot chicken. One of Mom's favorites."

After agreeing it could probably be reheated for a few minutes, he slid it in the oven, which left them staring at each other once again.

"How's the patient?"

"Good. Happy to see you. How's the doctor?"

"Good. Happy to see you."

They shared new smiles, and he opened his arms, and she limped into a careful embrace. Oh, how good it was to be here, to hear the thump, thump of his heart, to feel a sense of assurance that might even tip her into confidence.

"I saw Rose today," he murmured, lips grazing her hair. "Apparently she thinks I'm your beau."

"How funny that she should think that," she murmured, eyes closed as she drank in his scent of spiced oranges.

"I thought so, too. Although it's even funnier that everyone I've come across today seems to hold the same impression."

She drew back from her careful one-armed hug. "Really? That is most peculiar."

"Isn't it?"

His gaze swept to her lips, and a little thrill pulsated down her spine. Would he kiss her again? Now?

But instead he pulled away. "I left something in the car. I'll be right back."

"Okay."

She busied herself with retrieving plates and silverware and popping garlic bread in the oven. Garlic bread went with everything, didn't it? It was a kind of universal food, suitable for nearly every occasion. As was chocolate. And ice-cream. And—

"Roses?" She stared at the pink blooms before her, smiling. "Oh, you are quite the romantic, aren't you?"

He grinned, his cheeks turning pink. "I don't suppose I should tell you that Rose's friend Dorothy told me today I should give them to you."

Staci laughed. "No, I don't suppose that you should."

"Consider it unsaid then."

She hobbled to where Gran kept the vases and filled a square crystal vase with water. "Why would she feel you need to do this?"

"I don't know. Maybe your grandmother said something."

He shrugged. "I was passing the hospital gift shop and she asked me why I looked happy, and—"

Oh. Her heart glowed. "Thank you." She limped back and gave him a one-armed hug. "I'm glad you were happy today."

He stared into her eyes, and again she could feel the attraction pulsing between them.

A sloshing sound broke the connection as he hurried to turn off the faucet. "That reminds me. I better make sure the tree's bucket in the garage hasn't tipped over. Be back in a moment."

She busied herself with arranging the rose stems then finished setting the table as he lugged in the tree complete with bucket of refilled water.

"It's so lovely," she admired when he'd positioned the tree by the front window. "A perfect shape. You chose well."

He grinned, dusting off his hands. "That's the other thing Dorothy told me."

"What is?"

"That I chose well."

She had a feeling he wasn't talking about the tree. "Was it indeed?"

"Uh huh. But I wasn't sure I should tell you."

"Were you worried someone might get a big head?"

He drew closer, and still closer, then pressed his lips into her hair. "I like this head just fine the way it is."

After dinner—most delicious, she'd need to beg Jenny for the recipe—she settled on the couch, as per his instructions, as he sat on the coffee table before her.

"Before we get to decorating, I wanted to give you something else," he said, drawing a small package from his jacket pocket. "I didn't want you thinking I needed advice from elderly ladies all the time."

He handed her a red-ribbon wrapped gold box, something that made her heart beat fast. "Oh, James. You shouldn't have."

"It's not much. But I hope you like it."

She pulled the red ribbon bow, and the gold cardboard sides gently collapsed to reveal a glass bauble filled with paper curls of printed words. She peered closely at it, recognizing some lines from Jane Austen's works. "This is beautiful," she breathed.

"I saw it the other day at Brandi's. I know you write historical novels, and Mom has always gone on about how Jane Austen is one of the best, so that's what made me think of you."

Tears pricked at his thoughtfulness. "You're very sweet."

"I know," he said meekly.

She chuckled, and the mood released into the ease of earlier encounters. Her precious bauble had to receive prime position at the front of the tree, near where she instructed the prized London ornament from her parents to be placed.

Her heart was full. How wonderful was this man, helping her in such a manner?

"What about now?" he called, peering from behind prickly branches.

"Just move that painted one of the manger scene to the center branch," she instructed.

"Here?"

"No, the next one along."

He unhooked the intricately decorated bauble and moved it once again. "Better?"

"Much." She smiled. "Thank you."

"Are you always this much of a tyrant when it comes to decorating?"

"I've never really decorated before," she admitted. "Not since I was a child, so it must just be my control issues asserting themselves."

"Control issues, huh?"

"Best you know what you're dealing with."

He placed the last ornament on the tree and moved closer. "Oh, I have a pretty good idea."

"You do, do you?" She sank more deeply into the sofa as he

leaned down, arms bracing either side so her face was only inches away from his.

"I've got a pretty excellent idea, actually," he murmured, his gaze dipping to her mouth. "Especially now we're here, with no spectators around."

And with that he closed the space between them and placed his lips on hers.

She could taste the sweetness and tang of apricots on his lips, could feel the whirling sensations as his lips possessed hers in a gentle, yet thorough, exploration. Her left hand crept up to his face, then curved behind his neck, tugging him ever so slightly closer.

He made a noise deep in his throat, something her heroes would often do—so it *was* true!—then tilted her head back, one hand cradling her head. He kissed her tenderly, yet possessively, as if her lips held secrets he longed to know.

Ooh! Her eyes snapped open. She should so write that down.

He pulled away, confusion in his eyes. "What is it?"

"Sorry," she said, reaching across to the coffee table for a pen and paper. "I just thought of something."

"While we were kissing?"

"It's a compliment, really," she said, grabbing the pen and writing down the phrase. "There! Done." She smiled up at him.

"I don't understand."

She tossed the pen and paper aside and tugged him closer again. "You're such an excellent kisser that I had to write down how you made me feel." She pressed her lips to his.

He inched back. "Seriously?"

"Well, yes. That's what I do. Inspiration strikes, words and phrases come, and I have to write it down before it's lost forever."

"You'd write about private matters in your books for anyone to read?"

"Well, it's not all true, you know. I do write fiction. I've never married an earl, for example."

At his look of uncertainty, she rushed to reassure him. "Look, if you don't want me to, I won't include it." She scrunched up the paper, stifling a sigh. "See?"

He chuckled, although it sounded uncertain. "I've never dated an author."

"Well, if it's any comfort, I've never dated a doctor."

"I guess we're even then."

"I guess we are."

He met her small smile with his own. "I suppose I should let the author go finish authoring."

"I suppose."

"But if you happen to get things finished, let me know? I'd like to do this again." His brows rose hopefully.

"Decorate another tree?" she said, purposefully misunderstanding.

"Spend time getting to know you," he murmured, eyes dark with intention.

Via kissing? Yes, please. "Then you'd better go, before you get to know how crazy this author gets when she's feeling the pressure."

"You've got my number?"

"You gave it to me before. Go. How about I call you if I can't get things done by six tomorrow night?"

"Sounds like a plan." He swooped in and brushed another kiss on her cheek. "I really like you, Miss Everton."

"And I really like you, Dr. Wells," she murmured.

He departed, closing the door behind him, leaving her to wonder at the magic of the evening, her story far from mind. And to wonder if this mutual liking could ever lead to something that was lasting.

~

"Did she like it?" Brandi asked eagerly the next day.

"She loved it. Thanks for your help." He smiled at his former almost-sister-in-law.

"Well, she's an author, and I figured she'd enjoy all kinds of bookish things. Have you read anything she's written?"

"No."

"I think we have some of her books here. When your mom mentioned her, I knew I recognized the name." She moved to the bookshelf and drew a couple of books from the shelf. "Here."

He stared at the covers, one, the pirate book he'd seen a few days ago, called *Secrets of the Wind*; the other cover was far more eye popping, and made him blush and look away.

"I, er, didn't know she wrote that kind of novel."

Brandi chuckled. "Yeah, I don't think it's as bad as what the cover makes out. Not according to the Goodreads comments."

"Goodreads?" There seemed very little good about that second book. Heaven forbid Dr. Hollis ever saw it.

"You don't know about Goodreads?" Brandi looked at him sympathetically. "Poor James. You have been living under a rock, haven't you?"

No, just been away, focused on matters of life and death. He kept that to himself.

She went on to explain that the Goodreads community generally held Staci Everton's books in high regard, that she was known for pumping out good fiction with realistic characters and settings that were great to escape into. "I mean, we're not talking Austen, but I'm sure her books would be kind of fun." She raised her brows suggestively. "You could get an insight into how she thinks, James, what she might consider is romantic."

"No thanks." He already had a reasonable idea. Roses. Candlelight. Kisses.

"Oh, come on." She glanced around, then lowered her voice. "I probably shouldn't tell you this, but you can buy them as e-books also. That way no-one will ever know."

"E-books?"

"Oh my goodness, James, I'm going to pretend you didn't say that. Look, you want to read her book, don't you?" She smiled. "Don't worry, nobody will ever know what you're reading. One of the blessings of technology these days. You want the first one?"

Well, he certainly didn't want the second. "Uh, okay?"

"Great! I'll load it on an e-reader you can borrow."

A few minutes later he was outside the bookstore, feeling like he'd participated in a conversation where he only knew half the words, and had been steamrolled into something guaranteed to have complications.

Yes, he wanted to know more about Staci's world, to learn about what went on in her pretty little head. But the thought of reading her words both tantalized and terrified. What if he came across more vivid descriptions of kissing, and he started wondering about whom she'd been thinking when she wrote such things? Worse, what if there were... other descriptive, revealing passages? He didn't know what to think.

"James?"

He started at Pastor McPherson's voice, pasted on a smile. "Forgive me. I didn't see you."

"I didn't expect to see you out shopping during the day." He glanced at the paper bag which held Brandi's e-reader. "Got time for a coffee?"

"Uh, sure." They moved past the Nuthouse, past the vintage toyshop, down the block and across to The Coffee Blend, each step James took increasingly laden with dread. What would Pastor McPherson say if he knew how Staci made a living? What would Dr. Hollis say? Would something like that count as a scandal, the likes of which might affect his future at the hospital?

He lifted a hand to Suzy as he entered the coffee shop, motioning to a booth.

"TDH for you?" she called.

He nodded. "And a glass of water. Thanks."

The pastor ordered and they sat at the same booth he'd sat with Staci two days prior. James glanced up. The string of mistletoe still beckoned.

Pastor McPherson saw where his attention was and chuckled. "Want to switch booths, huh?"

"I'm good." He doubted Suzy would be teasing about kisses today.

They chatted in general terms about the weather, about the tree lighting, about the Christmas lunch. "You planning to volunteer?"

"I need to check my schedule at the hospital." And check on Staci's plans. Was she planning to return to Chicago?

"No pressure. Your mom has been a great support these past years. We usually have plenty of volunteers."

James nodded, turning as Suzy approached with their coffees.

"Howdy pastor, good to see you again. And Dr. Wells, how's that lovely girl of yours?"

"Staci?" James questioned.

"How many do you have?" she teased.

"Only one," he said, heat creeping up his neck. Now was definitely not the time for Dr. Hollis to overhear.

"Tell her I hope she can find you some more mistletoe, okay?"

Yeah, definitely glad Dr. Hollis wasn't here.

"You and Staci Everton, huh?" the pastor said.

James nodded, sipping his coffee to avoid answering.

"Well, well. That's mighty interesting. Mighty interesting, indeed."

"How so?"

The pastor sipped his hot chocolate. "Oh, you've both been

in my prayers. In different prayers," he hastened to add, eyes twinkling.

"So this isn't some divine matchup?"

"Well, I can't comment on that. Let's just say I think it's nice to see people find happiness at Christmas." Pastor McPherson sat back in his chair. "Have you told her yet about your future plans?"

"Regarding Africa?"

The pastor nodded.

"I can't, because I still haven't heard."

"And what if they say you're cleared to return?"

James sighed. "That's the question. I still don't know."

"Forgive me, but she doesn't really strike me as being Africa-friendly."

"I don't think she'd be unfriendly, but I know she's not used to traveling, or what it means to live abroad." He traced the woodgrain in the table. "I don't want to ask her to give up what she's used to."

"Would she go if you asked her?"

"Maybe. I don't know."

"Would you cope staying here if the answer is no?"

James smiled without humor. "Maybe. I don't know."

"Seems you have a predicament."

"You can say that again. But I'd prefer you didn't."

Pastor McPherson chuckled. "I'll be praying. For the both of you this time."

"Thanks." He drained his coffee, eyed his pastor. "There's something else. You know she writes romance?"

"She told me so herself. Historicals for the secular market, right?"

James nodded, relieved he wouldn't have to go into long explanations. "I just saw her books in Brandi's bookstore, and the covers are, uh, kinda not what I'd expected."

"And this is a problem because…?"

He lowered his voice. "Because if the hospital board was to find out that we were, well, dating, then there might be questions."

The pastor's brows arched.

James tugged at his collar. "Dr. Hollis has told me he doesn't want any scandal attached to the hospital. I get the feeling he's pretty conservative and wouldn't approve of her books."

The pastor's graying head tilted. "I'm not Reginald Hollis, but he's always been very big on traditional family values. I've heard him give addresses and seen the way he's voted before."

"Well, if you can add some prayers into these areas as well, I'd really appreciate it."

"Of course, my friend. Will do."

But the tension would not leave him, even as the pastor paid and left, and James was left wondering how to proceed, when progression in this relationship might lead to broken hearts and dreams.

CHAPTER 17

*L*ord James stood by Fiona's side as she spoke to the king and
queen, beseeching them to dispense funds to help the poor
within the land. His presence beside her imparted strength,
their discussions earlier had bestowed wisdom, and she felt her respect
grow for this man who had in turn engendered respect from her royal
parents. Their approval for him had spilled into approval for her,
something that whispered ease to her heart, and hope to her soul, that
in this festive season, she might have finally found that which it
seemed she'd forever searched for. Acceptance. And true love.

Staci sat back in her seat, rereading the words, a small smile
on her lips and ease in her heart. The past week had been one of
long days writing, and magical evenings. Her book had seemed
to write itself, the inspiration flowing fast, often into the wee
small hours. How could it not? Not when she was feeling such
emotions that spilled onto the page. And not when she'd felt as
though the words and phrases were whispered to her heart.

She'd had to change some things, but already could feel
Fiona's story holding some of the best writing of her life. Fiona
had purpose, had passion, but refused to let emotions get in the
way of her principles. Her principles—ones Gran could be

proud of—were hopefully those her readers could understand, could relate with, be inspired by.

Night after night Staci had finished at six, saved her work and sent James a text saying she was free. Night after night he came over, and ate dinner, working their way through the casseroles Pastor McPherson had organized and every takeout option Muskoka Shores had on offer, and talked about all things under the sun.

Last night she had tried to help by offering to make salad, but after one look at her attempt to cut tomatoes one-handed he'd firmly shooed her to the couch.

"Go," he'd pointed, "I cannot let it be on my conscience when you do yourself an injury."

"But I know a good doctor," she'd protested.

"Oh, you do, do you?" he'd asked, drawing near, humor curling the corners of his mouth.

"Yes," she'd murmured, savoring his delicious scent. "Dr. Hines is really very good."

He'd chuckled, moving into to kiss her cheek, where she marveled at his touch again. "Is she the only good doctor you know?"

"I might know another," she whispered as his breath feathered her skin.

James was a good doctor. A good man. A good son. He'd make a good husband.

Breath caught. She'd pulled back, pushing his chest gently away. "So, are you making dinner, Dr. Wells?"

"Slave driver," he'd grumbled, moving back to the kitchen, tossing smiles and jokes to where she'd sat curled up on the sofa, watching him, marveling that he wished to cook her dinner. How different he was from Alex, Alex who barely knew what she wrote, let alone had ever cooked for her.

That had been last night. She wondered what tonight would bring.

The doorbell rang. She hurried to answer it, the plaster cast on her wrist making her movements awkward. "Hello, you."

"Hi."

He looked weary tonight. She tugged him inside. "Are you okay? You seem tired."

"Yes to both. Today was tough. We lost a patient on my watch."

"Oh, James." She wrapped her good arm around him, held him tight, praying silently. "I'm so sorry."

"Thanks." His voice was muffled into her hair.

Emotion caught her chest. What a good man James was, caring for his patients so. She'd witnessed his compassion before, when he'd shared about some of the losses he'd experienced in Africa, but never had she seen him appear so raw.

He pulled back, scrubbed at weary eyes. "It's hard, you know? Sometimes we can almost think we're infallible, that we have all the answers, and then something like this happens and we're reminded that we're only human."

"Would it help to talk about it?"

"Probably not." He sighed, then glanced up, lips twisted to one side. "Maybe."

She tugged him down to the couch, listening as he shared, heart grieving for what he did and did not say. The imagination that could so often get her in hot water could easily sympathize with the impact on the patient's family, compassion further stirring as she saw how this loss—and others—had affected James, had eroded hope, and brought an element of self-doubt. How he needed someone who could encourage and remind him that not all of life was bad. Someone who could stand by him and be the strength he needed when he had little of his own.

"And so a local family is facing a very different Christmas now."

She threaded her fingers through his hand and gently squeezed. "I'm so sorry."

"I can feel it."

"What?"

"Your sympathy." He glanced down at her. "You really seem to understand. Thank you."

She managed a tremulous smile. What was she supposed to say—you're welcome?

He saved her from having to say anything, pressing a kiss against her brow. "That compassion must be why your books are so good."

"I beg your pardon?"

He tugged her a little closer. "I think readers feel like they can relate and identify with your characters, like they're real people."

"What? I'm sorry, but how would you know?"

"I have a confession to make. Brandi told me to read your first one."

"Brandi did?"

He nodded. "She recommended your books as realistic and a good escape."

"You're kidding, right? I thought she didn't like me."

He gently tugged at a flyaway curl. "It's a good thing you're not insecure."

"I know," she agreed. "Imagine if I was."

Amusement rippled through his chest. "I have to admit, I've been curious for a while about your books."

Staci's conscience panged. While she hadn't fully described all the content of her novels, she had told James enough that he knew not all of them would be considered appropriate for a church ladies' book club. "I don't think I'm the kind of author your missionary friends would enjoy reading."

"You might be surprised," he murmured. "I enjoyed it."

"Are you serious?" He'd actually read her work?

James nodded.

"Which one?"

"*Secrets of the Wind.*"

Thank goodness he'd said that one, and not one of the later books.

"I have to confess that when Brandi told me it had pirates I was imagining Captain Hook, but it's more like Captain Jack Sparrow."

"Except without the Johnny Depp vibe."

He nodded. "Do any of your other pirate books have a Keira Knightley vibe?"

"No!" She shoved him. "Why? Do you like that sort of girl?"

"I like this kind of girl," he said, and swooped in for another kiss.

"And you really did enjoy it? You're not just saying that?"

"Not insecure at all," he murmured, smiling.

"I think it's connected to having a vivid imagination," she confessed. "So, did you?"

"I'd say reading 300 pages in one go means I thought it was an enjoyable experience."

"Really?" Was there a bigger compliment? "You read it in one night?"

"Well, it was too good to put down. And once Captain Horner appeared, well, you had me hooked." He chuckled. Sobered. Eyed her seriously. "You really have a gift with words, Staci."

Her spirit sang at the respect she saw in his eyes. How wonderful that he believed in her. Had any man, save her father and Granddad, ever believed in her so? "So you didn't mind the, um, more passionate scenes later?"

"They were married, so it was not unexpected."

Relief oozed across her chest. "I'm so glad you thought so. I still get the occasional letter from readers who don't understand why that sort of thing should be in there. But I figure if they're married and they love each other, then they should be passionate with one another."

"Yes, they should."

He eyed her so intently she couldn't help but wonder what intention he had. This talk of marriage—No! She dropped her gaze. She really needed to tamp down this excessive imagination. Surely it was too soon to think of anything of a permanent nature?

"I, er…"

She glanced up again.

He shifted fractionally away. "I wanted to…" he tugged at his collar, as if it was too tight, "I wanted to talk to you about something."

"I'm all ears."

She waited, but he seemed hesitant.

"Would it be easier after dinner?" she finally asked. "Serena Williamson—have you met her? She's the assistant pastor's girlfriend—she dropped off another casserole, which I've had heating in the oven."

He exhaled. "Yeah, food would be great."

He said nothing more, only enquiring about her wrist as she popped more medication. "How is the writing going?"

"It's almost there. One chapter more, then the fun of editing can begin."

"Do you find it fun?"

"No, not really. I enjoy writing the first draft when a story feels full of possibilities. But later it can be a real struggle to get the words I thought were gold into their proper place." She smiled, glanced up at him. "Just warning you that I'll need you to be extra kind in upcoming days."

"Noted."

"And I might start craving chocolate."

"Got it."

"What, no comments about being unhealthy?"

"I wouldn't dare."

She kept the conversation cheerful during their meal,

sensing he needed a boost in spirits, as well as time to gather his thoughts so he could share. When they'd finished the meal she motioned to the sofa, where they could sit and admire the twinkling lights on the Christmas tree—or pretend to, if his words, as she feared, might be too hard to hear.

"So, you wanted to tell me something." She forced up her lips. "Call me insecure, but I get the feeling it isn't good."

"Ah, Staci." He picked up her hand, looked at it. Sighed. Then looked at her. "It's not *not* good. It's just unknown."

"What is?"

"I've been putting off telling you, but I'm expecting a letter soon which will tell me about my role in Africa."

Breath suspended. Her chest grew tight. "I didn't know you'd decided to go back there."

"I never said I wasn't."

"But..." She shut her mouth. He didn't need her to complain; she knew this was hard for him, otherwise why had he hesitated before? She couldn't blame him for her own misunderstanding.

"I'm sorry I didn't say anything to you before."

"That must be hard waiting." She wanted to be a good girlfriend, sympathetic and understanding. Hadn't he praised her compassion earlier? But everything roared within that she was about to be rejected, abandoned, that this time together would prove little more than a holiday romance.

"It *is* hard. And even if they say I can return I still need to decide if that's what I should do."

She nodded, swallowed. The fact he even had to ask this question made her wonder just how he saw her. Was it selfish to wonder if she had any rights at all?

"I love..." *you*, his eyes seemed to say, "spending time with you, Staci. But I have to wonder if..." his words trailed away.

"If what?"

His phone buzzed, and he snatched it up, glanced at the screen and sighed. "I've got to go. It's an emergency."

But he hadn't shared what concerned him so. *Be the good girl-friend*, she told herself. "We can talk later."

He shook his head. "I suspect this will take a long time." He pushed to his feet. "I'll call tomorrow."

"Okay."

But as she watched him leave, she knew it wasn't okay. Not really. She couldn't help but worry for their future. Because for the first time since they'd started dating, he'd left without a kiss.

JAMES PLACED his bag by the dining table, then moved to the fridge and removed the plastic-wrapped meal Mom had texted that she'd saved for him. He microwaved the pasta bake and grabbed a knife and fork. Outside, the pad of snow against the window broke the stillness of the night. Even Penny had only glanced up then turned her head away, unconcerned by his late arrival. Two minutes later he'd slumped in his seat, eating but not tasting food, as memories from the past mingled with more recent overwhelming failure.

"Jem?"

He glanced up at his mother. She was dressed in PJs and a robe. "It was terrible, Mom."

She smiled sympathetically, in a way that reminded him of Staci last night. He blinked, scrubbed at his eyes, then pushed his fingers through his hair as he willed the images away.

The hospital committee frowning at him. Flashback to three months ago, to others who'd judged and found him wanting.

"Mr. Ogilvie was perfectly fine when he was checked by Dr. Hines earlier." Dr. Hollis's beetling brows had pushed together. "Can you explain what happened?"

"I'm afraid not, sir."

Sometimes there was no medical reason. Sometimes people's hearts just stopped.

James had done all he could to retrieve life. His compressions had started almost immediately, and he'd needed to be dragged away before he'd stopped. The memory of something similar in Tanzania had kept him awake half the night. Had made him question whether this was a job which he had any right to do.

"They want me to take time off, Mom."

"That might not be a bad idea. You could spend time with Staci—"

"She's still got a deadline."

"I'm sure she'd be happy to spend more time with you."

He got that feeling, too, but, "Dr. Hollis told me I should be careful."

"What do you mean?"

"After the committee meeting he came and spoke privately to me. Told me I needed to limit the distractions, to ensure I'm focused on work."

"Haven't you been?"

"I thought so." He shrugged. "Apparently someone saw me down the street on my half day off, and overheard part of my conversation with John McPherson. They felt it was their duty to report it to Dr. Hollis."

"What were you saying?"

"I was talking about Staci, about the books she writes, and asking John's advice. He seemed to think—and it's now been confirmed—that Dr. Hollis would think her books too scandalous." He dredged up a smile. "Dr. Hollis has told me I need to rethink my relationship with her or reconsider my role at the clinic and hospital."

"What?" Indignation sparked in her eyes. "He can't say that."

"Well, he did."

His mother huffed out a breath. "What are you going to do?"

"What can I do? I can't—I literally can't—afford to not work. After my bouts of burnout, I can't see anyone willing to offer me a different job. Not that I'd ever be likely to see one if Dr. Hollis won't offer me a reference. And I still haven't heard from the mission board about Africa."

"Would you want to return there?"

He thought about it for a long moment, toying with the pros and cons. "I've been questioning things, wondering about that. To be honest, I don't think I do."

She exhaled. "I'm so relieved."

"Mom."

"No, not for the reason you think. Of course I would want you living nearby, or on the same continent, at least. What mother wouldn't? However, I also know that regardless of where you live, that it is God who has to protect you." She gently rubbed his shoulder. "But I think for your sake, for your own mental health, it's important for you to learn to balance hard work with things that give you joy. I'm not sure how much respite your work over there truly offered."

"It gave some."

"But not quite enough."

No. Days off held more intention than reality, a drive to a mountain pass certain to draw attention not just to peaceful vistas but the endless need.

"James, I think you need to be kind to yourself, to not consider your time there a failure."

"I didn't—" His words failed at her raised-brows look. Yeah, okay. His mom knew him well.

"You didn't fail, honey. You succeeded in doing something very few people ever do and made a very real difference to many lives."

Her words soothed the jagged edges of his heart.

"I think you should look back on that time in Africa and remember that you helped so many people. Help which you can offer here, too."

"If I have a job."

"This hospital isn't the only hospital nearby."

"I know. But Dr. Hollis was the main reason I got this one here." Whether James had got the position due to family connections or 'small-town boy returns', or sympathy about what had happened to James's brother he didn't know. But James knew that he didn't want to go through all the rounds of applications and interviews again.

"Perhaps you can stop working at the hospital, and just work at the clinic," Mom suggested.

"Reduce my hours? Sure. That'll help me pay off my debts and buy a house. Some catch that makes me."

She was quiet for a long time. He could hear Penny's faint snore from her basket. "Is this fear of a loss of your job the only thing preventing you from pursuing a deeper relationship with Staci?"

"I don't know. Maybe."

He didn't dare think about Staci for too long. She was like a shooting star he'd never reach, glittering into his existence then sure to leave his orbit, especially when she truly knew who he really was. A mess. Complicated. Haunted by the lives of those he'd failed. He had nothing to offer her. She offered everything to him, and these past days as Christmas Eve drew near it was getting easier—and harder—to keep her at arms' length, not knowing how to explain the many complexities that made up his life. What was the point in getting more serious with someone who was guaranteed to leave him anyway?

"I'll be praying for you. For you both." His mom hugged him. "Just remember, fear isn't the answer, James. Love is."

Yeah? Well, how could love get him out of this situation?

he End.

Staci leaned back in her seat, eyeing the screen. A miracle, right there. Something she'd had her doubts over, something she'd struggled and wrestled to make happen, but she'd reached the end of her manuscript and it was done.

"You're not exactly perfect, though," she muttered to the story on the screen. Still, with a bit—okay, a *lot*—of polishing, it would be good enough to submit. And with still a week until her deadline, she'd have enough time.

So this called for a celebration.

She grabbed her phone, and swiped to the contact favorites, only realizing at the last minute that she shouldn't call James as he might be with a patient. Far better to text him, which he could read when he had time.

Celebrating the end, she typed with her left hand. *Dinner out tonight, my treat. Have a good day! Staci xx*

After all his support and kindness these past weeks, and especially with the challenges his job brought, James deserved someone to take care of him for a change.

When no reply immediately came, she pushed up from her

seat, gladness at the finish still coursing through her veins. The desire to celebrate—to do something now—wouldn't be assuaged.

She moved out to the kitchen, spied Gran's apron hanging near the door. "Ginger cookies!"

A few minutes later the Christmas carols were cranking, and the scent of ginger and brown sugar wafted through the air. Gran loved ginger cookies—or ginger biscuits, as Granddad had called them—and baking would be a nice treat for when she returned in a few days' time, as well as providing sufficient distraction. Maybe she could make some as thank you treats, for Jenny and Mitch, and for the next door neighbors. Maybe she could even prove to James just how domesticated she could be.

Every few minutes she'd check her phone, to see if there was a message. But no. She typed again: *Not taking no for an answer. 7pm. Be here.*

She bit her lip. Was that too bold? Oh, what did it matter? She was a twenty-first century woman. And with such an invite he couldn't accuse her of insecurity and lacking confidence.

As the cookies baked, she made another call. "Gran?"

"Darling girl! How are you?"

"Pretty good now. I just finished my story."

"You did? Oh, that's wonderful. Congratulations!"

"It's so nice to have it done, especially as it is a little different from what I wrote before."

"And you think your editors will be happy?"

"It's a lot more sweet than the others, but the characters and plot are things people will care about, and the message of forgiveness always resonates."

"I'm so happy you're writing such books now. The others may have paid the bills, but it sounds like this is one that will encourage and inspire, and that's something that you can be proud of."

"I am, Gran." Gladness filled her chest. "And now all I want to do is celebrate."

"Oh, I wish I could celebrate there with you."

"You'll be here soon," she reassured. "I'm hoping James is free and we can go out for dinner."

"I'm sure he would love to. Poor thing."

Her pulse spiked. "What do you mean?"

"Oh, I saw him earlier, and he seemed rather stressed. Going out for dinner would be a good break."

There came a sound of muffled voices, then Gran spoke again. "Dorothy is here, says hello."

"Hi, Dorothy," Staci called. Gran was so popular. "I better let you get back to your friends."

"Well, congratulations, darling. I'm so pleased for you. All my love."

"All of mine to you. Bye!"

Staci ended the call, happiness bouncing inside, begging for release.

She sniffed the air. The cookies were done. Slid them out onto the cooking racks and eyed them. Hmm. Maybe the darker brown edges could be covered with frosting.

She was searching through Gran's cupboards for ingredients to make frosting when her phone pinged a message. Spinning, she almost toppled over on her bad ankle in her attempt to snatch the phone.

Congratulations, but can't tonight. Sorry, James.

She stared at the words. Seriously? A few taps and his phone was ringing. Ringing. Still ringing.

"Come on, pick up," she muttered. He had to be there. Hadn't he just texted?

But when his phone went to voicemail, she didn't leave a message. Was he ignoring her? She couldn't think of what to say that didn't sound accusatory.

Then Gran's words from earlier filtered in. That's right. He'd been stressed. Maybe the pressure of work meant he was too busy.

She rang his phone again. This time when it went to messages she spoke. "Hi, James. It's Staci—which I'm sure you know if you checked the number of who called. Anyway, I'm sorry you can't make it. Maybe we can do something tomorrow night instead? I… I'd love to see you. Okay. Call me!"

She ended the call, worrying her lip. Had that sounded perky enough, and not desperate?

"Not insecure at all, are you?" she mocked herself.

The next few minutes she spent trying her best to hide the burnt bits of the cookies with the frosting, before deciding there was no way she was ever going to be secure enough to offer these as any type of thank you gift, nor offer these as proof of domesticity. She bit into one. Still tasted as it ought. It just wasn't very pretty.

Her phone buzzed, and she grabbed it, relief filling her as she saw the name onscreen. "James! Hi, I was just thinking about you."

"Hey, Staci. Look, I'm really sorry, but I won't be able to make it tonight."

"Oh." She'd known it, but the disappointment still pierced. "Is it work?"

"Not exactly, although it's related to it."

"Sounds mysterious." She rose, limped over to the kettle, and switched it on. Looked like tonight was going to involve editing, not celebrating.

At his continued silence, she pressed, "Is everything okay?"

A beat. "Yeah."

"That didn't sound too convincing, Dr. Wells."

"I, um, probably should go."

"Oh. Okay. Well, what about tomorrow night? Will you be free then?"

He sighed.

She sensed his withdrawing, felt the fear rise. "James?"

"Er, yes."

"Is something wrong?" A memory stabbed. "You said the other night we need to talk. Can we talk then?"

"We do need to talk," he finally admitted. "I'll see you at seven tomorrow night. But this will be my treat. Okay?"

"Okay." She tried to sound upbeat, but anticipation was fast being surpassed by a deep, disquieting fear.

SATURDAY MORNING WAS SPENT WRITING, then cleaning, then tugging out her best dress before deciding it would not really suffice and calling a taxi to take her downtown to Merrill's Fashion Boutique, a place which might have been fashionable twenty years ago but did not exactly scream fashion of today. Still, she managed to find a basic black dress that fitted well, and more importantly that she could put on herself. That, combined with the knee-high boots and green velour wrap was probably as nice an outfit as she could find in Muskoka Shores. Especially for someone with her injuries.

The afternoon was spent having another careful shower complete with plastic-bagged arm, then she dressed, and did slightly wonky makeup. Still, James had seen her at her worst, and too much makeup would doubtless shock him, so she kept it to a minimum. She peered at her reflection. Sighed. It would be nice for her green eyeliner to not look quite so smudged. A draw of her brush through curls and she was set.

He arrived at seven, prompt as usual, and she answered the door and drew him inside.

His jaw sagged. "Wow."

"Wow yourself." He was dressed in a suit sans tie, adding a casualness that appealed even more. But even the fancy attire couldn't hide the weariness in his eyes. Her heart softened. Poor man.

"Ready to go?"

"Yes, indeedy."

He helped her into the car—a car, not his usual truck. When she pointed this out he simply said, "Dad said I should." He grinned in a way reminiscent of earlier interactions. "That makes me sound like a teenager, doesn't it?"

"It's important to respect our parents."

"Well, they were right. It wouldn't have been right to take you to Alphonse's in the truck."

God bless his parents.

She asked about his day, heard about the clinic, and wondered as he relaxed just what he really wanted to tell her. She sensed it wasn't pleasant, but knowing him, knowing he would likely stiffen up if she pushed, made her hesitate to ask as she normally would.

The car turned into a drive, the Muskoka Shores Resort name lit on the stone wall, the avenue of trees drawing them to a series of large stone buildings. "This looks fancy."

"It is."

He escorted her from the car and they were guided inside to the restaurant, from which piano music could be heard playing softly. Christmas trees glittered in white and gold splendor. Oh! That was another line she should write down. She fished out her phone and was about to dictate her note when the maître d' approached.

"Bonsoir, mademoiselle and monsieur. Welcome to Alphonse's. May I take your coats?"

James helped her from her coat, his solicitude, his touch, evoking the expectancy they always did. But something was not quite right. She could read it in his eyes, which had not looked directly into hers at any time this evening. But she couldn't spoil tonight. Not yet, anyway.

They were led underneath twinkling lights to a white-draped table filled with silverware centered by glowing candles and a tiny square glass vase containing a red rose. Her pulse heightened. Was he nervous, as this was to be his avowal of love? What else did a red rose symbolize?

But if that was the case, why was he looking at the menu, and not at her?

"This is very lovely," she began. Would he pay attention to her?

"I'm glad you approve," he murmured, eyes still on the leather menu.

"Of course! How can I not? I'm just a little worried that I might embarrass you."

He glanced up at her quickly, and her heart froze. *Was* he embarrassed by her? What had happened?

She tried out a laugh. It sounded creaky. "I just meant that with my arm bound that eating might get tricky and I'll probably make a mess." That was all. That was what he thought too. Wasn't it?

"I can help you," he said, as if mechanically.

"That could be romantic," she said, smiling in a desperate attempt for playfulness.

His gaze dropped.

As did her heart. "James, is something wrong?"

"No. Not at all." He still didn't meet her eyes. "Let's order, shall we?"

His haste in ordering, his lack of conversation, none of it made her feel she could truly relax. Did he want to leave?

Their first starter arrived: garlic *escargot*. The special forks were effective at retrieving the little snails, although she obviously still lacked left-handed skills, which necessitated his help in securing their shells, which provoked some very welcome laughter.

"Just as well it's pretty delicious," she said.

"That which is a challenge is often worth the wait."

She eyed him, waiting as the waiter removed their plates and placed the second course down. When he'd gone, she said softly, "I hope you mean that."

"Mean what?"

"About the challenge being worth it."

"Why do you say that?"

She speared a piece of lettuce. "Because I get the impression that's what you think I am right now."

"What?"

Staci placed her fork on the plate with a clatter that drew heads. She ignored them, eyes focused on James's face, as she said in a low voice, "I've asked you several times now what the problem is, and each time you either ignore me or deny it, but never once have you looked me in the face. James, something is wrong. What is it? What's happened? Have I done something to upset you?"

"You could say that," he muttered.

Uh oh. "What? What is it? Tell me. Please."

He studied his Beef Wellington for what felt like a minute, while she nervously sipped at her glass of wine. Whatever he was about to say, she suddenly felt quite sure she did *not* want to know.

"I… I was talking with my boss."

"Dr. Hollis?" Oh, look at her being the good girlfriend and remembering her boyfriend's boss's name.

"And he wants me to be careful."

"Is this about your patient?" What did that have to do with her?

"He wants me to stay away from anything that might bring the hospital into disrepute. He mentioned your books. Something called *The Corsair's Bride*."

Oh dear. Not one any good person should ever read.

"Staci, when he described it, I didn't know what to think."

Shame washed over her. Flame had insisted she spice things up, so she had, to a hot chili rating of nine. "I'm not exactly proud of that one."

His gaze narrowed. "But you said before, how you write from experience…" He broke off, looking suddenly uncertain.

Her shame was immediately swallowed by shock that he would think she was that lax with her morals. "You don't honestly think that's written from my own experience, do you?"

"Then how—?"

"Well, some of it—a *lot* of it—is imagination, simply imagining what could be."

"But that's the thing. It's not really the sort of thing people would expect from the w—girlfriend of a doctor in a small-town community."

Wait—had he been about to say wife? She stared at him, sorrow streaming through her chest. He probably wouldn't dare think that word anymore. At least in relation to her.

"Staci?"

She licked her lips, tasting the sour-sweet note of French dressing. "But I don't write like that anymore," she said in a small voice.

"But won't your publishers still expect it, and your readers?"

"Maybe. But that doesn't mean they can't learn to have different expectations of a Staci Everton book."

"You're going to write sweet and wholesome now, are you?"

"Yes. That's exactly what this new book is."

He didn't look convinced, brow lowered, as he studied his plate. "I've been thinking about all this, and I just don't think I'm comfortable with having our private moments out there in black and white for all the world to see."

"But they're not out there for everyone to see. My books aren't exactly bestsellers, James," she felt compelled to remind him. But for once the thought of her non-bestseller status didn't hold its usual sting.

"I... I'm wondering if maybe this has been a mistake."

She blinked. "What?"

"I... I think we should go." He turned, summoned a waiter, who looked disappointed at their proposed departure before dessert.

That made two of them, Staci thought indignantly.

She kept her lips pressed together, reserving her anger for when they were back inside the car. "I don't understand you at all. This isn't fair. How can you invite me out to such a fine restaurant," she gestured to the stone entrance walls they were passing, "then insist we leave? What is it? What do you mean is a mistake?"

He said nothing for a long time, only concentrating on the snowy road, something she did appreciate, although everything within her demanded explanations.

Minutes felt like they'd stretched to days by the time they were passing through Main Street. But for once the pretty storefronts of Muskoka Shores held no charm.

A few minutes later they were on Elm, on Maple, were pulling into Gran's drive.

"Are you going to talk now?"

He killed the engine, glanced across. "Want to go inside?"

"Not if you're going to drop another bomb on me."

He shook his head, and helped her limp inside, even going so far as to help her remove her boots. She felt a bit funny with her sock-covered stockings, but he'd seen her lack of fashion sense before.

"Do you want some tea?" She felt she should offer. "Or hot chocolate?"

"No thanks." He stared at his hands, seating himself beside her on the sofa.

She counted to ten, then twenty, then finally asked again, "James, what is wrong? You mentioned a mistake. What is it?"

He finally met her gaze. "Us."

Her chest grew tight. No. "What do you mean? I thought things had been going really well."

"So did I. Until recently, when I realized our jobs, our work, can never be considered compatible."

"I still don't understand."

"Staci." He glanced up at her. "I really care for you, which is why this is hard. My job here is dependent on me staying scandal-free. I'm sorry, but I can't see a future. And it doesn't change the fact that I've got nothing to offer you."

"But I really like you," she whispered, emotion welling in the back of her eyes.

"I like you, too, but," he kneaded his forehead, "it's not fair to you to continue this."

"So you're breaking up with me?"

"I…" He swallowed. "I'm sorry, Staci, but I can't continue to see you. Can't run the risk of falling more in love with you when I have nothing to offer."

More in love with her? Hope sparkled, a distant, shining light, before the rest of his sentence crashed down into reality. "You keep saying that, but what do you mean nothing to offer?"

"I have no house," he said harshly. "No savings. I've spent it all on training and my work overseas. I've got nothing."

"I don't care about those things." What could she say to convince him? His earlier words tiptoed across her mind. Did all this mean he had thought himself in love with her? *Please, Lord.* Maybe there was still a way to see a Christmas miracle occur. For if he'd considered it once, he might be persuaded to consider it again…

"Correct me if I'm wrong, but does the hospital board only accept perfect candidates?"

"Nobody is perfect," he muttered.

"Exactly. But it seems you think they want perfection, a blameless record."

"I think Dr. Hollis wants someone who is not associated

with someone's name that appears in the first page of Google searches for racy romance novels."

Oh. They might have something there. "James, I'm sorry, but I can't change that."

"I know."

"So what do you want me to do?"

He shrugged.

"I can't change the past, James. None of us can. But we can change and make sure the future is different. Can't we?" Frustration soared at his continued silence. "I don't even know why this is a problem. We haven't even said I love you. It's not like we're getting married."

He flushed, dropped his eyes even as he pushed to his feet. "I have work tomorrow. I should go."

She pressed her lips together as he neared Gran's front door. How could the evening of celebration and romance have turned so badly so quickly? In a last desperate attempt to salvage the evening, she called after him, "Thank you for tonight. It was fun." At least the first half had been.

He nodded, but still didn't meet her gaze. And the front door closed, the sound of his car started, the crunch of the driveway grate indicating he had gone away.

CHAPTER 19

iona watched the carriage leave, the rumble of wheels seeming to strike deep within her soul. From far away the church clock struck three echoey booms, the sound of a coffin being nailed shut. Too melodramatic? Staci placed an asterisk next to it, rubbed at her weary eyes, and resumed the alterations. So much for thinking this story was done. *She would not look back, she would not, even as a small part of her wondered if her heart might be breaking.*

No, no, no. Staci pressed the delete button, one she'd used more often than she'd wanted in recent days. Fiona might be a medieval-era girl, but she possessed some modern sensibilities. She *wouldn't* break her heart. Hearts didn't break, after all. They merely were bruised for a really long time, as if the inner workings—the ventricles, or maybe the aorta—were clogged or damaged, and couldn't function properly after all.

But hearts *didn't* break, she thought savagely, so Fiona's wouldn't. And neither would anyone else's.

It had been nearly a week since the French restaurant debacle. A week of unanswered calls, of awkward visits with Jenny, of Gran finally coming home. A week of confusion, of frustration, of putting on a brave face. A week of rewriting the last chapters. A week of tears leaking onto her pillow. A week when she'd seen James exactly once, at church, before he'd disappeared with Joel, Serena, and Joel's sister Toni. Maybe she should make an appointment at the clinic. He'd have to speak to her then, wouldn't he?

She still couldn't quite fathom what had happened, why he'd seemed upset but hadn't fought for her. How serious had his attentions really been? Had she underestimated his feelings? Maybe when he'd murmured that he'd never felt this way before she should've realized that perhaps he actually hadn't. Maybe his kisses had possessed so much potency because he wasn't used to spreading them thin. She wished she could enjoy his kisses again. Wished he didn't think of this—them—as a mistake.

Not that she was any better. 'Mistake' seemed to be her middle name. Regrets at her former way of life gnawed her dreams, shadowed her days. She'd prayed and sensed God's peace, so she didn't despair. At least with her career. She even sensed she should return for this year's Flame Christmas party. She'd received the last-minute invitation yesterday. The emailed invite, anyway. Attached to an email from Max explaining— once again—that Flame couldn't afford her to delay her submission.

This time the email demanding she submit didn't faze her. She'd written what she felt she should write, and if they didn't like it, well, she would have met her contractual obligations, even if a little part niggled at the thought it might be rejected for not meeting their 'usual standards.'

Whatever. With the rewrites of this chapter and the next, and a final read through and check for errors, she'd soon be finished. It might not be her best work, but it felt a better work, cleaner, if not exactly highly polished. It was amazing how much she could write without the distractions of a certain doctor, whom she'd only seen at a distance at the church service last Sunday.

A knock came at the closed bedroom door. "Come in," Staci called.

"Staci?" Gran's sweet face appeared. "Have you thought any more about Christmas?"

Regret gnawed. "I'd really like to stay," for Gran, if nobody else, "but this seems to be my best chance to speak with both my agent and publisher about the future. It's not often they're in the same city, let alone at the same party. But as soon as it's done," and she'd sorted out other Chicago commitments, "I promise to return. That is, if you don't mind a roomie."

"You know you're welcome for as long as you want."

"Thanks Gran." Staci pressed a kiss to the top of her head.

"Now, where did I leave my glasses? Have you seen them anywhere, dear?"

Staci's teeth edged her bottom lip. And this was one of those necessary commitments, why she'd felt to rent out her lakeside apartment. Gran's memory seemed to have sharply declined since her hospital stay, and Staci could not fathom abandoning her last remaining family member to live on her own and had determined to look after her as long as she could. Her eyes prickled. For as long as Gran lived.

"Staci? Have you seen my glasses?"

"Um, your glasses are on the chain around your neck, Gran."

"Oh! What a duffer I am." Gran sighed. "You must think me a very silly woman, sometimes."

"Not at all, Gran."

"When did you say you were leaving again?"

"Thursday." That would give Staci a full day to make what arrangements she could before the party on Saturday night. "I'll come back after the Christmas day service on Sunday."

"You will?"

"I'll be pretty late, though, and will have to miss the charity lunch, but I feel like this Christmas I need to start things properly again by going to church in the morning."

"Oh, I'm glad! I didn't realize you were attending a church in Chicago."

She wasn't, but it didn't mean there weren't any to join. "I'm sorry I'll miss Pastor McPherson's Christmas Day message."

"Oh, well. I'm sure he'll stick it up on that interweb thing— oh, what was it called, he mentions it every week, along with those blessed cards he wants visitors to fill out."

"Is it a blog?" Staci suggested.

"No, no, it's a listening thing. Has something to do with these new-fangled coffee machines I see advertised all the time."

Staci stared at her. "I've got no idea."

"Oh, come on dear. You're modern and up-to-date. What do you call those things used in coffee machines?"

"A filter?"

"No, no, no. Oh! Pods, that was it."

Staci chuckled. "Do you mean a podcast?"

"Yes! Oh my, if he's said it once, he's said it a thousand times. I don't think he understands that most of us don't know how to find the silly thing."

"Would you like to know, Gran? I'd be happy to show you."

"No, no. I heard it once, that's enough."

Another reason to be concerned. Gran usually loved dissecting sermons and rereading her notes taken during the service, taking the time to look up every Bible reference. But the hospital counselor had said she might be prone to bouts of confusion, so Staci could only hope and pray this was one of those times.

The doorbell rang. Staci hobbled to the door and peered through the peephole. Then wished she hadn't. Why had she decided today to wear her holey and slightly baggy red checked leggings? She'd wanted comfort, not class. Now she wished she'd made more of an effort.

"Are you going to open that thing or am I?" Gran tutted, moving to the door.

"I've got it, Gran," Staci said, and swung it open. "Hello, Dr. Wells."

"I've come to check on the patient." From the way he didn't look at her, she supposed he meant Gran.

"Well, as you can see, she's doing well." She gestured to where Gran stood, her face wrinkling into smiles.

"Dear boy!" Gran stretched out her hands. "How are you? It seems an age since we've seen you."

"Hello, Rose," he said, thawing slightly. "You're looking well."

"I'm looking old, that's what I'm looking." She grimaced. "But never mind me. Anastacia is looking very well, don't you agree?"

A muscle ticked in his jaw. Still he didn't look at her. "Yes."

"How can you say that when you've barely glanced at her? Annie, say hello to the young doctor there."

Staci summoned a smile to her lips. "Hello," she said, parroting more softly, "to the young doctor there."

His gaze slid to hers for a moment, a moment she was sorely tempted to pull a face or do something equally startling to jerk him from this aloofness. But she refrained, maturity winning out. If he held onto this unreasonableness, then that was his problem, and it wasn't her responsibility to jolly him along. She'd endeavor to treat him as per normal.

"I don't know if I ever thanked you for putting up my tree," Gran said. "It's been so long since I've had a real one, and the scent fills the house just like I remember from years ago."

He unbent enough to give her a small smile. "I'm glad you like it, Rose."

"Oh, we both do, don't we, Annie?"

Staci finally met his gaze. "Love it."

He flushed and looked away. "Now, Rose, I just wanted to check…"

His voice lowered as he continued talking. Staci remained beside the door. His presence here was unexpected. Gran had been seen by a nurse just yesterday, who had proclaimed her quite well, especially considering her advanced age. She frowned. Surely he could have found the nurse's report easily enough. Why *was* he here?

"Very good. Well, I best be going again," he said, once more avoiding Staci's gaze.

Was he that embarrassed by her? A peek at Gran revealed she seemed just as surprised by the lack of any attention shown to Staci.

"Say hello to your mother and father for us," Gran said.

"I will," he promised.

Gran glanced between them. "You know, for two people who seemed to be getting on so well it looks like you've never met each other. I find that very strange."

"I'm sure many people consider authors strange," Staci said, glad to see red filling his cheeks. "Even those authors considered sweet and wholesome."

"Oh, that's right," Gran said, turning to James. "You cannot know the number of times I've had my conversation interrupted by Annie as she writes down a turn of phrase. I can imagine some might find it frustrating, but if it allows the creativity to flow, then I guess it's for the greater good."

Staci was torn between wanting to thank Gran for supporting her, and chagrin at suspecting James thought she'd put her grandmother up to saying such things. Judging from his facial expression, he still wasn't convinced.

He cleared his throat. "I should be going."

"Oh. Will we see you again?"

"I beg your pardon?"

"Will we see you again soon?" Gran repeated.

"I suppose so, at church."

"Oh." Gran looked disappointed. "That won't work. Staci will be away."

He turned to her. "You're leaving?"

"I'm going back to Chicago. I've got a meeting with my publishers."

He stiffened, his face blanking to impassivity as he nodded.

Such unconcern spurted something from within. "You should probably go, then. I wouldn't want Dr. Coffee getting worried he might be portrayed in a book one day." So her propensity for immaturity hadn't entirely gone away.

"Anastacia Fiona Everton," Gran protested.

Staci ignored the disappointed look in her grandmother's eyes and stared into gold-flecked green eyes. "You don't need to worry about ever being included in one of my books, Doctor. I prefer my heroes to want to try to understand their ladies."

Something flashed in his eyes, and his lips pressed together.

She faked a smile, curtsied, turned, and limped away.

THE CLOUD CLINGING to him since his last interview with Dr. Hollis had darkened with his mother's morning news. Staci had left town. She'd left without a goodbye. Not that he could blame her. She was probably relieved to get away from him. Mom and Dad had asked about her, but he couldn't answer, couldn't explain. He was doing the right thing, wasn't he?

"Dr. Wells?" Larissa's voice came across the intercom. "A visitor for you in the foyer."

His pulse jumped. Had Staci returned? Had she forgiven him? He hurried through the doors, scanned the hospital foyer for the red curls. Saw Rose Everton, sans granddaughter.

"James Wells, what is this I hear about you?"

James released a silent sigh, wishing Rose's voice was not so carrying. What if the rest of the people in the hospital foyer heard? "Did you wish to speak to me, Mrs. Everton?"

"You know I do, young man."

"Then perhaps we could adjourn to the cafeteria."

He sent a message via Larissa that he was taking his break now, and accompanied Rose to the cafeteria, where he purchased her a cup of tea and a scone, and they sat in a far corner table near a window where they could not be overheard.

"I'm sorry, Rose. I really am."

"Are you?" She peered at him closely. "For if you truly were sorry then it would not be hard to mend things."

"I'm afraid it's not so easy." He briefly explained his reasons.

"Do you truly think her so shallow that she would care about your ability to provide? You know she has an apartment in Chicago. She has her work and has done quite well for herself."

"Exactly. And I have nothing."

"Don't be so silly. You have *you*, your kindness, your compassion, your faith, your sense of humor. Don't you think that means so much more to her?"

"Kindness doesn't pay the bills, Rose."

She sipped her tea then placed the cup down carefully. "I can understand a man likes to have his self-respect, my husband was just the same. But that's not all, is it? Staci never explained either."

A pitiful shot of relief streaked through him. Staci had proved herself kind to the end.

"What really happened, James?"

He gazed out at snow-burdened trees. "I can't go into that."

"Can't, or won't?"

He played with the fraying tinsel in the table decoration, sad testament to the fact Christmas was so near, an occasion he'd dared hope might actually be merry.

When he glanced back, it was to see Rose's face had softened. "You don't want this any more than she did, do you?"

He pressed his lips together.

"You cannot know how much it grieves me to see my only living relative sad."

Okay, he really didn't need the emotional manipulation. He felt guilty enough already.

Her eyes narrowed. "Is someone holding something over you? Is that it?"

"I cannot say anything more."

"That tells me enough." She sighed. "Well, I'm very sorry that you can't see all of Staci's most wonderful qualities."

"I assure you I do," he murmured.

"Really? For if that was the case—"

"Oh, hello Rose. Dr. Wells." Dr. Hollis studied them, brows upraised.

James froze, as Rose murmured a greeting.

"I trust you've had a chance to think about what we discussed earlier, Dr. Wells."

James couldn't look at Rose. "I have."

"Oh, Dr. Hollis, did you hear? My dear granddaughter, my only living relative, has gone back to Chicago."

"Is that so?" Dr. Hollis said politely, gaze fixed on James.

He nodded.

"Then I guess what we discussed earlier is resolved," Dr. Hollis said. "Good day."

James met Rose's gaze, saw the moment the truth leapt to her eyes. "Do you mean to tell me that Reg Hollis is behind this?"

He didn't mean to tell her anything. "I cannot say—"

"—else you'll lose your job, I see how it is. Well!" Her eyes narrowed. "Is this something to do with her books? I know the man is narrow-minded to a fault, but I never—"

"Rose, I do not want you to think I care more for my job than I do Staci, because I don't. I," he swallowed, "I love her."

She sighed, her features soft with tenderness. "I knew you to be a sensible man. She is a darling, isn't she? So clever, so capable and kind, yet filled with self-doubt. Reminds me of someone else I know."

He didn't have to look beyond a mirror to guess who she meant. "I didn't know what to do. And she was wanting to return to Chicago anyway, and I didn't think she'd miss me."

Rose Everton made a "Pshaw" sound.

"Look, I know I didn't handle things well. But if I don't have a job here, then I'll struggle to find one elsewhere. Dr. Hollis gave me a job when no-one else would, and I'm determined to stick it out until I've got enough savings that means I'm not forced to live off my wife's earnings."

"Your wife?" Her eyes widened. "I didn't realize things had progressed so seriously."

"They didn't progress nearly as seriously as I wanted to, not because I didn't want them to, but because I couldn't afford to."

"I understand now." She nodded. "Well, we'll have to see about this."

"What do you mean?"

She smiled suddenly, straightening in her chair. "Didn't you listen to the sermon last Sunday? Isn't Christmas about God's gift of undeserved grace and mercy? Have you been praying, young man?"

"Yes, ma'am," he said meekly.

"Have you been believing?"

Well, not really.

She pulled herself straight and eyed him firmly. "I think it's time you start believing in Christmas miracles. Understand?"

"Yes, Mrs. Everton."

Her smile drew out his own. Maybe there was a way to go forward after all.

~

HE DIDN'T LEARN what going forward might entail until at the end of his shift, later that evening.

Dr. Hollis called him into his office and handed him a letter. "This came for you, via the hospital mail."

James nodded, ripped it open. Read the words with a disbelieving heart. "The mission board is happy for me to return."

"Yes."

James looked up sharply. "You knew?"

"I suspected. It was on my recommendation."

He had? Talk about miracles. Unless—"Do you want me gone?"

"On the contrary. I want you very much to stay. You are proving to be quite popular, both here and at the clinic, and that's always good for business. And now things have been resolved with your author friend," he pursed his lips as if in distaste, "then I trust you will consider staying on."

James stared at the piece of paper. "I had thought I would say no, if the board offered me another chance. But now…"

"But now what?" Dr. Hollis frowned. "Don't you want to stay here at the hospital?"

James met his look squarely. "I had thought so, but things are different now. I don't like the feeling of coercion, being forced to give up my girlfriend for the sake of the hospital's reputation. Nor do I like the fact that some might consider my work tainted, simply because of books Staci had written in the past. It does not speak very well of Christian grace, does it, sir?"

"Yes, but—" Dr. Hollis spluttered.

"I love Staci, sir. And I recognize I've let fear get in the way of telling her." He rose, offered a small smile. "I do appreciate all you have done for me, in giving me another chance, but I fear I will have to offer my resignation."

"Now don't be hasty, young man."

"Hasty?" a new voice called. "Who is being hasty?"

James pivoted as Dorothy Hollis walked into the room.

Her face lit as she saw him. "Oh, dearest James. How are you?" Without waiting for an answer she turned to her husband, sinking into the chair James had just vacated. "I do hope you are not making James make any hasty decisions, Reginald."

"He wishes to leave."

"Is this because of poor Staci? Oh really, Reginald."

Dr. Hollis held up his hands. "My hands are tied. I can't stop him."

"You can and you very much *will* stop him," she admonished, turning back to James. "I'm sorry my husband has been saying silly things. You must forgive him. 'Tis the silly season after all."

"I'm sorry, Mrs. Hollis, but I don't know what you mean."

"Let's not beat around the bush. Did my dear husband tell you to end your relationship with Staci or else you'd lose your job?"

"Now really, Dorothy," her husband complained.

She cut off his words with a hand. "I do not need you to answer, Reggie. You have obviously said more than enough." Her gaze centered on James. "Well, Doctor? Is this what he said?"

"Not in so many words."

"Hmm, but that was the general gist of it, yes?"

"You could say so."

"I never knew such a sanctimonious…" She sighed. "Forgive him, please, James."

"I fail to see what this has to do with you, Dorothy," her husband muttered.

"It has everything to do with me," she snapped, drawing upright. "When my dearest friend informs me that her only living relative has been forced to move away because my narrow-minded husband has the temerity to tell a young doctor he must make such a choice between her and his job, well, I knew I couldn't stay away. Especially when this involves one of my favorite authors."

Dr. Hollis gasped. "What?"

"Staci Everton has long been one of my favorite romance authors." She turned suddenly to James. "Have you ready any of her novels?"

"Only the first."

"Hmm. I'd skip the second until you're married." Her eyes gleamed. "But you'll probably enjoy the others."

"I didn't know you read her books," Dr. Hollis said to his wife, brows raised in surprise.

"That's what e-readers are for."

"Dorothy, I have to say I'm very disappointed—"

"Do not *dare* to say you're disappointed in me, Reggie," she said, narrow-eyed. "For if you do then I shall have to start recounting long and hard about all the ways you have disappointed me. Is this any way to treat a vulnerable young man? Bribery? Bullying?"

"Now, Dorothy, I really must insist—"

"Do you not have any concept of what this hospital is meant to be? A place of mercy, a place of grace, just like my father intended it to be," she snapped.

"Your father?" James asked.

She nodded proudly. "My father was a doctor who first established the clinic decades ago, then later helped establish the hospital when he realized townspeople shouldn't have to travel to the city for healthcare. It amalgamated with the government health services a couple of decades ago." She glared at her husband. "And I shouldn't have to remind you that he was none too fond of my choice when I begged him to accept you."

"Dorothy, this is hardly the time or place to mention such things."

"This is *precisely* the right time and place to discuss such things," she insisted. "For if you judge this man"—she pointed to James—"then you have obviously forgotten how you were treated mercifully by those who could have judged you."

Talk about awkward. James glanced out the window. It was dark, but he could see snow falling. What was Staci doing? *God, be with her.*

"Reginald," Dorothy's voice had softened, "Rose tells me that Staci is meeting her publishers about her new book. It has a very different feel, a very different purpose."

"Is this true?" Dr. Hollis asked James.

He nodded, remembering some of the passages she'd read aloud, wanting his input. "She said she wants to write something that honors marriage, that helps people see love as a commitment. She was so glad to think so many of her previous readers might have a chance to understand how love can be portrayed as bigger than feelings."

"Love is bigger than feelings." Dorothy nodded. "Well said."

A warm glow filled his chest. James thanked God for Dorothy's most unexpected support, but he sensed from the way Dr. Hollis still frowned at him things weren't sorted yet.

The chairman of the hospital board cleared his throat. "Dr. Wells, it appears that perhaps I have been a little hasty."

"Reginald, you have been extremely hasty," his wife corrected. "Dear James here is owed an apology, as is Staci too, I fear."

Dr. Hollis turned pink.

"That's really not necessary," James began. "I—"

"Oh, I think it is," Mrs. Hollis continued. "And I do hope you will reconsider staying on. Muskoka Shores needs people like you, Dr. Wells, people who understand the world is not always easy, nor comfortable, but can help others see how blessed they are, and their contribution to the wider world is important."

James's throat tightened.

"And it certainly doesn't hurt to have such a personable young man be here. I declare the hospital seems so much brighter knowing there's a chance one might see you here."

Now James could feel his own cheeks grow warm.

"Dorothy, please," her husband muttered.

She chuckled. "Now, Reginald, didn't you have something to say to Dr. Wells here?"

Dr. Hollis turned to James, and with an air of long suffering said, "I trust you will overlook my unfortunate remarks from before."

"And?" his wife prompted.

"I hope you will choose to work here."

"And?" Her brows rose.

"And I was wrong in asking you to give up Miss Everton. Please forgive me."

Bands strapping his chest flung free. "Thank you, sir. I'm happy to put this in the past if you are. And I will definitely reconsider working here—"

"Oh, good!" Mrs. Hollis said, clapping her hands.

"—but not before I've spoken with Staci."

"Very sensible," she approved, standing, and looping her arm through his. "Finished for the day? Care to walk me out? Of course you will, you're such a nice young man after all. See you at home, Reggie." She steered James outside her husband's office, closed the door, and squeezed his arm. "Well done, dear boy."

"I should say well done to you," James said, gratitude threatening to burst his chest. "Mrs. Hollis, thank you so much."

"Oh, it's all your own hard work that got you there," she said, patting him on the arm. "Besides, Reggie needs to learn he can't always have his own way."

He grinned.

"Now, do you think you could persuade Staci to put me in as a character in one of her books?"

He laughed, and thanked God, and knew Christmas miracles could come true after all.

CHAPTER 20

Staci stood sipping a virgin margarita at the top of the Sears tower, or whatever name it was going by now, trying to pretend enjoyment in Flame's Christmas party. So far the evening had progressed exactly as she thought it would: festive cocktail dresses and drinks aplenty, and people trying to one-up each other, even as they pretended to be humble. Funny. It didn't seem to bother her so much now. She had nothing to prove to this crowd, no desire to impress those who felt they needed to be impressed. The night had gone surprisingly smoothly, but that may have been because she was yet to have The Talk with Bronwyn and Max. She silently exhaled, committing it to God again, and tried to look interested as a newbie author gushed about working with Max and receiving an endorsement from Davis Scott.

"Staci."

She tensed. Turned. Sure enough the Great One himself. "Max."

He air-kissed her cheek—new company policy, perhaps?—acknowledging his acolytes with a nod. They were probably too young even for him. "Stace, I feel we really should talk." He steered her into an alcove.

"Let me guess," she said. "It's about my latest book."

He frowned. "I'll confess it took me by surprise."

"Yes, I was surprised I got it finished and sent off before the due date, especially given the circumstances." She lifted her cast-bound wrist.

"Yes, well." He glanced away. "Let's just say it certainly had a very different feel to what I'm used to seeing from you."

"I thought it was time for a change."

"Well, the thing is, I'm not entirely certain this will be a change your readers will respond positively to. Where was the romance? Where was the drama?"

"Oh, there was plenty of romance, just the innocent kind. And as for drama," she said, with another none-too-subtle glance at her cast-bound wrist.

"I understand it's been a trying time for you—"

"Do you, Max?" Staci interrupted. "Do you really? See, I'm not convinced that you do. I met your deadline—was actually ahead of your deadline by several days—and produced a book I'm actually quite proud of, despite you showing next to no compassion for my situation."

"I thought I explained—"

"Is this really how you think you should treat one of your long-standing authors, Max? Someone who has been loyal to you, despite other publishers offering better deals, and you ignore the fact she was taking care of her grandmother, the only family member she has left"—gosh, she hated talking about herself in third person, but it seemed to be the language Max understood—"a family member who at one time it was thought might likely die, and *then* she was incapacitated herself, thus making this author's submission of a book *ahead* of time all the more remarkable!"

Staci drew in a breath, conscious her voice had risen, and

that they had a small audience. She forced a smile she hoped appeared sweet. "I understand that you're following instructions, but I don't understand how you can treat your authors so badly when you claim cost-cutting as a reason." She gestured—with her left hand—to the expensive surroundings. "I don't understand how you can claim to need cost-cutting measures when Flame hires a place like this." Her eyes narrowed. "Or is this some sort of farewell party for us all?"

He paled, but before anything more could be said, she felt her wrist being grabbed, and she was spun around to meet the irate gaze of Bryan Flanagan.

"I'd appreciate it if you could keep your voice down."

"I'd appreciate it if you removed your hand," he did so, "and were honest and upfront for once. Have you read Fiona's story yet?"

"There hasn't been time, but I know from what Max has said it's not up to your usual standard."

"That's because it's better," she declared, tossing her head.

"That's exactly right," another voice came. Bronwyn's voice. Her agent stepped forward. "I need to speak with you and Max immediately."

"This is a party, Bronwyn. We don't talk shop here."

"Except it seems we do. This is important, Bryan, and if you don't wish to talk privately, then fine, let's talk here."

Staci stared at her agent. Why did Bronwyn look so grim? She'd assured Staci that her work was excellent, even more so than usual. What was wrong?

"Have it your way, then," Bronwyn said, when Bryan refused to budge. "I'm not sure if you've caught the latest in the Twitterverse, but it seems there is some question over the authenticity of your golden boy's work."

"What? Davis? You're mistaken."

"Am I? Maybe you've missed the side-by-side comparisons

as readers note the similarities between that and an obscure 1960s book set in England."

"Like anybody cares."

"Apparently somebody does." She mentioned the name of a Big Five publisher. "Apparently they're very interested in how someone could write something using the exact same phraseology. Their legal teams are looking into things, and I wouldn't be surprised if they sue."

"I don't know what you mean," he sputtered.

"I'm sure you soon will." She smiled, a glint in her eye, as she surveyed the hushed room which now sprang into whispers and hastily drawn phones from bags and pockets. "Now, getting back to my client here. I feel it best to inform you that after Staci's Fiona book we shall be seeking publication elsewhere."

"What?"

"Of course, that is subject to your agreeing to publish this book, as is, without substantial changes. If you can't recognize true talent then we'll be more than happy to return the advance and go with another publisher immediately. In fact," she turned to Staci, "I think that is what we should do. Your book is not of the standard Flame is known for, that is true, being of much higher quality. I really don't think we want our names associated with such circles once the true extent of this debacle becomes known."

Staci eyed her agent, striving to keep the panic at bay. "Bronwyn?"

"Walk with me," she instructed, guiding Staci to a column near the door. "I'm sorry for the theatrics in there, but it's true. Davis Scott has been discovered as a fraud, which means this ship is gonna sink, baby, so we need to jump off quick."

"But my story—"

"We'll break the contract, don't you worry. I spoke to some other publishing heavyweights this afternoon, getting my ducks lined up in a row. You can give back the advance and we'll get your story back pronto. You do have the money, don't you?"

She would once her apartment was rented. "I'll get it to you."

"Good. Then we'll shop you to someone else." She mentioned the name of another Big Five publisher. "I was speaking to one of their editors the other day, and I've a feeling they'll be more receptive to your story for a new line they're establishing, something called Sweet and Wholesome."

"You don't think my back catalog will be held against me?"

"I think they'll see you as a versatile author, someone who can write to spec, and on time. I should think they would be thrilled to have you."

"Really?"

"Really. Staci, your writing just keeps improving, and now, adding this subtle faith element? Genius. Your work will appeal to your usual readership plus hold the possibility of attracting new, faith-based readers. *Fifty Shades* is over. Readers want clean reads."

"You really think so?"

Bronwyn cleared her throat. "Staci, I don't know if I've ever mentioned this, but I used to attend Sunday school. That last story was something even my Sunday school teacher couldn't object to. It's got heart, hope, and such an inspiring message of forgiveness. If people can't respond to that then they must be dead inside."

"You liked it?"

"Loved it. Now stop fishing for compliments. I see another client of mine I'm going to have to free from Max's snare."

Staci watched her march purposefully across the room to speak to a now visibly upset Davis Scott-endorsed newbie author. *Lord, help her.*

"Staci."

At the sound of that voice she closed her eyes. No. It couldn't be. It had to be a dream.

"Staci, please."

She swallowed, refusing to spin around. Not that she could even if she wanted to, as her ankle had apparently decided this very moment to give her grief. She waited until he moved in front of her. Raised her brows at the tall, curly-haired man with the gold-specked green eyes.

James held out his hands.

She restrained hers and put them on her hips. Well, put one hand on her hip, as the other remained in its cast. "Hello." Why was he here? Why was her heart racing? Oh, why couldn't she see a chair—her ankle was killing her.

"I, uh, hope you don't mind my being here. I—"

"Why *are* you here?" she interrupted. Tonight was not the night for weak and helpless damsels.

"Your grandmother, Rose, told me where you were."

"Did she now?"

"Please." He moved to grasp her elbow, but she edged it away. His hand dropped, his face fell. "I think you think I've been a bit of an idiot."

"No," she said. "I *know* you've been a bit of an idiot."

He stared at her, before giving a wry chuckle, a sound that broke past her defenses and scraped amusement from her too. "Can we talk?"

"Only if we sit down. My ankle is killing me."

"May I?" He gestured to her long gown, and she nodded, and he swept her up once more to the surprised enjoyment of those nearby. "Where shall I take you?"

"Gretna Green," she said promptly.

He laughed, and she basked in the sound, in the vibration of his chest. "I have a confession to make," he murmured.

"What's that?"

"Rose let me read Fiona's story."

"Did she now?"

He placed her on a seat—something that appeared more like

a golden throne—and sat beside her carefully. "You don't seem too concerned."

"Why should I be?" she said, smoothing the folds of her green skirt. "Not when I told her she could."

"How did you know I'd ask to read it?"

"I hoped. I prayed. I trusted God that you'd see reason. And judging from the Gretna Green comment, it seems you have."

"Did people really run away to get married there?"

"Don't you trust historical authors to deal honestly with the facts?"

"I don't know too many authors. Only you." His eyes darkened, he grasped her hand. "You made me your hero."

"I used your first name for my hero," she corrected softly.

"But you didn't change it. You could have, but you didn't. It made me hope you might forgive me." He glanced down, gently squeezed her hand, then looked up. "I'm really sorry for how I treated you before. I don't have any excuses."

She caressed his fingers. "*I'm* sorry for being ungracious."

"You weren't ungracious. Just confused, and rightly so. I was pretty confused myself."

"But you're not now?" Hope trembled within.

"I…" His gaze fused with hers. "I missed you."

"I missed you, too," she whispered.

"I'm sorry for getting carried away. It was Dr. Hollis and his insistence that your previous books might taint the reputation of the hospital that confused me."

"I'm sorry my previous books embarrassed you."

"You've done nothing to embarrass me. I should have remembered that God is into second chances." He gestured to the twinkling lights and Christmas decorations. "Especially at this time of year. Please, say you'll forgive me."

"Of *course*, I forgive you."

Relief lit his features then he drew her close in a bergamot-scented hug.

Oh, how sweet was forgiveness! Her smile threatened to burst her cheeks as she nestled closer. "So you have your job back?"

"Only if you say yes."

Breath suspended. "Say yes to what?"

"Say yes to loving me, for I, dear Anastacia Everton, love you."

Her heart filled with astonished joy. He loved her? "You do?"

"I love you most ardently," he whispered, quoting her own words, his breath dancing along her cheek.

She closed her eyes, savoring this dream-come-true, speaking the words from the depth of her heart. "I love you, too, James Wells."

"We make a good team," he whispered.

"The best," she murmured. "I think we should keep this team going for a while longer."

"Me too."

He turned his head, and once again her lips met the fire of his. Oh, how easy he was to kiss! How wonderful it was to be restored to a proper relationship again.

"I missed you so much," he murmured against her cheek. "I don't know what got into me before."

That made two of them.

"You know, it wasn't until I read your new book that I realized just how powerful a piece of fiction could be. Who knew that fiction could speak truth to me?"

"So it wasn't too boring for you?"

"Not at all. I have to admit, I did like the bits with the scorching kisses."

"Did you now?"

"I did." And he backed it up with a scorching kiss of his own.

"Well, well, well! So the good girl's going bad." Bronwyn stood, arms crossed, a smile tweaking her lips.

"Not bad," Staci insisted. "This is all good."

"Really?" Bronwyn held out her hand to James. "Hi. Bronwyn Matthieson, Staci's agent. I don't believe we've met."

"James Wells. Staci's boyfriend," he said, with just the slightest intonation at the end that made it a question.

His hooked eyebrow and pleading eyes made her smile and press her lips against his cheek for reassurance. "Indeed he is." She turned to Bronwyn. "James is a doctor who works in Tanzania."

"Worked," he corrected softly.

Staci's gaze swung to him. "What are you saying?"

"I've decided to stay in North America."

"Really?" Hope lit her heart.

"Really."

She threw herself at him and hugged him fiercely, murmuring against his shirt, "Are you sure?"

"One hundred percent."

She closed her eyes, gratitude filling her chest. She knew there was more involved in his decision than her, but she was so thankful. To God. And to James. And to God for James.

Bronwyn cleared her throat. "Where did you say you were?"

"Tanzania," James supplied.

"It's a country on the east coast of Africa, between Kenya and Uganda and half a dozen others. He worked as a medical missionary there," Staci explained, eyeing Bronwyn's face for reaction.

"My uncle was a missionary," Bronwyn said. "In Peru. He always brought back the strangest looking carved animals."

"I don't know about carved animals," Staci continued, "but I do know James has excellent taste in fiction," she said, snuggling up to him.

"Have you read her latest work?" Bronwyn demanded.

"It's really good," James said.

"Her best yet," Bronwyn said, nodding. "I didn't think I could care about a romance with barely any kissing, but that kiss after they were married, whew! What a doozy!"

"Yes, it was."

Bronwyn eyed them. "It's enough to make me wonder if Staci has been writing from experience."

Staci stiffened, but James's chuckle put paid to any fear, as he wrapped his arm around her. "Remember, Bronwyn, you can't believe everything you read."

"Hmph! Well, that didn't look like fiction to me," she said, before wandering off.

"Is this fiction?" Staci asked.

"It feels rather real to me."

And to prove it, he once more captured her lips with his own.

"Come back to Muskoka Shores for Christmas," he whispered.

"For Christmas?"

"For me." His eyes were tender. "And for forever."

Happiness bloomed within her, and she nodded.

He kissed her sweetly. "Happy Christmas, Staci."

"Happy Christmas, James."

And she snuggled into his arms, thanking God for Christmas miracles, and knowing this would be the happiest of Christmases, indeed.

THE END

If you enjoyed this book, then make sure you read the next in the Muskoka Romance series, *Muskoka Hearts*

A NOTE FROM THE AUTHOR

Thank you for reading *Muskoka Christmas*, the second book in the Muskoka Shores Christian contemporary romance series. This book is based on my visit to the beautiful Muskoka region of Ontario, Canada, and springs from Muskoka Blue, the sixth book in the Original Six contemporary romance series, that enters on Sarah and Dan's romance story (grab your copy of *Muskoka Blue)*. If you've enjoyed this book, please check out the pictures from my visit to Muskoka on my website at www.carolynmillerauthor.com

Reviews help other readers find new-to-them authors, so if you can spare a moment to write a quick review at Amazon / Goodreads / your place of purchase, I'd be very grateful.

Enjoyed this taste of Muskoka? Then make sure you read the next book in the Muskoka series, *Muskoka Hearts*.

If you enjoy Christian contemporary romance you may want to check out the books in the Original Six hockey romance series, a sweet & swoony, slightly sporty Christian contemporary romance series.

The Breakup Project
Love on Ice
Checked Impressions
Hearts and Goals
Big Apple Atonement
Muskoka Blue

Romance and hockey fans may also want to read *Fire and Ice*, the first book in the new Northwest Ice series, releasing in 2023.

I'd love for you to check out my other books and to sign up for my newsletter at www.carolynmillerauthor.com where you can be the first to learn all my book and contest news, and discover more behind-the-book details and photos.

A huge thank you to the following people for their encouragement and eagle eyes: Bea, Brittany, & Becky - I appreciate you all so much! Big thanks to the ladies in my Facebook group, Carolyn's Books & Friends, for all your support in helping promote my books.

ABOUT THE AUTHOR

Carolyn Miller lives in the beautiful Southern Highlands of New South Wales, Australia, with her husband and four children. A long-time lover of romance, especially that of Jane Austen, Georgette Heyer and LM Montgomery, Carolyn loves to write contemporary and historical romance that draws readers into fictional worlds that show the truth of God's grace in our lives.

To find out more about Carolyn's books, and to subscribe to her newsletter, please visit www.carolynmillerauthor.com

You can also connect with her at

ALSO BY CAROLYN MILLER

The Original Six hockey series
The Breakup Project
Love on Ice
Checked Impressions
Hearts and Goals
Big Apple Atonement
Muskoka Blue

Muskoka Romance series
Muskoka Shores
Muskoka Christmas
Muskoka Hearts
Muskoka Spotlight

Northwest Ice hockey series
Fire and Ice

Trinity Lakes collection
Love Somebody Like You

The Independence Islands series
Restoring Fairhaven
Regaining Mercy
Reclaiming Hope
Rebuilding Hearts
Refining Josie

Historical:

<u>Regency Wallflowers</u>

Dusk's Darkest Shores

Midnight's Budding Morrow

Dawn's Untrodden Green

<u>Regency Brides: Legacy of Grace</u>

The Elusive Miss Ellison

The Captivating Lady Charlotte

The Dishonorable Miss DeLancey

<u>Regency Brides: Promise of Hope</u>

Winning Miss Winthrop

Miss Serena's Secret

The Making of Mrs Hale

<u>Regency Brides: Daughters of Aynsley</u>

A Hero for Miss Hatherleigh

Underestimating Miss Cecilia

Misleading Miss Verity

'Heaven and Nature Sing' from the Joy to the World Christmas
novella collection